Love and War

Love and War

Latoya Nicole

www.urbanbooks.net

Urban Books, LLC
300 Farmingdale Road, NY-Route 109
Farmingdale, NY 11735

ISBN 13: 978-1-64556-097-5
ISBN 10: 1-64556-097-X

First Mass Market Printing September 2020
First Trade Paperback Printing June 2019
Printed in the United States of America

10 9 8 7 6 5 4 3 2 1

Distributed by Kensington Publishing Corp.
Submit Orders to:
Customer Service
400 Hahn Road
Westminster, MD 21157-4627
Phone: 1-800-733-3000
Fax: 1-800-659-2436

Love and War

by

Latoya Nicole

Dedication

"You're my morning star, shining brightly beside me. . . .Our love will shine bright in the night like the stars above, and we'll always be together."

The first time I heard Mary J. Blige sing that song, I said I can't wait to find a man to love me like this. I have searched high and low, and yet, that love seems to evade me. On January 31, 2011, that love came to me out of nowhere. I didn't realize I would find it in my daughter. Ever since you came into my life, I have experienced love like I never thought I could. When you look at me, you don't see my mistakes; you don't see the pain I have gone through or our struggles. You see the best mom in the world. You see love and a protector. That is the greatest love ever. You have made me better, and I will always be grateful to you. Don't ever forget that if no one else in this world loves you, Mommy does, and I *always* will. Miracle Monet Riley, you are my heart and soul. Don't you ever forget that.

Acknowledgments

Curly B. Edwards, we have been through so much together one couldn't even imagine. You have known me since I was a little girl, and we have always been close like family. But when I started dating your son, you treated me as if I were your own. Remember how we stayed up all night playing cards? Jack and I would be whooping all on y'all, and you would be so mad. I have never seen one person fire that many partners in one night. LOL. You even stood out there and fought with your girl. You never let anyone mess with me, and I didn't play about you, either. It hurts me to see you struggling, but I know God has you. Just remember, I love you, and I will never forget what you did for me. Get well soon. God has the last word. To my Edwards and Davis family, stay strong. I love y'all.

To my supporters, you guys don't have to have my back like you do, but every release, you are right there cheering me on. Auntie

Acknowledgments

Marsha, Steph, Shunta, Shenitha, Elmie, Vella, Shonda, Amanda, Erica Densley, Zatasha, Kb Cole, Juanita, Dawn, Paris, Ash, Panda, Amb, J Diorr, Jennifer, Tres, Ebony, Jonelle, Derrick, and anyone else that is right there with me sharing and promoting every release. I thank you from the bottom of my heart.

To my readers, we have come a long way, and I am still pushing forward. You guys make me what I am, and I want you always to know that I am forever grateful. Keep believing in me as I continue to climb my way to the top. I love you, and I appreciate you. Make sure you share and tell a friend.

Like my author page on fb @misslatoyanicole
My fb page Latoya Nicole Williams
IG Latoyanicole35
Twitter Latoyanicole35
Snap Chat iamTOYS

Chapter 1

Baby Face

"Hey, nigga, you heard from 'Blaze'? He knows we supposed to be meeting at the office." Sick and tired wasn't the word when it came to my baby brother, Blaze.

"You know that nigga probably knee deep in some pussy. Quit acting surprised." My brother Quick was never bothered by Blaze's bullshit.

"Nah, he gon' be surprised when his ass don't get a cut of the money."

"You know that nigga will spaz out. You know he would fuck around and set your house on fire. I don't know why you insist on fucking with that crazy-ass nigga."

"Yea, I know, and you know I ain't fooling with his ass. I'm too pretty for the bullshit. I'll see your ass in a minute and try to get in touch with your brother." Hanging up the phone, I jumped in my silver Maybach and headed over to the office. Before you get it twisted, I'm not no nine-to-five-ass nigga. I was a part of one of the biggest crime families in Chicago. My name is Zaire "Baby Face" Hoover. At the age of 29, I was the oldest of all my brothers, but I look like I'm about 16. I blame that shit on them good-ass genes. My mother is black, and my daddy is Puerto Rican. Because I had good hair, I switched the shit up. Right now, I'm wearing it low, but you can still see I have good hair. I figured if I got that good shit, why not show it? Shit drove the ladies crazy. Grabbing my phone out of my pocket, I thought it was Blaze, but it was my baby brother, "Shadow."

"Where the fuck y'all at? I swear I'm the youngest, but I'm the most responsible."

"Your ass always complaining. You act like an old-ass man. I'll be there in five." Not giving him a chance to respond, I hung up on his ass. That nigga nag more than a bitch, and he was only 22. He was the only one engaged to be married. It's not that I didn't want that shit; I just haven't found it. A nigga approaching 30, I was ready for the family life. I wouldn't be like Shadow's ass nagging all the fucking time, though. He better nag at that bitch. I didn't want to hear it.

Pulling up to the office, I was hoping every-body else was here. I didn't want to listen to that shit by myself. Looking at the sign on the building, I stood there to reflect on everything we had accomplished. Hoover Inc. Run by four brothers out of Cabrini-Green Projects. We now have a nightclub called Hoover Nights, a strip club called Diamond in the Rough, and we owned real estate all over the city. To an outside pair of eyes, everything would look and seem legit, but we funded that shit robbing banks. We were untouchable, and it was time to make our next big score.

"Nigga, why the fuck are you standing out here gazing and shit?"

I turned around. "Quick" was looking at me like I had lost my damn mind. I hadn't even realized I was still staring at the sign.

"Cus I can. Bring your ass on before Shadow start preaching to us about the necessity of time." Laughing at our baby brother, we walked through the door.

"This shit is getting ridiculous. Do you know how much we could have accomplished had you been on time? You motherfuckers are jerking off, and I could have been doing something more productive with my shit. Time is money, and if you niggas don't start paying me for my time, I'm going to stop attending." Quick and I looked at each other and damn near passed out from laughing so hard. "I'm glad y'all think this shit is a game."

"Dude, you sound like an educated thug. We here to discuss robbing Fifth Third Bank, and you in this motherfucker talking like we about to take an exam." Shadow was ready to fight Quick. He was sensitive.

"If I knocked your ass out, I bet you wouldn't be talking that shit." He was the fighter out of the four of us. Don't get me wrong, all of us could throw them hands, but Shadow's ass could have made a career of it.

"Your black ass always trying to fight. Ain't nobody scared of your angry ass. Let's get started. We can fill Blaze in on the shit when he gets here. We don't want to waste any more of Shadow's time." This nigga was really still standing there breathing all hard and shit. Not paying him any fucking attention, I went on to discuss the robbery. "The plan is set for Thursday. We will meet up here at nine and then head out. This bank is in the middle of everything. We need to be in and out. As you know, it's hard as fuck to drive downtown, and I ain't trying to be no sitting duck in traffic. Shadow, you already know you are to stay in the car."

"Why the fuck do I always have to stay in the car? I'm better in my shooting than any of you niggas."

"You know damn well Quick is the better shooter, I'm the mouthpiece, and Blaze knows how to get in the vaults if they don't produce the key. Everybody has a part, and you are going to play yours. Now, as I was saying, we will not be in the back longer than sixty seconds. Anybody that is still in that motherfucker after that will be left. Do I make myself clear?" Both of us looked at Quick when I said that.

"Fuck you looking at me for? I be on time."

"Nigga, please," Shadow and I said at the same damn time.

"If we allowed you to, your ass would be in there shooting for hours. We can't do that shit downtown, nigga. In and out, are we clear?"

"Yea, nigga, damn. Y'all better emphasize that shit to Blaze's ass. Y'all know he will be in there trying to set the whole damn bank on fire." Quick was laughing when he said it, but we all knew it was the truth.

"Don't be talking about me when I ain't here. I'll set your fucking curls on fire. Play with it if you want to." Blaze finally made it to the meeting. Grabbing my hair, I moved away from his ass. Everybody in the room knew he would do it.

"Hey, nigga, my shit lying down today. Where the fuck you see some curls?"

"Nigga, quit acting like as soon as the heat hit that shit, it ain't gon' curl up like some sweaty pussy hair."

I hated this nigga Blaze; he didn't have no chill.

"Glad to see you could finally join us."

We all looked over at Shadow and busted out laughing. This nigga was dead-ass serious about his time.

Chapter 2

Blaze

"Damn, baby, suck this clit. Right there. Don't stop, daddy."

This bitch was getting on my nerves with all this talking. "Bitch, I know how to eat pussy. Damn. Now, can you nut so I can stick my dick in? I got somewhere to go."

Looking at me like she wanted to say something smart, she thought better of it when I looked up at her. My eyes were a pretty grey, but them bitch's was ice cold.

"Fuck, I'm about to come. Yes, baby. Yes." Her body started shaking, and I couldn't be happier. Grabbing my condom, I slid that bitch on and slid my dick in her now-ready pussy. As soon as I got inside of her, I knew this was a mistake. This bitch's pussy was loose as a goose. When I tell you I didn't feel anything, I didn't feel shit. It felt like my ass was fucking air. Slamming my dick inside her, I tried moving my hips side to side to feel something. Then this bitch started screaming for dear life.

"Oh God, this dick is so fucking good. This is your pussy, baby."

She knows damn well she didn't feel my dick because I couldn't feel that motherfucker. If I didn't already know it was there, I would have thought I lost that bitch in the waves. I started slamming my dick like crazy and shuddered some. Rushing a nut, I needed to get up outta this bitch right now. I rolled over like I was worn out and she had the best shit ever.

"Too bad I gotta go; I was gon' give you an all-nighter." Smiling at her, I got up and threw on my clothes. Removing the condom, I stuck the shit in my pocket.

"Why you doing all of that, baby? I have a garbage can." She looked offended.

"I know, baby. It's just something for me to keep until I see you again. I gotta remember this good pussy." This bitch looked shaky. Like she might try to turkey base my shit. "I'll call you later after my meeting." I kissed her on her jaw and went to walk out the door.

"Hoover, nobody does it like yooouuu."

Did this bitch really start singing the vacuum commercial? Simple bitches. Laughing, I damn near ran out of her shit. Jumping in my Rover, I looked at my phone and saw that I had twenty missed calls. I called Quick back because I didn't want to talk to Baby Face's ass.

"Nigga, you know Baby Face madder than a motherfucker. He says your ass always late."

"I know, nigga. I was fucking that bitch from the bank. I had to get the key to the vault just in case shit didn't go as planned."

"Damn, your ass living the life. You get to fuck fine-ass bitches and finesse them out of they shit."

"Nigga, she fine, but that ho's pussy was trash. I would have rather fucked the janitor."

Busting out laughing, Quick could barely talk. "I'm surprised you didn't set her shit on fire for it being that whack."

"Bye, nigga. I'll be there in a minute."

Zayn "Blaze" Hoover. I'm sure you can tell how I got my nickname. I was the fire-starter. Been that way since I was a kid. My mama couldn't stand that shit either. My dumb ass would just sit around the house striking matches and flicking lighters all day. One time I went too far, and I got my ass beat.

"Blaze, quit flicking that damn lighter and come eat."

As I got up to go in the kitchen, Quick's ass tripped me, and I hit the wall and busted my lip. "Ma, look what Zavier did. I'm bleeding."

She barely looked at me. "Boy, you are all right. Now sit your ass down before you get that shit everywhere." Everybody was laughing, but I was pissed. I was tired of my little brother getting away with everything. He was gon' pay today. Waiting until they all were sitting down watching Martin, I walked behind the couch and flicked my lighter.

Pretending I tripped on some old shoes, I attempted to throw the lighter into Quick's lap. But my aim was off, and it landed in Mama's good wig. Before I could say anything, that damn hair caught fire so fast that I couldn't say shit. She jumped up beating the hell out of her head.

"Mama, just take it off." Baby Face was yelling at her, but I think she was trying to save her good hair. When she finally got that fire out, she beat the hell out me for three days straight. Every time she thought about it, I got my ass beat.

Now at the age of 26, my fire infatuation is much bigger. I will set a motherfucker on fire in a minute. Looking at me you would never know it, though. I was a pretty-ass nigga with tats all over my body. I tried my best to look like the street nigga I was. I didn't want motherfuckers to see me and think shit was sweet. Niggas knew our name, though, and they knew not to fuck with us. As Fabolous said, "I'm a movement by myself, but we're a force when we're together." Walking in the building, I heard these niggas were in here talking shit.

"Don't be talking about me when I ain't here. I will set your fucking curls on fire." When I said it, I looked over at Baby Face, and that nigga got the fuck out of the way. He knew I would flick my Bic in a second.

"Glad to see you decided to join us," Shadow spat at me, and the nigga was dead-ass pissed I was late.

"Nigga, I had to get the key. Y'all be blowing the fuck out of me acting like I ain't working when I'm out here getting this pussy."

"Don't blame that shit on work. Your ass fuck everything under the sun, and now you wanna say it's because of work." Quick started laughing . . . until he saw me eyeballing his hairline.

"You are too old to be still fucking like you crazy. Get you a good woman like I did. The shit is easier." Shadow would kill anybody's buzz.

"Nigga, I'ma start calling your ass Deacon Frye. You be on that other shit ever since you got engaged. You got engaged, not us!" Everybody started dapping it up when I said that comment. "Somebody tell me what the move is. I'm trying to head over to the club tonight. I need to go get ready."

"Which club?" Shadow asked looking weary.

"Hoover Nights. We know you not allowed in Diamond in the Rough no more."

"Shut the fuck up. She knows that's my shit. I wish she would tell me I can't go in my shit, but I'm down for the club tonight too." We laughed because we knew this nigga was fronting.

"Shid, we all in that motherfucker then. Baby Face, tell this late-ass nigga the plan so we can get out of here." I reached in my pocket and pulled the condom out I had just used on that bitch and threw it in Quick's hair.

"This jerk-ass nigga play all his fucking life," Quick said, walking off pissed. The rest of us laughed, and I listened to the plan.

Chapter 3

Quick

Leaving the office, I was trying to get the damn nut out of my hair. Blaze's ass was always doing stupid shit because he knows we gon' let that shit slide. That nigga really would set your ass on fire and not think shit of it. The nigga set my face on fire when we were kids.

It was late at night, and my brothers and I were up talking shit like always. When I heard tapping on the window, I looked out and saw it was this girl named Zatasha. Blaze was in love with her ass, but she wouldn't give him the time of day. She wanted the kid, and I was feeling her fine ass too. We had been creeping for a month, and I had planned on telling my brother before someone else could. Looking around to make sure Blaze wasn't paying attention, I went outside. We talked for a few, and I told her I would holla at her later. After we hugged and kissed, I turned around to go in the house . . . and Blaze was looking out the window. When I got inside, I tried to explain it to him, but he didn't want to hear it.

"Bro, I'm sorry, I didn't know how to tell you."

"It's all good. She a friendly-ass thot anyway." *He shrugged his shoulders and got in bed and went to sleep. I was out not too long after him. Then I woke up from the pain. This nigga was sitting there with the lighter up to my face, just cooking my shit. It doesn't look bad, and most people think it was a birthmark, but it wasn't. That nigga wake and baked my ass.*

That's why I knew not to fuck with that nigga. He was certified crazy, and he didn't care who he set on fire. The shit was all a game to him.

Not paying attention, I ran right into this chick that was just standing there.

"My bad, gorgeous." Turning on my charm, I smiled at her, showing all my pearly whites. "What's your name?"

"Alaysia."

She didn't ask me my name, but a nigga like me was going to tell her anyway. She was about

five foot ten and thick as New Orleans grits. She
had her hair cut in a short style, but the shit was
sexy as hell on her. Her brown skin looked like
it was glowing. Staring into her big pretty eyes, I
damn near forgot to respond. Not one to chase
a bitch because I have asthma, I decided to go
about this a different route.

"My name's Quick. Me and my brothers about
to go home and get ready to go out tonight. It
would be nice if you would join me."

"Where y'all going?"

"Hoover Nights. I'll have them put you on the
list."

"Okay, so you want to take my number down?"
She was looking confused because I didn't ask
for it.

"Naw, baby girl. If you show up tonight, then
I'll give it to you." She was looking a little upset,
so I decided to soften it up some. "If you don't
have my number, you can't cancel. When you
show up, I'll give it to you . . . and more."

"Okay, well, I'll see you tonight and add a plus
one to the list with my name." After watching
her thick ass walk away, I jumped in my Benz
truck and headed to the house to get ready. All
the way home, I tried my best to get Blaze's nut
out of my hair, but the shit wasn't budging.

As soon as I pulled up to the crib, I went in
and started laying my shit out. If Alaysia did

decide to come, I wasn't gon' let her outdress me. I was a conceited nigga. I decided to wear my black Gucci blazer and a white tee, black jeans, and my all-black Christian Louboutin high top sneakers. I was a hood nigga to the core, but I did try to add some class to it when I stepped out. Making sure I laid my 9 mm on the bed to top off my outfit, I was set. I didn't leave the house without my heat. Chicks be mad as hell because I fucked with my heat lying right by me just in case these bitches tried something. Blaze was the fire-starter, but I was the nigga with the happy trigger finger. It was worse when I was younger. Everybody else in the hood would be fighting, and my ass would pull my gun out and lay a nigga down and keep eating my ice cream. That's how I got my nickname Quick. Baby Face gave it to me. I could hear him clear as day, *"Nigga, you act just like Eddie Murphy on* Harlem Nights. *I'ma start calling your ass Quick."* I thought he was joking, but the day I shot Blaze, everybody started calling me that, and it stuck.

I was 14, and Blaze was 15, but we always hung around Baby Face and his friends. Back then, I was just Zavier Hoover, and my brother was the only one that would call me Quick. The nigga Blaze was trying to show off, and he kept fucking with me.

"Zavier, why you got on my shoes? Dirty ass always in my shit." Blaze was trying to get a laugh out of the crowd.

"Don't front on me, nigga. Mama bought these for me, and you know it."

"Look how big them motherfuckers is. You know damn well them ain't your shoes. Take my shit off." They were his shoes, but I didn't like the fact that he was trying to play me in front of his homies. Standing there looking at him, I had fire in my eyes. This nigga grabbed my foot and pulled them off. Everybody around was laughing their asses off. Not finding shit funny, I reached in my waist and grabbed my .22. Right in the middle of his laugh, I shot his ass in the top part of his foot.

"Now, nigga, neither one of us can wear the motherfuckers." That was the last day anybody called me Zavier. That was the night Quick was born.

To this day, I didn't argue with niggas. I don't have time. Either you gon' shut the fuck up, or you gon' get shot the fuck down. My phone started ringing as soon as I jumped in the shower. I hated to miss a call, so I jumped back out. Who the fuck is this?

"How the fuck did you get my number?" I didn't know who it was, but if I gave it to them, then they would be stored. I didn't play the phone games.

"I see the gentleman is now gone, and the hood done came out." Racking my brain trying to catch the voice, I got tired of playing.

"Stop playing on my shit before you find out how I got my name. Now, who the fuck is this?"

"Alaysia." Now, I know damn well I didn't give her my number.

"I'm sorry, sweetie, but how did you get my number?"

"I googled the company you were coming out of today, and a list of numbers came up. I tried one and lucked up." I know this shit should have been a red flag for me, but my dumb ass was turned on. I like crazy bitches, and this one was screaming psycho than a motherfucker.

"If you would have waited until tonight, I would have given it to you."

"I know, but I wanted to show you that I don't allow no nigga to shut me down. If I want you, then you are mine. Now, gon' and finish getting ready. I'll see you in a little while."

Laying my phone back down, I jumped in the shower with a brick-hard-ass dick. Yea, this bitch was bat-shit crazy, but crazy bitches have the best pussy. I couldn't wait to show her what type of nigga she was fucking with. She thinks she's in control, and I will let her think it for now, but I'm not my baby brother, and no bitch was gon' lead me. As long as we were together, *I* would be the one wearing the pants. I don't mind crazy, but I hate a chick that don't know she is the woman in the relationship.

After washing my ass and my hair, I climbed out of the shower and threw my clothes on. I couldn't wait to see Alaysia's thick ass.

Chapter 4

Alaysia

Hanging up the phone with Zavier Quick Hoover, I looked back over my notes. While I was making sure I knew everything there was to know about him, someone knocked on my door.

"Can I come in?"

It was my partner Tate. We had a relationship outside of work—personal and business. I was Officer Alaysia Hampton. I had been on the force four years now, and the check just wasn't cutting it. My partner came to me about two years ago with a plan on how to make more money. We knew every dealer, hustler, and criminal out there in these streets. The plan was to utilize what their illegal activity was. If you sold drugs, we would catch you in a deal and then blackmail you. The shit had been working for us. The Hoover Gang thought no one knew they were behind all of the bank robberies, but they weren't as smart as they thought they were. One of the girls Zayn Blaze Hoover fucked over came in one day and told us everything. Thank God she came to my partner, and now, we have our next lick. This was the big time, and we could retire off this shit. We would control which banks they would rob and then take half the cut. When the time was right, the Hoover boys wouldn't know what hit them.

"Yea, baby what's up?"

Leaning down, he kissed me, then sat on my desk. "How did it go? Did he bite?"

"Of course, he did. I'm going out with him tonight. I'm going to take my sister with me. I couldn't get you on the list, but make sure you are in the building. We are going to their club Hoover Nights."

"I will definitely be there. You know downtown is out of our jurisdiction, so make sure everything runs smoothly."

"I know, baby. Lock the door. I need a quickie before I go home and get ready." Doing as he was told, he locked the door and started unbuckling his pants. The sex with Tate was great. He was my first, and I loved everything about him. His dick wasn't really that big, but by him being the only nigga I have ever fucked, it was perfect for me. Sitting on the desk, I leaned forward to take him in my mouth.

"I love the way you suck this dick." Every time he would compliment me, it turned me on. Since he wasn't that big, it was always easy for me to deep throat him. The only thing I hated was he didn't last long. If I sucked his dick too long, he would nut, and that would be it. I always had to time it right to make sure I got some meat inside this pussy. I have never come or had an orgasm from sex, but the shit feels good. I think my pussy only comes from getting eaten. I could feel him tightening up, so I stopped. Pulling my pants down, I leaned over the desk and allowed him to hit that shit from the back. In four minutes, it was over, and I was cleaning myself off with wet wipes.

"I will see you after I leave the club, Tate. Please, be careful. I love you."

"Love you too, baby."

I rushed home and ran my shower. Grabbing my wine-colored, red-fitted bodycon dress and my black knee-high boots, I jumped in the shower and got my hygiene together. Once I started getting dressed, I realized you could see my panty line and decided to go commando. I applied my lip gloss, and I was ready. I never wore makeup, and I prayed I never had to. Jumping in my Lexus, I picked up my sister Elise from her house. She jumped in the car talking shit.

"Damn, bitch, it took you long enough. What was your ass doing? You almost made me sweat my hair out."

"Girl, shut up. I had to wrap up paperwork."

"Which one of the brothers are single? I'm trying to get this kitty played in tonight." I couldn't do shit but laugh at her crazy ass.

"Three of them are, and one is engaged."

"I'll take the engaged one for two hundred, Alaysia. Niggas get a shot of this pussy and tend to get clingy. Give me the one that already has a bitch, and I can send his ass back home to her ass. What's his name?"

"Shadow. He's the youngest. Your old ass will be in cougar city if you fuck with him. He's only 22."

"Call me what you want, just don't call me late to get that dick."

I couldn't take anymore of her ass. I turned my music up and got my mind ready for this next lick. Giving my keys to the valet, I was impressed already, and I haven't even made it inside. The line was around the corner, and more cars were pulling up. There were two separate lines, and I assumed the shorter one was for VIP or people on the list. After waiting five minutes, it was my turn to give my name to the security.

"I'm on the list. Alaysia plus one." He looked at the list and started speaking into his headset. My sister looked at me all confused, but I had no answers for her.

"Let me find out we not on this damn list, and I'm going home. You won't have me looking stupid going from the important line to the bum section." Since she decided to say the shit out loud, the girls in the next line copped an attitude. "Is there a problem? Trust me, this ain't what you want. Move around." My sister was a hothead, and this is why I barely came outside with her. No one would ever know she was born and raised in the damn suburbs.

"Excuse me, what's the hold up?"

The man didn't even respond to my ass. About to walk away, three more security guards walked up to the ropes.

"Miss Alaysia, follow me, please," one of them said. Elise's ass was looking impressed as we were escorted by security. I couldn't believe all these people were inside, and the damn line was still around the corner. The men led us upstairs, and we ended up in an empty section that overlooked downstairs.

"This will be your personal VIP section. The bottles are yours, complimentary of the owner. If you need anything else, your waitress will get it for you. Enjoy your night." He walked off, and the other two security guards remained outside our ropes.

"Bitch, you done hit it big time. Too bad your ass about to rob his ass blind and take all his money."

"Bitch, shut up before someone hears you." I walked over to the rail and looked out over the club. I was trying to locate Tate when I spotted the Hoover Gang being escorted in. "Elise, come look at this shit. These niggas are made." She walked over, and we stood there watching them like we were some damn groupies. All four of them was fine as fuck. Each one had their own looks and ways about them, but every one of them would drive the women crazy. My eyes landed on Quick, and my pussy jumped. This nigga oozed sex appeal. He was looking fine as fuck, and his birth mark made him look more distinct. He didn't look all that black, and you could tell he was mixed with something. He had his hair curly tonight and combed back, and his no-nonsense look made my kitty jump. He was about six feet of pure "I'll fuck your ass right now." He wasn't as muscular as his brothers, but a bitch didn't mind. He was sexy as fuck, and I would have to make sure I got this shit over with soon. Tate would not like me being alone with him too much.

"Which one is Shadow?" Elise wasn't kidding, and I don't know why I thought she was.

"The darker one with the low fade."

This bitch started pulling her skirt up trying to make it appear shorter. I walked away from the banister and acted as if I didn't know they were there. There was no way I would let him look up, and he see me drooling like a damn groupie. Taking a seat, I sent Tate a quick message, just in case he didn't see me. It was too late to turn back now. The game was on.

Chapter 5

Shadow

I don't even know why I agreed to go out with these niggas. I had been waiting here for two hours for our meeting. Then we had to wait for Blaze's ass to finally get there and explain the plan to him. I already knew my girl was going to be pissed. I walked in the door and tried to play it off, like it was nothing, and started getting my clothes ready. I could feel her standing in the door waiting on me to look up. I continued to act like I didn't see her ass.

"Zavien, you just gon' act like you don't see me standing here?"

I finally looked up. "Hey, baby, what do you have planned for tonight?" I walked over to kiss her, but she pulled away.

"I planned to kick it with my man, but it looks like that's a no-go."

I could already feel the nagging coming, and I decided to try to avoid it. "Baby, we have some meetings with some potential clients tonight. I have to go. You know I'm the smart one out of the crew, and it's at Hoover Nights, not the strip club." I added that last fact in, hoping it would ease her mind.

"Nigga, a ho is going to be a ho, whether she sliding down the pole or popping it on the dance floor."

"If I wanted them, I wouldn't be with you. Let me get dressed. You know I hate to be late."

"When are you going to climb out of your brothers' ass and be your own man?"

She was starting to piss me off, and I could tell that's what she was going for. When I was a kid, I followed up behind my brothers everywhere they went. I wanted to be just like them. That's how I got my name. Zavien Shadow Hoover. Most people assumed it was because I was the darkest one. I'm 22 years old, and I got engaged last year. My fiancée was everything a man could dream. Shirree Taylor, a brown-skinned beauty in my eyes. She wore her natural hair in a flat wrap. She had big, pretty, doe eyes. When she talked, I would watch her lips, and my dick would get hard. She had a petite frame with just the right amount of curves. Most of all, she loved

a nigga. The moment I saw her, I knew I wanted
to marry her. My brothers clowned the shit out
of me right at my own party when I announced
the engagement. I had never been more embarrassed in my life. I didn't say a word, but not
because I was scared. I knew it would only add
fuel to the fire, and Blaze's ass is ignorant. He
would have sent the whole house up in flames.
Shirree was so hurt that I didn't stand up for her,
but she didn't know my brothers like I did. This
was how we fucked with each other. If I had tried
to jump Blaze's badass, they would have gotten
more ignorant just to get under my skin. Ever
since then, she's been throwing the shit in my
face. She knows it pisses me off when she does
that, but tonight, I wasn't biting. Her nagging is
half the reason I haven't set a date yet. Don't get
me wrong; I love my girl. I just think since that
night, she lost respect for me or some shit. We
haven't been the same; well, she hasn't. I'm the
same nigga I've always been.

"Get fucked up if you want to."

I walked away from her and jumped in the
shower. I had to find a way to make things right
between my bitch and me, or we were going to
be engaged forever. It's like she was determined
to make a nigga miserable. All I wanted was her
ass, but I wouldn't be disrespected in my own
house. I needed this drink I was about to have.

After throwing on my Gucci cardigan and jeans, I slid on my Tims and grabbed my keys. Knowing my brothers, they would all be in their Phantoms, so I jumped in mine as well. We always do the same thing. Whoever arrives first parks in front of the club, and the others line up behind him. You know I was there before everybody else, but thankfully, these niggas were right behind me. We all jumped out, and the hoes went crazy. Smiling and waving like we were famous, we headed in. I guess in Chicago we were famous, though. Our family ran this city, and we didn't plan on stopping any time soon. Our security made way for us to walk through the club without having to bump into anybody. They didn't allow anybody to get close. I guess the DJ got wind of us being in the building, and our song "B.M.F." by Rick Ross hit the speakers.

"I think I'm Big Meech, Larry Hoover. Whippin' work, hallelujah. One nation, under God. Real niggas gettin' money from the fucking start." Anytime my brothers and I walked in, this was the song the DJ played.

"Yo, show some love to my niggas. Hoover Gang is in the motherfucking building," the DJ screamed over the mic. The girls started running over immediately, only to get their feelings hurt by security. I looked up at our VIP section and saw two girls in it.

"Who are they up in our shit?" I looked over at my brothers.

"This bitch I met today, and I guess her plus one."

These niggas were always trying to impress some hoes. We walked up to the area and let ourselves in the ropes. My brother introduced everybody.

"Alaysia and plus one, these are my brothers. That's Blaze, Shadow, and Baby Face." We all nodded our heads at them, and I noticed the plus one was staring at me as she brought her dress up.

"Does plus one have a name?" I decided to ask. My rude-ass brothers would have called her plus one all damn night.

"I'm Elise, and you are?"

"Shadow." She was cute, but I could tell she wasn't my type. I didn't like loudmouthed bitches unless we were fucking. The bottles looked like they hadn't been opened, so I grabbed one. I handed the ladies a cup and then my brothers. The night was just beginning, and I was determined to get fucked up. I hadn't been out in a while, and I needed this night.

We were all having a good time when Elise came and sat on my lap and started grinding. Quick and his girl were in the corner caught up in a conversation, and Baby Face and Blaze were leaning over the rail drinking and watching the club. They were probably watching some bitches, but bottom line, they weren't over here with my ass. Reaching her hand underneath the table, she started grabbing my dick. Normally, I would have stopped her, but I was feeling myself, and I was feeling good. The liquor had me going, and she had me brick hard. That's why when she unzipped my pants, I didn't move. She hovered over me as she slid my dick out, and then slid right down on that motherfucker. The fact that she was fucking me with all these people around was turning me all the way on. Grabbing her hips, I tried to take control because she was fucking the shit out of me. I was trying not to be noticed, but she was bouncing her ass up and down on me so hard I couldn't do shit but enjoy the ride. Once she started tightening her muscles on my dick, I was a goner. Before I could realize I was about to nut, it was already shooting inside of her.

"Damn, plus one, you don't play no games, do you?" Blaze and Baby Face were just sitting there watching us. Before she could respond, shots rang out in the club. Pushing her up off me, I grabbed my gun and ran over to my brothers.

"Nigga, if you don't put your dick up, somebody gon' shoot that motherfucker off." Blaze laughed at me while I fixed myself. More shots rang out. It was time to get the fuck up out of there. I grabbed Elise, and Quick grabbed Alaysia, and security led us out the back door. We stood there waiting for them to bring us our cars.

"I'll make sure you get home safe. You can't get your car. I'll have them drop it off to you," Quick explained to Alaysia.

"But I drove with my sister," she whined.

"I'll make sure she gets home."

"I bet you will." Alaysia didn't look too happy when she responded. Our cars pulled up, and each of us got in. As soon as we pulled away from the others, Elise grabbed my dick out and began sucking the shit out of that motherfucker. I was about seven and a half inches, but she was swallowing that motherfucker like it was two. I almost forgot I was driving and went to lean my head back. Fuck. Let me get it together before we crash. I pulled over on the side of the road and let her have her way with that motherfucker.

This girl had a big appetite when it came to sex, but I had to get my ass home before my girl started tripping. She had just ridden me to the moon and back, and now she had my dick back in her mouth trying to revive it. He was dead and done. It was looking like a day-old Vienna sausage, and her ass was *still* sucking.

"Elise, he ain't waking back up. I need to drop you off and get my ass home." Sitting up, she wiped her mouth off and started adjusting her clothes.

"I'm sorry. It's been awhile, and the shit was bomb. I don't know how to act when I get good dick." There was no way I was going to believe she hadn't had sex in a while. She was too lit.

"It's all good. If I didn't have to go home, shit would be different. He still would have been asleep, but I would have let you keep trying to wake his ass up." She smiled at me as I continued to drive her home.

Pulling up to her spot, we hit an awkward silence. I decided to speak first. I reached in my glove box and grabbed a pen and paper.

"My battery's dead, but write your number down, and I will hit you up tomorrow." She grabbed the pen and started writing. I prayed my phone didn't start ringing. There was no way I was giving this bitch my number, and I had no intentions on seeing her again. It was fun for one night, but that's all this would ever be. She leaned in to kiss me and climbed out of my car. I jumped on the expressway and did 80 in a 60 all the way home, hoping that Shirree was already asleep when I got there, but knowing her ass, she was gon' be waiting for me at the door. That was the least of my problems. I had to figure out how the fuck to jump in the shower without her getting suspicious. If she was asleep, I would take one in the basement where she couldn't hear me. Please, Lord, let her ass be asleep.

Chapter 6

Alaysia

I didn't expect to get snatched up out of the club like that. I wanted to make sure my man was straight, but it would look too obvious if I took my ass back in a club where they were shooting. Sitting in the car with Quick, I was glad that he turned his music on. That gave me time to pull my phone out and check on Tate.

Me: Hey, baby, are you okay? Did you make it out of the club safely?

Tate: Yeah, I'm headed to your spot now. See you in a little while.

Me: No, he is driving me home right now. I don't want us to run into each other. I will call you when he leaves.

Tate: Make sure you do. Be safe.

When I put my phone back in my purse, Quick was looking at me. Trying to play it off, I placed my hand on his leg, hoping it would distract him.

I didn't know if he saw my messages or not, but I wasn't going to tell on myself. Grabbing my hand, he placed it on his dick, and I wasn't sure, but the motherfucker felt big as hell. I didn't want to encourage him, so I just let my hand lie there without moving it. Closing my eyes, I attempted to play asleep. Leaning my head back, I hoped he got the drift and realized wasn't shit shaking, and he could go on about his business. Feeling that the car stopped, I opened my eyes and grabbed my purse . . . only to realize I wasn't at home.

"This is not my house. Quick, where are we?"

"I said I would make sure you got home safe. I didn't say when." He didn't even allow me the chance to respond. The nigga just jumped out and walked over to my door and grabbed me by my hand.

"Quick, I need to go home." He tilted his head to the side and studied me for a minute.

"For what? You have a man? I don't do bitches who got niggas. The shit is too messy." Letting him slide with the bitch comment, I had to make an executive decision.

"Let's go." I would stay, but I wouldn't have sex with him. Needing him to trust me, going home wasn't an option. I could tell by the look on his face that if I left, I would lose him. They were about to be our biggest score. I could not allow him to walk away. When I walked into his place, the shit looked plain as fuck. How are you driving around in a Phantom, but you don't even have a TV in your place? It was a small house, and it was barely furnished.

"You live here?" I couldn't believe they supposedly had all this money, and this nigga's shit look like he got Section 8.

"This is just one of my places. It's closer to downtown, and I didn't feel like driving all the way home." In other words, this nigga done took me to his ho house. He doesn't trust me enough to let me know where he lays his head. Walking upstairs, he went and got in the shower. Debating on whether I should text Tate, I decided against it. He would only tell me to get the fuck home. This wasn't a part of the deal. Getting in his bed, I tried to force myself to sleep. I heard the shower stop, and I closed my eyes. I could feel his presence standing over me.

"Get the fuck out of my bed in them sweaty-ass clothes. Who the fuck raised your ass? Take a shower. There's some clean shit you can put on in the dresser. Towels are in the closet."

I opened my eyes, and this nigga was standing there in all his naked glory putting on lotion. He didn't even look up at me anymore, and I'm glad because my eyes were glued to his body like Gorilla Glue. He wasn't real big, but he was muscular. The complete view was nothing short of amazing. This nigga's dick was the biggest I had ever seen. Granted, I had only seen Tate's, but, damn, he was twice his size. That alone had me wet. I didn't think my coochie could take all of that, but it was damn sure good to look at.

Jumping up, I smacked my lips and stomped off into the shower. I didn't have an attitude, but I wanted him to think I did. Quick needed to stay his ass away from me. *Far* away from me. The whole time I was in the shower, I whispered to myself, "Stay focused. Stay focused." The shit wasn't working because I kept picturing his dick in my mind. Jumping out of the water, I hurried and threw his T-shirt on, not wanting him to get any ideas. When I walked out of the room, the nigga was in the bed butt naked and snoring. The fuck? Nigga ain't gon' even try to get the pussy. This some new shit here. Climbing in the bed, I felt appalled that the nigga went to sleep on me. Well, they say be careful what you ask for, but the shit was definitely a blow to my ego.

My eyes were still closed, but I could feel the sun on my face. My body was shaking because

Tate decided to wake me up with some morning head. Moaning, I opened my eyes so I could see my man eating his morning breakfast. Looking down, I started to panic. I forgot I spent the night with Quick. Conflicted, I didn't know what to do. My body was on fire, and I had never felt this way before. Tate was damn good, but this was a different kind of feeling. This shit was making my soul shift. I think my veins were coming this shit was feeling so good. Noticing that I was awake, he stood up and reached for a condom. Knowing I couldn't allow this to happen, I slid out of bed.

"I'm sorry, Quick. I can't do this." This nigga continued to put his condom on. Grabbing all of my stuff, I attempted to walk out of the door when the nigga grabbed me by my neck and slammed me against the wall.

"Where the fuck you think you going? Did I *say* you could leave?" Using his tongue to separate my lips, I struggled to turn away.

"You gon' rape me?"

Pushing my head to look down at his dick, he snapped at me. "Do it look like I need to rape a bitch? You gon' do it because you *want* to." I still tried to get away from him, so he grabbed me and slammed me against the dresser. Using his feet, he slid my legs apart while he held me down on the dresser. My body betrayed me when he slid his fingers inside my wet spot. Shit started running down my legs like I was pissing on myself. Wanting so badly to leave, I couldn't. Tate has never made my body react like this. My clit felt like it was about to bust open it was so swollen. By this time, I was praying he would put his dick inside me. As if he could hear what a bitch was thinking, his fingers were replaced by his meat. Sliding it up and down my slit, I braced myself for its entrance. When I say a bitch wasn't ready, I wasn't ready. It felt like my insides were ripping, he was so big. Trying to adjust myself to take it all in, he slammed me back down and made me take all of it. Nigga didn't even give me time to get used to it; he started tearing my ass up.

"You still want to leave? Huh? You want to go?" Now he was talking shit.

"No, don't stop." I don't know how I was going to fuck Tate after this. Shit, I don't even think I *want* to. This nigga was laying it down, and all I could do was scream and moan. My coochie finally got used to it, and I started throwing that shit back.

"That's right, baby, fuck this dick." The slaps on my ass caused me to nut involuntarily. My body started shaking, and I could feel his doing the same. After he released, the nigga slapped me on the ass and threw his pants on.

"Your car is outside. We gotta get up out of here. I got a run to make." This nigga was all energized, and all I wanted to do was lie back down. Getting my shit together, I walked out the door feeling bowlegged. This nigga done fucked me so hard, my kneecaps reversed. I couldn't wait to get home and lay my ass down. Giving me the most passionate kiss ever, he opened the door and helped me in my car. "I'll call you later, baby."

Pulling up to my crib, I got aggravated when I saw Tate's car. After fucking Quick, it made me realize I been getting cheated all this damn time. I was not in the mood to be looking at this little-dick nigga. I laughed to myself as I got out of my car. As soon as I stepped into the house, the questions started coming.

"Where the fuck have you been, and why are you walking like that?" He was pissed.

"Baby, I was thrown to the ground in the club. I hurt my damn hip and leg. I'm tired and sleepy. The nigga wanted to talk all damn night. He interrogated me like he was the damn police. I just want to lie down."

"Don't brush me off like I'm getting on your nerves. I was up all damn night worried about your ass. You could have sent a text or something."

"Baby, this was your plan. I didn't want him getting suspicious. Damn, are we gon' argue about this all day? I'm sorry, but I didn't want to jeopardize our shit."

"Did you fuck him?" Trying to look shocked, I almost bust out laughing because my coochie was *still* throbbing.

"Are you really going to ask me some shit like that? Have I *ever* fucked one of our marks?" His expression told me he was about to say something to piss me off.

"Why? This is a big mark. These niggas get pussy thrown at them every day. He not about to let you in on his shit, and you ain't giving it up."

I tried to play hurt. "I can't believe you want me to sleep with another man. That was *not* a part of the plan. I thought we were supposed to catch them in the act and then blackmail them?"

"Plans have changed. I been looking into these niggas. There's no way for us to catch them slipping if you aren't around. You need to stay around. I'm sorry to ask you this, but it's for us. It's for our future." He was pleading with me, and I wanted to laugh in his face. Like nigga, I pray he keeps fucking me.

"I have to sleep on this one. Let me lie down, and I will get back to you later."

Kissing me on my forehead, he headed to the door. "It's for us, baby. Just remember that."

When he walked out the door, I shook my head and went and climbed into bed. He has no idea what he is asking for. This was the first time I came from getting fucked, and I couldn't stop thinking about it. Smiling as I went to sleep, I hoped I had a dream about Quick.

Chapter 7

Blaze

"You sure this motherfucker is striker plated? Nigga, I will kill your ass if you give me a stolen car with stolen plates." I stopped by the chop shop to holla at my nigga, Vito. We always get our cars from him before a robbery. The last one he gave us was hotter than a bitch's pussy with gonorrhea.

"I checked it twice. This one is good, and it's on the house. My bad about the last one. I'll leave it on the lot, and you can pick it up when you need it."

"Don't play with me, boy. You know I will have your shop looking more Cajun than a-motherfucker." Dapping him up, I jumped back in my whip. We were about to hit up Fifth Third Bank, but my ass was hungry. I pulled up to my favorite soul food place called Priscilla's and jumped out. I blocked the entryway because they always have me in and out.

"You know you can't park there, right?" Looking over at some lame-ass nigga, I kept it moving. "I'm saying, when I come out, I don't want to try to get around this big-ass car, because you parking in the wrong spot."

"Nigga, get the fuck outta my face." Walking in the door, I tried to ignore his ass.

"You mad cus you doing some fucked-up shit. I tell you about young dumb niggas."

Laughing, I cut the line and went straight to the register.

"Hey, Blaze. You getting your usual?"

"Yea, baby girl. Make it quick. I gotta get up out of here."

"You know I always take care of you. Hey, Fred, bring me a fried chicken, yams, and mac." I handed her a fifty.

"Keep the change." In two minutes, they were bringing my food out.

"See you next time, Blaze."

Flashing my smile at her, I walked back through the crowd. The nigga from the parking lot was smacking his teeth. I was going to let him live, but I decided against it since his ass don't know when to shut the fuck up. I walked out and went to my trunk. Grabbing a towel, I walked over to his car and opened the gas tank. I lit the motherfucker and jogged my ass back to the car.

By the time I hit Roosevelt Road, I had heard the explosion. Laughing, I wish I didn't have shit to do, or I would have stayed to see his face. Niggas just don't know when to shut the fuck up.

As soon as I walked into the office, my brothers started in on my ass.

"It was you, wasn't it?" Shadow was pissed off as usual.

"What the fuck y'all talking about?"

"Nigga, somebody blew a nigga's car up in Priscilla's parking lot." Quick was laughing like he already knew it was me.

"Naw, I ain't did shit." I pulled out my food and started eating it.

"Nigga, if I don't know shit else, I know Priscilla's. Something is wrong with your ass. Hurry the fuck up and eat, nigga, so that we can get this show on the road." Baby Face barked out orders as usual.

"Let me get a wing, bro."

"Here, Quick, damn." Handing him a wing, I ate my food, then got up and changed my clothes. "Y'all niggas ready?"

"Fuck, yea." Quick's ass was always ready.

"Let's go." Walking out the door, we saw a chick walking to her car. The bitch was bad as fuck. She was in between brown-skinned and light-skinned. Her hair was cut short on the sides and the back. She was about five foot five and thick, how I like my bitches. Passing up my brother's truck, I walked over to help her in the car.

"Let me get that for you." She looked up at me, and my dick jumped. She was even prettier up close.

"You don't look like the type that opens doors."

"I'm not. So shut the fuck up and let a nigga try to show off." Most bitches would have been offended, but not her. She laughed as if I were making a joke.

"OK, but don't take all day to ask for my number. I got shit to do." Smiling, I pulled out my phone.

"I'm Blaze. I'm in a rush myself. So, what's your number?"

"I'm Drea." After she gave me her number, I told her I would hit her later and jogged back to the truck.

"Who the fuck stops in the middle of a bank robbery attempt to get a number?" Baby Face shook his head as he pulled off.

"Me, nigga, that's who. Now, drive and let's get this shit over with."

"You ain't gon' do shit but fuck her and duck her."

Quick was right. I didn't trust these hoes, but I will fuck these hoes. I didn't date the same bitch longer than a week. All the hoes in Chicago were the same to me. They see a nigga with money and go out of their way to trap his ass. These bitches steal, could barely fuck, can't cook, and have a house full of kids they want you to take care of. I was straight. I loved my life the way it was, and I had no intentions on changing. Some niggas not meant to be tied down. I was like a bad lace front . . . You can't hold me down.

After changing whips, we pulled up to the bank and threw on our masks. Pulling our hoodies on tight, we grabbed our guns and the bags and jumped out of the beater. Shadow stayed in the car like always.

"Everybody get on the fucking floor. If you move, I shift your hairline back," I yelled, pointing my guns at the customers. Quick jumped up on the counters to make sure the tellers didn't hit the silent alarm. "We have one minute. Let's get it." Baby Face walked to the vault with the key I had given him and went in to grab the money.

"Bitch, quit blinking so much. You making me nervous." I couldn't tell if the ho was trying to signal someone or if she had a condition. "Thirty seconds." Screaming loud enough so my brother could hear me in the vault, I walked around the room to make sure nobody tried anything stupid. I stood over this bitch with a fat-ass booty. She was lying down, but her shit looked like it was still standing up.

"Nigga, quit looking at ass and focus," Quick yelled at me.

Putting my attention back on everyone else, I glanced back at her ass one last time.

"It's time, my niggas, let's roll." Baby Face came running from the back with the bags full, and we headed toward the door. When I passed the bitch with the fat ass, I leaned down and smacked that motherfucker.

"Bitch, I would fuck you raw and make you swallow my babies."

"Nigga, let's go." Quick was holding the door for me. We jumped back in the beater, and Shadow drove off.

"What the fuck took y'all so long? We never go over time."

"This nigga Blaze wanted to play in a bitch's booty hole and shit."

Laughing at Baby Face, I wish I had met her somewhere else because I would definitely be hitting that shit tonight.

As soon as we got back to the office, I jumped in my car and called Drea. I was going to fuck somebody tonight, and I preferred it to be her.

"What you got planned later?"

"Nothing. Was just sitting around the house." Her voice was soft, but you can tell she had a little hood in her.

"Text me your address. I'ma come grab you in like an hour. Is that cool?"

"Yeah, I'll be ready." Hanging up, I flew my ass home so I could shower and change clothes.

Chapter 8

Drea

I tried to play it cool when I met Blaze earlier. That nigga was "throw your draws in the garbage" cus he got them too wet, but I didn't want to come across thirsty. He was dressed in all-black, but something about him screamed money. Not that it mattered to me, though, because I was set for life. My husband was damn near a king in these streets. Andrea Edwards was my name, and I am 25 years old. My husband G Money and I had only been married six months when he got murdered. Being the only person that knew where all his money was, I got it all. Knowing how people are, especially my brother, I played it cool like I didn't have much. My mother only had two kids, I was the youngest, but you couldn't tell by the way my brother acted. Michael "Slick" Edwards. The nigga was a snake. He didn't care who he crossed to get what he wanted, but at the end of the day, I loved him. He was the only family I had left. I let him live with me after he got out of jail, and I regret that shit every day. My house is always filled with niggas while they go over get-rich-quick schemes. There is no doubt in my mind if he knew how much I really had, he would rob me blind. Making sure my shit looked nice, I knew I couldn't deck my shit out because he would start putting two and two together. Texting Blaze my address, I got out of my Lexus and went into the house. As usual, my brother and his friends were in there talking about some bullshit.

"Nigga, I'm telling you, we need to hit the spot tonight. If we wait, they gon' know it was us." "Slick" was trying to convince his homies to do some bullshit.

"Slick, your ass never think shit through. That's why shit always going wrong. You need to have a plan first." I agreed with his friend Pooh silently as I made my way through the front room.

"Sis, I need like $500. Me and the crew wanna go out tonight, but they scary ass don't want to rob the store. You got me?" Knowing I really didn't have a choice, I agreed.

"Yeah, I got you. I'm about to go out myself. I got a date."

"He better not be no fuck nigga. You know I don't play about my sister."

"I know, I know. Let me go get ready before I don't have a date at all." Walking in my room, I closed the door and locked it. I had some money stashed in my house, but I never wanted Slick to know that, or he would hit it every time he wanted some. Knowing that nigga, he would probably take it all. Taking out $500, I started grabbing clothes to get ready. I didn't know where we were going so I grabbed some jeans and a see-through white tank, a burgundy bra, and my burgundy Guess heels. I wanted to be dressed for whatever.

By the time I was done getting ready, my phone had gone off. It was Blaze letting me know he was outside. Grabbing my clutch, I walked out of my room and locked the door. My brother and his friends were still there, but they were just sitting around waiting for me.

"Here. Try not to spend it all, Slick. Money don't grow on trees."

"Thank you. Let me walk you out and make sure you not leaving with a clown-ass nigga."

I shook my head and allowed him to walk me out the door. Blaze was in a black Maybach, and he had that bitch shining. I wish I could stunt with my money like that, but I had to play it cool if I didn't want everybody begging. Sitting down in the car, I got ready to close the door when my brother screamed out to me.

"Be safe and have fun." He was never this nice about me leaving with a nigga. When I looked up, he had this look on his face I couldn't recognize. It was almost as if he were happy. I couldn't focus on him right now, though, I was about to enjoy my date.

"Hey, handsome, I see you upgraded from earlier." He was looking and smelling fine as fuck.

"You looking pretty good yourself."

"Where are we headed?"

"Out to eat at The Godfrey downtown. You been there?"

"Naw, I haven't, but I love to eat, so I hope your ass ain't a cheap nigga."

"I should have known your ghetto ass haven't been here, and anything over fifty dollars you paying for it yourself."

We both started laughing. Any other bitch would have been mad or offended, but from my experience, the niggas that talk the most shit be the sweetest. He was funny to me, and I didn't mind the shit talking.

"I'll dine and dash on your fine ass before I pay a bill." He looked over at me to make sure I was joking. I'm guessing he has had that experience before.

"I will set your ass on fire if you embarrass me like that." I laughed, but for some reason, he didn't. I shrugged it off, and we continued our back-and-forth until we got to the place. The shit was beautiful. It was on the roof, and it was set up all classy and shit. They had a live band, and it was actually kind of lit. The crowd was mixed, but I didn't care because I was with the finest nigga up there. Something about him just seemed right. Nothing felt forced, and everything just flowed. I could get used to this.

After we finished our food and the bill came, I reached for it, and he laughed.

"I'm not that nigga that won't let you pay. You reach for it again, you stuck with that motherfucker." I grabbed the bill and laughed at him. "You think I'm playing, but if you don't have enough, your ass gon' be washing dishes, cus I'm telling you now, I'm not paying that motherfucker." Glancing down at our $300 bill, I reached in my clutch and pulled out my debit card. Sliding it in, I set it back on the table and continued our conversation.

"I'm still waiting on you to tell me why you don't trust bitches."

Staring at me for a few moments, he had this look in his eye. His once ice-cold grey eyes seemed to soften.

"They only after one thing. My name. I don't have time for the bullshit, and I like the way my life is now. Everybody not meant to be in a relationship."

"Everybody after your name? Blaze?"

"You don't know who I am?"

"I know that you are Blaze. That is all that you told me. *Should* I know?" While he studied my face to see if I was lying, I pulled my phone out.

"What are you doing?"

"Shit, I'm googling Blaze. You won't tell me who you are, and I need to know who I'm around." The waitress brought my card back; I signed and left a twenty-dollar tip. "I think I have a right to know who I'm seeing."

"Baby girl, you don't know how good it is to hear that shit, but I'm nobody. Just a nigga trying to make it like everybody else. You won't find shit on Google with your slow ass. Come on." We left, but I was still curious about who he was. I would definitely find out. He had me fucked up if he thought I was going to be around here hugged up with a nigga I didn't know. When I got home, I was going to make sure I did some digging to find out. All I had to do was ask my brother because his ass knew everybody, but I didn't want him in my business like that. Tomorrow, I would do my searching, but tonight, I would enjoy my date. We headed to the lakefront where we sat and talked the night away. I was feeling Blaze. I just hoped he was feeling me too.

Chapter 9

Baby Face

Since all my brothers were busy, I headed to the bank to deposit our earnings from the clubs last night. They were doing damn good, and I was happy we were bringing in so much that we were able to clean our dirty money. However, as soon as I walked in the door, I got irritated. The motherfucker was packed, but my view was great. The girl standing in front of me was thick as hell. Most people would consider her a BBW, but I would call her ass country thick. She looked like she was slugging midgets in the back of her dress. Her hair was fire red and in some kind of big, curly 'fro, but not that nappy shit. It was big-ass curls. Wondering if it was real, I was rubbing my fingers in it before I realized what I was doing. She turned around with fire in her eyes . . . until she looked into mine.

"That's rude as fuck. You do know that, right?" She was trying to act mad, but her eyes told a different story. She was beautiful and not in a fake kind of way. Her hair was real, and I loved that shit.

"I'm sorry. I was just wondering if your hair was fake since it was so big and pretty."

"You could have asked. I don't even know you, and that's just something you don't do."

Loving her feistiness, I wanted to get to know her better. "What's your name? Let me guess . . . Red."

"That's so cliché. It's Juicy, and yours?"

"Having a fat ass and the name Juicy ain't cliché?"

Thinking it over, she laughed. "I guess you're right, but my name was Juicy before I got all this ass. I was a chunky li'l girl. You still have not told me your name." Knowing she was going to say my name is cliché, I damn near gave her a fake one.

"Baby Face."

Laughing at me, I already knew it was coming. "That shit is *definitely* cliché, but it fits you."

"Juicy fits you as well. By the way, that is one big ass." Trying to contain myself, I almost smacked that motherfucker when she turned around to move up. It jiggled every time she moved. We stood there talking shit and laughing until it was our turn in line. I finished before she did because they already knew what to do with my shit, so I stood there and waited on her. Walking out of the bank I was thinking there was no way I was letting her get away without taking my number . . . until she pulled her phone out.

"That's your phone, Juicy?"

She looked up at me like we were still in joking mode. "Yup. You don't like my phone?" She was laughing, but I was dead-ass serious.

"I don't do Androids. I'm sorry, babes."

When she finally realized I was serious, she snapped. "Are you serious? I know your ass is not that stuck-up."

"Stuck up like a dick first thing in the morning. I hate that green text shit, and then I have to explain what emoji I'm sending because y'all don't get them. Slow-ass text and shit. I need to see that bubble and know you responding to me. Won't act like you ain't get my shit."

By this time, her face was as red as her hair. She was pissed. "That's some girly-ass shit right there, but you can have that."

Before I walked off, I decided to piss her off a little more. "You too good looking to be walking around with that thot-ass phone. When you upgrade, come holla at me." Before she could respond, I walked off. My phone rang as I jumped in my Maybach.

"What's up, Blaze? Where y'all at?"

"Chilling until later. I'm going to the strip club tonight."

"I'm rolling with you. I need to see some ass to get my mind off this chick I just met."

"You didn't get her number? Her ass must have been flatter than a twelve-year-old boy's chest."

"Naw, her ass was fat as hell. She had a fucking Android phone."

"Hell, naw, I would have set that bitch's nipple on fire. Fuck she thought this was."

Laughing at him, I'm glad it was him I was having this conversation with. He was the only brother that shared my feelings about an iPhone.

"I'm gon' meet up with you later. I haven't been there to check on the girls in a while."

"A'ight. Bet. I'll hit up the other two and see if they want to roll." Hanging up, I rode to the house to catch a nap. We didn't go to the strip club that much, but when we did, it was always lit. We had the baddest hoes, and they knew how to work that pole. Maybe tonight I would finally let them work my pole. I was backed up, and I'm too fly to be out here jacking my dick off, wondering if I had fucked up because I couldn't get

Juicy's thick ass off the brain. Maybe I should have gotten her email. Laughing at myself, I lay it down to take my nap.

Somebody was about to get this good dick in they life. Trying to talk myself into it, I lay down because everybody knows I'm picky. "Tsunami" is not allowed to go inside of any and everybody. Once I put it on they ass, bitches be losing their minds, and I'm not with the drama. I'm the laid-back brother, but I will shut shit down. Finally dozing off, I hoped I dreamed about Juicy's fat ass.

Waking up to Tsunami brick hard, I jumped my ass in the shower to calm his ass down. You ain't getting no pussy tonight, so sit your ass down. After I washed my ass and brushed my teeth, I grabbed my clothes to get dressed. Being a slim nigga, I had to make sure I stayed fresh to death. Chicks was after the heavier-built niggas nowadays. Rocking my Gucci cardigan, jeans, and gym shoes, I threw on a pair of Gucci shades as well to be extra. Since I had on red and black, I jumped in my all-red custom G-Wagon. Not being able to find that right chick was having me in a funk. Nobody wants to hit 30 single than a motherfucker. Well, at least *I* didn't. A nigga was looking for his Bonnie, but that bitch was hiding from a real nigga like me. Getting fly always made me feel better. It was what I did best.

Driving to Diamond in the Rough, I turned on some make-me-feel-better music. Lil' Wayne always had me feeling cocky. Bumping "I get it in," I headed to the club. When I pulled up, I saw my brothers' Phantoms parked in a row waiting on me. I didn't even know them niggas was coming for sure. Without even hearing him, I bet Shadow's ass been talking shit the whole time.

Pulling up last in the line, we got out, doing our normal Hollywood routine. It's a lot more ratchet here because all the chicks are normally looking for a come-up, and they don't care who knows it. We were escorted straight to our VIP section, which gave us the perfect view of the club and the ladies. We were behind the stage, but it sat up over them like a DJ booth. I loved it because it really gave the illusion that we were making it rain when we threw money at them.

"Baby bro, how the hell did you convince Shirree's crazy ass to let you come out to the strip club tonight?" He hadn't been to the strip club in over a year.

"I told her ass I was going, and there wasn't shit she could do about it." Laughing, we knew the nigga was lying. "For real, though, I told her ass we had a meeting at Hoover Nights. Just so y'all know in case she asks." Shadow was pleading with us to lie for him.

"You know I'm gon' tell her ass the truth and set her lashes on fire if she says anything smart." Shadow knew he had to keep his girl from around Blaze for a while because he would do just that. The DJ started speaking into the mic.

"Y'all know what today is—Amateur Wednesday. Any girl from the audience can come on stage and see if they have what it takes to get these niggas to make it rain. Y'all get an hour before the pros come out here and show y'all how it's *really* done. Any takers? Aww, shit, the birthday girl thinks she has what it takes. Help her to the stage." He started playing "Hammer Time" by Big Sean and Nicki Minaj when I saw her. I would never forget that ass or her hair. Juicy got her thick ass on the stage and started dancing like it's what she did for a living. Not even realizing I was in a trance, I walked over to the rail and reached in my pocket. Knowing I was coming to the strip club, I made sure I brought five stacks of one-dollar bills. I was generous, but I wasn't into giving strippers all my money. Pulling out the five stacks, I started making it rain as she twerked and slid up and down the pole. I made sure I gave her every last dollar and not just because I wanted her, but she earned every damn bill. Walking over to my brothers, I was hoping they brought more money than I did.

"One of y'all give me some more money."

"Nigga, you just gave her ass two mortgage payments." Blaze was talking shit as usual.

"That's the girl from earlier. Give me some more money, nigga; damn." He reached in his pocket, and his cheap ass gave me two stacks. Not having time to argue, I took it and walked back to the banister. The DJ was boosting it up.

"Aww, shit, girl, you better shake that ass. You got a Hoover boss loving that shit." She never paid attention to where the money was coming from until he said that. She turned around and looked me dead in my eyes right before she went down in a split. I started throwing the rest of my money, never taking my eyes off her. When the song ended, I was low-key pissed. She put on one hell of a show, and if I wasn't trying to get with her, I would have tried to hire her ass. As good as she danced, she probably already worked at another strip club. Walking over to security, I told him to get her and her friends. Sitting back down, I waited until she came up. When they got up there, she looked even better up close. She had on all-black, a see-through black tank, some black booty shorts, and some red heels. After I introduced her to everybody, security brought her money up, and I handed it to her.

"Maybe now you can buy a new phone."

"Is that why you threw all your money at me? Sorry, baby, I am *nobody's* charity case." She handed back to me all of my money. This nigga Blaze actually sat there and grabbed all of his money out of the pile.

"You're not a charity case, sweetheart. You earned every dollar I threw at you. Let me talk to you for a minute." When we sat down, she laid her purse and phone on the table. "I had no right treating you like that, but I meant what I said. If you want to date me, you need a new phone. Is that too much to ask?"

"Yeah, it is, for a nigga I don't even know if I'm going to be talking to in a week. You telling me, every girl you met had an iPhone?"

"Actually, they did. Everybody has their thing; this is mine, and I'm asking you to just do this one thing for me. I'm worth it, babes." She looked like she was thinking it over when we saw a big-ass flame.

"Problem solved. I burned the bitch up. Now, you don't have a choice. Get you a new phone, shorty. This shit has been cremated." Trying my best not to bust out laughing in her face, I looked over at her phone, and Blaze's ass had it sitting in a cup of alcohol, and that motherfucker was cooking.

"Really? This the kind of goofball shit y'all do? It's my motherfucking birthday, and I'm sitting here getting insulted over a fucking phone."

"You better calm that shit down, shorty, before I torch that motherfucking wig on your head."

I knew Blaze was going to go in, so I tried to smooth it over. "Let me take you tomorrow to get you another one. I'll pay for it, and I'm sorry we ruined your birthday." Looking like she wanted to cry, she reluctantly agreed. Trying to lighten the mood, I pulled her to me.

"Can I get a private dance? Gon' and twerk that shit for a nigga like you was just doing down there."

Smiling again, she got up and started grinding on me so good I almost came in my fucking jeans. She was going to be mine. I would make sure of that . . . after she got her new phone, though. Something about her was driving a nigga crazy, and I was ready to see what it was.

"My hair is real, though, asshole. Don't act like I didn't hear that shit," she yelled over to Blaze.

"Them eyelashes ain't, and if you keep talking shit, your ass gon' be looking up at Baby Face like Mike was looking at Joe leaving that Pepsi commercial." Looking over at me, I could tell she wanted me to defend her.

"Juicy, please, let it go. I swear that nigga dead-ass serious, and I can't be with no bald-headed chick with patches." She laughed, but I was dead ass. I hope she didn't say shit else to him, or she would see he was too. Thankfully, she didn't say shit else. I enjoyed her bouncing her ass up and down on my dick. She was going to be mine, all right.

Chapter 10

Shadow

Ever since the other night when we went out to Hoover Nights, my girl has been tripping. When I walked in the house, she was waiting for me at the door. Walking right past her ass, I went upstairs and lay down. There was no way she was going to let me get in the shower. As soon as she started in, I tuned her ass out and went to sleep. I woke up the next morning to a million *who is she* questions. I was too young for this shit, and I just wanted peace in my home. My girl was the shit to everyone except herself. No bitch could compare to her ass, and all I wanted was her, but she didn't see that. The nagging and constant complaining was getting on my fucking nerves. When a nigga comes home from a long, tiresome day, all we want is peace and happiness with our girl. A home cooked meal and some sex. That was all we needed. We were simple.

All the extra shit is what makes a nigga stray. I'm not even the cheating type, but Shirree's ass done had me on restriction since that night. Me being drunk and horny, I decided to text Elise. I had no intentions on ever seeing Elise again, but my girl had been working my nerves for the last week. The next day after the club, I went to my car and got Elise's number. We have been texting each other ever since, but I had seen her.

Me: What you doing?

Elise: Nothing, just lying around.

Me: You want some company?

Elise: Sure.

Me: Text the address. I'm on the way.

Letting my brothers know I was about to head out, I jumped in the Ghost and was out. Sober enough to drive but too fucked up to pay attention to my surroundings, I drove to Elise's house without a care in the world. When I got to her door, I rang the bell and waited for her to answer. She opened it, and she was butterball naked. My dick went brick immediately. Seeing how it was pushing against my jeans, she wasted no time pulling him out. Walking over to the couch, I sat down because I wasn't gon' be able to keep my balance. As soon as she put my dick in her mouth, I was in heaven. My girl was a beast in the bed, but Elise handled my curve

better. She knew how to suck it just right so that
the whole dick could still go down her throat. As
good as her shit was, I would rather be home
with my girl, but right now, I needed to nut, and
I came where I knew she would be ready to give
me what I needed. My dick swelling up brought
me back to why I was here. This girl had me
ready to come, and she had only just started.

"Wait a minute, baby. I want to feel that pussy.
Bend over." She turned around and bent over
on the floor. Praying I didn't get carpet burn, I
kneeled and rubbed my dick up and down her
pussy. As soon as I stuck the tip in, someone
kicked in the door.

"What the fuck! Shirree, baby, what are you
doing here?"

"I knew there was another bitch, but you lied
to my fucking face. I hope she was worth it
because I'm *done*."

"Can you let me explain?" I hadn't even realized that Elise had turned back around to
face me and that my dick was still standing at
attention.

"Explain *what,* Shadow? How you were about
to fuck another bitch raw?" Not even realizing
it, this was the second time I was about to fuck
Elise without a condom. The liquor had my ass
tripping. Still kneeling there like a dumb ass

with my dick out, Elise's disrespectful ass didn't even care that my fiancée was standing here hurt beyond measure. She started sucking my dick.

"Baby, I'm drunk. I swear I didn't mean this shit."

"Nigga, you must be high. You gon' actually sit there and let this ho keep sucking your dick in my face?"

Fuck! My dumb ass forgot to tell her to stop. "Shirree, I promise you it's not like that. This is the first time this has ever happened, and I didn't even get it in." The look on her face scared me.

"Nigga, you got three seconds to get this bitch's mouth off your dick, or I am killing both of you motherfuckers."

I can't believe my dumb ass still forgot to stop her. "Elise, baby, can you stop? I need to talk to my girl."

Shirree walked over and slapped the taste out of my mouth. "'Baby'? You gon' sit here and call this bitch 'baby'? You can have this ho." She turned around to walk out. As I stood up to go after her, I realized Elise never stopped sucking my dick. Once my girl was out of the room, and my focus returned, I realized my dick was brick hard, and my veins were bulging.

"You have to stop. I need to go after her." I don't know if it was the liquor, lack of sex, or bomb-ass head, but I sat there and allowed what happened next to go on. Elise stood up over me and pushed me back. Before I could respond, she slid down on my dick and started riding the shit out of that motherfucker.

"You already put out; you may as well get the pussy." Made perfect sense to me. I wrapped my hands around her waist and guided her up and down on my dick like there was no tomorrow. It would probably be a long time before I got some more pussy, so I better make this count.

"Fuck, ride this dick, girl." She squeezed her muscles as she went up and down on my shit. Slapping her on her ass as she rode me only made it worse. Before I knew it, I was shooting my nut up her pussy like she belonged to me. Damn near unable to move, she slid off me, and I closed my eyes.

"Get me a towel." Once I felt the warmness on my dick, it took me about five seconds to realize it wasn't a towel; it was her mouth. Thinking my dick was out for the count, that motherfucker rose up like Lazarus.

"We have to stop; I need to go home." But that shit fell on deaf ears. All I heard was moaning and slurping sounds causing my dick to hit the back of her throat. Knowing I was about to get killed for this stunt I was about to pull, I said the words anyway.

"Turn over." Like last time, she did exactly as she was told. As I slid my dick inside her asshole, I wondered what was going through Shirree's mind when I didn't run out after her. I was dead-ass wrong, but right now, I was about to get this last nut. I would face the consequences later.

When I finally got home two hours later, I had the dumbest look on my face because I didn't know what to say. Every time I got ready to leave, Elise would start sucking me off, and I swear my dick stood up every time. From this day forward, I was done drinking. I couldn't believe I had done this dumb-ass shit, and my girl caught me. Walking in the house, it scared me because it was too quiet. When I got up to the bedroom, I opened the door and out of nowhere . . . *Bang!* This motherfucker shot at me.

"Are you crazy? Put the gun down before I beat your ass."

"You got five seconds to get the fuck out of my house before I kill you where you stand. Your bitch ass sat there and let her suck your dick in my face, and then you stayed another two hours to finish what you started. I am done, and if you want to walk out of here alive, I suggest you leave me now."

Shirree wasn't a physical person. That's why she didn't attack Elise, but seeing her stand here with a gun pointed at me, I knew I had crossed a line. I was not about to let my fiancée walk out of my life, but tonight was not the night to try to get her to listen. She was hurt and pissed, and I was tipsy and smelling like sex. It would be best for both of us if I just left right now. Walking to the closet, I grabbed a few things and threw them in my Gucci duffle bag. No, I wasn't walking away from my fiancée, but I needed a damn good excuse and plan before I tried to win her back. Walking out of the bedroom, I turned to her one last time before I walked out.

"I love you, baby, and I am sorry. I will fix this." *Bang!* The crazy bitch shot at me again. Jumping in my whip, I drove to the only place I knew I could at this time of night. As I stood on the porch, I thought about the dumb shit I pulled on the only woman I ever loved.

"I knew you was going to come back." Pulling me inside, Elise grabbed my dick out of my pants and started sucking on this motherfucker like it was her last meal.

"Fuck, girl, you are going to get me killed." Not only was I shocked I came back over here, but I was even more shocked my dick stood back up for her, and the motherfucker stood right up like we didn't just fuck for two hours. As soon as she started with the slurping and moaning, I felt my nut rising. Fuck my life. After all was said and done, and the liquor began to wear off, I realized how much I truly fucked up. I prided myself on being faithful to my girl. Her attitude has been fucked-up lately, but she was the only chick for me. She had my back like no other, and I knew I had just hurt her deeply. Not knowing how I was going to fix this, I knew that leaving Elise alone is where I would start. This bitch had to kick rocks before she made me lose my fiancée.

Chapter 11

Drea

My date with Blaze was nothing short of amazing, but I'm still pissed he won't tell me who he is. That was okay, though, because I invited my bitches over tonight, and I knew they would help me figure it out. They were more like my sisters instead of my friends. They were there for me when my husband died and stayed by my side when my mom passed away. I never had to wonder if they were real or not. We been down with each other since we were kids, and nothing would change that. Paris owned a boutique downtown Chicago, and she was one badass stylist. Most people tried to throw shade because she was a BBW, but that ho would outslay a slim chick any day. Panda was the hairdresser. Working at a shop out west, she had so many clients we could barely get some free time out of her ass, but no matter what, she would come and slay our shit whenever we needed her. Ash owned a day care. I don't see how she did it because those kids were bad as hell. I tried to help her out one day and help her teach since she was short staffed, but I ended up the one learning the lesson. I knew then that I didn't want any children. Walking in the front room, I could feel my temperature rising because my brother and his friends were in there—as usual.

"I'm telling you, it was that nigga. You know I don't forget a come-up." Slick was excited about a new lick.

"All I'm saying is, you been wrong before, and you not about to send me off." Pooh was here so much you would think he lived here.

"Nigga, I'm never wrong, and even when I'm wrong, I coulda been right," he said, laughing because he was trying to say my favorite line from *Get Rich or Die Tryin'*.

"What the fuck ever, my nigga. Just ask her." Tired of hearing them go back-and-forth, I finally let my presence be known. I needed them to leave so I could clean up for my company.

"I hate to break y'all's shit up, but my girls are about to come over, and I need y'all to find another spot to kick it tonight."

"We like bitches; why we can't stay?" My brother knows damn well he and his homies don't have a chance with my friends.

"Because it's girls' night, and my bitches bad and bougee. They are not checking for y'all." Picking up garbage, I looked back at them because they still hadn't moved. "Why are y'all still here? I allow y'all to kick it here every day. I'm asking for one, damn." Finally realizing I was getting pissed, my brother stood up and told his crew they were out.

"Let's roll. I ain't trying to hear this shit tonight. Sis, you got some money?" Rolling my eyes, I reached in my purse and grabbed what was in there.

"This it?"

Knowing it wasn't anything less than two hundred dollars, I got pissed. "You can give it back, or you can get a job. The fuck you think this is?" Talking shit under his breath, they left. Continuing to clean up, I cut the music on and tried to break out of the mood my brother put me in. Lighting candles and spraying my house,

I finished just in time. My bitches walked in, and I was happy as hell to see them.

"What's up, bitches?" Hugging each of them, I was excited, and it showed. "I'm surprised Joe let you unwrap your lips from his dick long enough for a girls' night." Ash, Panda, and I laughed, but Paris rolled her eyes.

"You tried it, but I sucked it so good, he fell asleep. He'll be knocked out until I get home." Her freak ass stayed fucking, and I didn't see how they had time for anything else.

"What's been going on with you, and what the hell is so important? I cancelled two heads for this get-together." Panda always complained when she had to cancel a client, but deep down, I think she was happy as hell to get away.

"Damn, let me get y'all some drinks first." Getting the cups and the liquor, I walked back over to my girls to explain how I needed their help. "So, I met this guy."

"Yes, bitch, yes. I'm so happy for you." Ash was the sweet, innocent one, and she wanted everybody in love.

"Gah, she ain't even said shit yet." Paris was about to get started, but I cut her off. I needed them to focus.

"He keeps saying it's refreshing to date a girl that doesn't know who he is and don't want him for his name. I asked who is he, and he won't tell me. All I know is his nickname, and I feel some kind of way that I don't know who I'm dating. He is fine as hell, and our date was amazing, but I need to know this nigga before we go any further." Looking around the room, I waited for them to respond.

"Well, are you gon' tell us his nickname? Damn. What we supposed to do? Walk up to every fine-ass man in Chicago?" Panda was looking at me like I lost my mind.

"My bad. His name is Blaze, and that's all I know."

"Zayn Blaze Hoover, age 26, has three brothers, and they own two clubs. Bitch, where the fuck did you meet him?" Paris's ass always knew the tea.

"I was coming out of the store, and he ran up on me. Scared the shit out of me too because the nigga was dressed in all-black. I thought he was about to rob me. How do you know him?"

"Bitch, what rock do you live under? My ass is a lame, and even *I* know who he is." If Ash knew, then I should be ashamed of myself.

"All they ass is fine, but, bitch, you got the craziest one. Did he tell you how he got his name?" Paris was waiting for me to respond, but I just shook my head no. "Bitch, he will set anything on fire if you piss him off. All of them are crazy, but he is a special kind of crazy. And he don't like bitches."

"He gay?" Panda, Ash, and I all screamed at the same time.

"Naw, he one of them mean-ass niggas that don't trust shit a bitch say. He fucks and ducks. Have your ass rethinking your life."

Thinking about what she was saying, maybe it wasn't a good idea for me to mess with him. Just as I thought I should leave him alone, my phone rang.

"Hey, cutie. What you up to tonight?"

"Hanging out with my girls."

"Can I see you once they leave?" Thinking about it, I decided to tell him my feelings face-to-face.

"Okay, I'll text you once they're gone." When I hung up, their asses were all smiling at me. "What the hell y'all smiling for?"

"Because I never thought you would date somebody else after G Money, but look at you.

I'm happy for you." Ash was acting like we just confessed our love.

We continued to turn up until Paris's ass had to leave. I immediately texted Blaze. Waiting on him to come over, I jumped in the shower. Even though I didn't plan on giving him any, I had been out and about all day, and I needed to clean this thang. After drying off, I rubbed lotion all over and threw on some pink shorts and a tank. Sliding on some footies, I felt relaxed.

As soon as I sat down, the doorbell rang. Walking to the door, I got butterflies in my stomach. When I opened it, I hated that I hadn't put on any panties. I was so wet the shit might start leaking down my legs. He was standing there with this sexy-ass smile, flicking a lighter. His grey eyes were making my heart skip a beat. My eyes stopped at his lips. Lord knows I wanted to suck those lips. Seeing that they were moving, I tried to focus on what he was saying.

"You gon' leave me out here in the cold, or are you gon' let me in, girl?" Blushing, I moved out of the way and allowed him into the front room. What I really wanted to do was allow him into my bed. "How did your girls' night go?" he asked while pulling me to sit down on his lap. Feeling his print through his jeans made me grind a little. I didn't do the shit on purpose; it was more like instinct.

"It was cool. How did your day go, Zayn?" Looking up at me, he studied me for a while and then pushed me off his lap. Standing up, he walked toward the door. "Did I do something wrong?" Confusion filled my face as he twisted the knob.

"You ain't no different than these other bitches. Lose my fucking number." He practically barked it at me.

"Excuse me?"

"You heard what the fuck I said," he threw over his shoulder as he turned to walk out the door.

"Fuck you then with your psycho ass." Now *I* was pissed.

"Keep talking, and I will set them saggy-ass titties on fire" was the last thing he said before he walked out the door and slammed it. He had me fucked up I thought, looking down at my breasts. My shit was sitting perfect, but what the fuck came over him? What pissed me off is the fact I had no idea what I did wrong, but to hell with him. That's what I was thinking, but my body was telling a different story. For some reason, seeing him pissed off turned me on, but I wasn't going to call his ass. Fuck him.

Chapter 12

Quick

"You did *what?*" Holding my stomach as I laughed, I couldn't believe this nigga, Shadow. "Hold on, don't tell me no more. I gotta see Blaze's face when you tell this story." My brothers and I were about to have a meeting for our next hit. This would be the last robbery we did for a while because it was going to be one of our biggest hits.

"Nigga, you think this shit is funny? This why I don't tell y'all shit." Shadow was taking his frustrations out on me, but I didn't give a fuck. This shit was epic. Just as I was about to respond, Baby Face and Blaze walked in.

"Just in time. Hey, I need y'all to hear this shit," I said, yelling over to them. I waited until they got closer. "This simple-ass nigga got caught cheating with plus one. Shirree walked dead in on his ass as he was about to stick his dick in."

Waiting on that to sink in, I continued with the rest of the story as Shadow looked at me pissed. "So, the nigga arguing with his girl, but he never put his dick up. Plus one's bold ass started sucking it while they were arguing, and this nigga didn't stop her." Everybody was laughing hard as hell . . . well, everybody but Shadow. "Then he kept fucking her for another two hours before he went home to explain." I couldn't help the tears that fell from my face as I laughed at baby brother's expense.

"What the fuck was you thinking, my nigga? Are you crazy?" Of course, Baby Face was all serious.

"I don't know, man. I was drunk." Dropping his head, Shadow told the rest of the story. "When I got home, she had a gun pulled out on my ass, but what pissed me off is she actually shot at me."

"Nigga, I would have burned that bitch's uterus up. She wouldn't be able to have a motherfuck-ing drop of piss come out, let alone a baby." This nigga Blaze was dead-ass serious. "Where did you go?"

"I went back to Elise's house." Shadow was damn near whispering by now.

"Who the fuck is Elise?" Blaze didn't know the girl's name.

"Plus one." We laughed as we all said it together. All jokes aside, baby brother may have really fucked up his happy home. I felt bad for him, but I would never tell his ass that.

"Enough about me, what's going on with you niggas?" Shadow was ready to change the subject.

"Speaking of simple, this nigga was about to set ol' girl's house on fire because she found out who he was." Baby Face caught us up on the newest bullshit of Blaze.

"Naw, it was how she did it. I just told her ass it didn't matter who I was, and I liked her because she didn't know me. The fact that she went out of her way to find out who I was, let me know she like them other bitches." Shadow and I looked at Blaze like he lost his mind. Looking at Baby Face for answers, he shrugged his shoulders.

"That's the dumbest shit I ever heard in my life." No matter how I replayed it in my mind, the shit still sounded stupid.

"It is what it is. Anyway, when are we hitting up this bank?" Blaze was back to the money.

"Tomorrow night. This is the first time we are going to take a bank while it's closed. We're going in through the door, and we're only in there three minutes. In and out, no bullshitting around. We should be able to grab all, if not most, of the money since there will be three of us in the vault. Shadow, you will stay outside and watch our backs. Blaze, you pick up the car at midnight and meet us here. Are we clear?" Everybody nodded in agreement. "Since we ain't got shit else to do, let's hit up Hoover Nights later." We needed the drinks, so we headed home to shit, shower, and shave.

Looking at myself in the mirror, I knew I was fly as fuck. Wanting to invite Alaysia, I changed my mind because I didn't know if baby brother wanted to see plus one. Maybe she will let me slide through after. Shooting her a text, I hoped she agreed.

Me: What you on later?

Alaysia: Nothing.

Me: Can I roll through?

Alaysia: What time?

Me: After I leave the club.

She didn't respond, so I grabbed my keys and jumped in the Ghost. I pulled up to the club, and Shadow was already there, so I just slid behind him. Five minutes later, Baby Face and Blaze made it there. Getting out together doing our normal routine, we headed in. With our song blasting over the speakers, we waved and made our way to VIP.

"Hoover Gang is in the motherfucking build-ing," the DJ yelled through the mic like always. As soon as we got in VIP, we went over to the railing to look out over the club. Scanning the room for the baddest bitches, one of them caught my eye.

"Hey, Blaze, is that ol' girl?" Looking at where I was pointing, this nigga had the nerve to get pissed. She was throwing that ass all over some lame-ass nigga. If we were at Diamond's, I would have thrown her all my paper.

"Yea, that's her. Bitch got me fucked up. Watch this." We all started laughing as he walked out of VIP with our security. This nigga was about to be on some bullshit, I could tell by his walk. When he got to the bar and dipped some napkins in a cup of liquor, I couldn't hold back my laughter.

"This nigga is ignorant." Grabbing my phone, I hit record as he walked up to the chick and lit the napkin. As soon as he reached her, he threw that shit right on her ass. The shit had me in tears because she was still dancing, not knowing her ass was on fire. That shit must have gotten hot because she jumped up with her eyes big as a prostitute's pussy. Crying real tears, I laughed as Blaze stood there with his arms folded as she came up out of her dress. Security put out the fire, and he whispered something to them and walked off. When he came back to VIP like ain't shit happened, I was no more good.

"Nigga, what the fuck is wrong with you? I thought you didn't want her?" I said, laughing as I waited for him to answer me.

"I lied. So the fuck what? Bitch got me fucked up." Turning my head as I heard the commotion, security was dragging her toward VIP, and she was fighting like a motherfucker. She had some hands too. It took three of them to get her up there.

"Let me go. I just want to go home." She was screaming at them.

"Sit the fuck down before I embarrass your ass." Blaze turned back to security and told him to go to the office and grab her something to throw on. Funniest part of it all is, the chick sat her ass down.

"Y'all got us fucked up. Where my bitch at? We will come back and shoot this motherfucker up." Some girls were going off trying to get in VIP.

"Shut the fuck up and quit causing a scene in my club, Paris." Grabbing her ponytail, Blaze started back talking. "This don't look like human hair, so if you don't want this horsy to start hee-hawing when this fire hit it, I suggest you shut your ass up and go sit next to your friend."

Rolling her eyes at Blaze, she slapped him in the back of the head.

"Don't play with me, Blaze, or the next time I style your ass, you gon' be looking like Prince in *Purple Rain,* nigga. Heels and all. Hey, y'all." She waved to us, and I couldn't do shit but laugh. Ash, Panda, and she walked in. It's a small world, and it's crazy this is their friend. I used to fuck with Ash back in the day, and I was digging her too, but one day, I looked up, and she was in a whole new relationship.

"Hey, Quick." She said it all soft and shit, and my dick got hard.

"Hey, baby girl." Leaving her be, I turned back to the club and watched the hoes shake their ass. We finally had enough, and we all started heading out.

"Shadow, where your ass going?" I asked, making sure my brother was straight before I got out of there.

"I'm gon' head to your crib downtown. Or is that where you headed?"

"Naw, you can go there. See y'all tomorrow." Checking my phone, I saw Alaysia had texted me the address. I texted her back and let her know I was on the way. Doing seventy all the way there, I finally pulled up. She was at the door which was opened as soon as I walked up.

"Why you still got clothes on?"

She started blushing. "Who said you were getting some?"

Not about to play these games with her, I walked in and closed the door. Grabbing her roughly, I picked her up around the waist and leaned against the wall.

"You still want to play this game with me?" She didn't say shit, so I slid my hands down to her panties. Moving them to the side, I started rubbing her clit. When a moan slipped out, I snapped.

"Shut the fuck up. You didn't want me to have none, so don't be moaning and shit." Undoing my pants, I slid my dick out and used that instead of my fingers. Using my body to hold her up, I reached in my pocket and grabbed a condom. Sliding it on, I pushed her panties to the side again and rammed my dick in. Looking at her, I could tell she was trying not to moan. Sucking her titties as I rammed my dick in her, she finally couldn't help it and started moaning like crazy.

"Tell me you want this dick." No response, so I slammed my dick in her as hard as I could. When she finally couldn't take it, she damn near screamed the words.

"I want your dick, baby!"

"Stop playing with me then." Not wanting to let her off the hook, I continued slamming my dick in her until she was coming all over that motherfucker. Using both hands to hold her waist, I fucked the shit out of her ass until I could no longer take it. Filling the condom up with my seeds, I damn near dropped her ass.

"You got some good pussy, baby. Quit being stingy with that shit." Letting her stand up, we headed upstairs. For a brief moment, I thought about Ash. That shit was in the past, though. Shorty moved on with her life, and I don't chase bitches. As soon as I lay down, I looked over at Alaysia.

"Come ride this motherfucker."

Chapter 13

Blaze

Looking over at Drea, I knew she had an attitude, and I didn't give a fuck. I never said I was an easy nigga to get along with, but I didn't tolerate disrespect. I'm that nigga, and mother-fuckers are going to treat me like I am.

"Fix your fucking face, Drea."

"Fuck you, nigga," she spat at me as she rolled her eyes. When I looked back at her, my dick got hard. She was pouting, but I swear she was the finest bitch I have ever seen. All I wanted to do was suck on her lips.

"My bad, baby girl, but I didn't like seeing you dancing all on that lame-ass nigga. Y'all had me fucked up." Getting mad again, I started snapping. "How the fuck you gon' come in my club and disrespect me like that? Who raised your ass?"

"Nigga, are you for real? How the fuck was I supposed to know that it was your club? The only reason I know your name is because Paris told me. My dumb ass was sitting there bragging on this nigga that I was feeling but didn't know shit about, and when I said your name, she told me she knew you." Looking like she was ready to beat my ass, she kept snapping.

"Then you got pissed for no reason and disrespected *me*. You said lose your number, and I did. Why the fuck you tripping?"

Feeling a li'l bad now, I softened up. "Cus that's my ass, and you not about to be throwing that shit unless it's for me." Still pissed, she wasn't ready to let it go.

"And my mother is dead. Don't reference her again, or I will shoot your ass."

Laughing, I reached over and grabbed her hand. My pops is deceased, so I know the feeling. Without saying a word, I drove her all the way home like that. Not ready to let her go, I kept her in the car talking to me, finally deciding to let her know who I really was. Well, minus the bank robbing. So I opened up to her. This was new to me, and I don't even know why I was doing it now, but my heart was telling me she was different. I ain't saying she gon' be my girl, but I may fuck her a couple of times before I leave her alone. She finally decided to call it a night, and I didn't want her to leave. My dick was hard, so I decided to shoot my shot.

"Can a nigga come in and spend the night?"

Laughing at my ass, she shot me down. "No, you can't. I need to go rub some cocoa butter on my ass to make sure I don't get any burns." She climbed out of the car but climbed back in and kissed me. "I had a nice time. Well, not at the club, but after." When she climbed back out, I had to stop myself from begging her to let me stay. Getting myself in check, I drove off and headed home. It was going to be a long night, but I didn't feel like fucking another bitch. I wanted Drea. She didn't know it, but I was going to get her ass to give in, whether or not she knew it.

The next morning, I got up and washed my ass. Throwing on some jogging pants, a white tee, and my Space Jam 11s, I headed out to get breakfast. Grabbing some for Drea and me, I headed to her house to surprise her. When I knocked on the door, her brother stared at me as if he knew me.

"Is there a problem, nigga?" Ain't no bitch in me, so I got that shit out of the way.

"Naw, we cool. Let me wake Drea up." He walked off, but something wasn't right with his ass. She came to the door embarrassed, but I don't know why.

"Blaze, what are you doing here? You done caught me lacking and looking a mess."

Smiling at her, I just followed her in the house. Keeping my eye on her brother, she led me in the room. Right before she closed the door, I heard him say, "I knew that was his ass." Making a mental note of that shit, I handed her the food, and we sat down to eat.

"Your brother lives here?" I asked, trying to figure out what it was about his ass.

"Who, Slick? Yeah," she said while rolling her eyes.

"What that nigga do for a living?"

"Beg me and petty hustle," she answered in between bites. Making sure I made a mental note of that as well, I continued my questions.

"Baby, where do your ass work? How is he begging you?"

"I don't work, and he begs for whatever he can. Your food is getting cold. You aren't going to eat?" I could tell she wanted me to change the subject, so I let it go for now. She must be embarrassed that she is unemployed. Digging into my food, I decided today I would be a gentleman. For once, I was going to do something nice. After we were done, I waited on her to shower and get dressed. Walking back out to the living room, I looked at her brother in disgust and walked out. How the fuck you, a grown-ass man, living off your sister, and she don't even have a job? Clown-ass nigga. When Drea was ready, we jumped in my Range Rover and headed to the mall.

"What are we doing here?" She was looking at me side-eyed.

"I did burn your dress up, and I want to buy you another one." She looked happy, but her words didn't match.

"You don't have to, baby. I'm good. Let's see a movie. My treat." I loved the gesture, but today was about her. Wondering where the hell this girl was at, she finally walked up.

"Hey, gah. You ready for your shopping spree? I can't wait to style you." Paris walked up, not wasting any time.

"What shopping spree?" Looking from me to Paris, she started shaking her head no.

"Can you just let me do something nice for you? I feel bad. Let me say sorry," I said. Reluctantly she agreed.

"You better say yeah, I get something outta this deal too, gah. Now, let's go." After going in about twenty stores, I started to think this may have been a bad idea to call Paris's ass. A nigga been here four hours, and I was ready to go.

"Whatever y'all don't have in ten minutes, you won't have. This shit is ridiculous."

Laughing at me, they put the last items on the counter, and I paid for them. Walking out of the mall, I felt like Benson carrying all of this shit. With a slight attitude, I dropped Paris and her bags off at her car and headed back to Drea's house. I needed a nap before we headed out tonight, so I decided to sleep at her spot instead of going all the way home.

"Do you mind if I crash here? I need to sleep before I go handle some business tonight."

"You can stay."

We got in her room, and I lay down in the bed while she grabbed her Kindle.

"What are you about to read?" Never being around a girl that likes to read before, I was curious.

"I'm about to finish this book called *He Ain't Perfect, but He's Worth It* by KB Cole. And since you're going to be asleep for a few hours, I'm going to either start *Cherished by a Boss* by A. J. Davidson or *Wishing He Was My Savage* by Trenae." Looking at her like she was crazy, I lay down.

"Girl, you said that shit like I know them people. The only thing I read is my money."

"Well, you asked," she snapped while rolling her eyes.

"I didn't mean to." Both of us laughed as she leaned against me while I closed my eyes to rest.

For a minute, I thought I was having a wet dream about Drea, but when I opened my eyes, her mouth was really on my dick. She was sucking it so soft and gentle, and the shit was driving me crazy. Now, I done had my shit sucked by a bunch of bitches, but this slow, passionate shit was doing something to me. I tried to think about something else, so I don't bust, but the shit wasn't working.

"Wait, girl, give me a second." Thinking she was about to stop, I exhaled, trying to gather myself. But she started placing soft kisses on my shit and licking real slow now. When she got to my balls and started humming, that was it for me. I couldn't hold it, and I nutted in her mouth. A nigga was about to feel bad for not warning her . . . until she swallowed that shit and kept sucking. She kept going until it was hard again, and I wasn't going out a second time.

"You got a condom, baby girl?" She pulled one from out of nowhere and used her mouth to slide it on. This bitch was gon' make me marry her ass tomorrow. Flipping her over, I needed to take control of the situation. Sliding my dick into her, I started hitting her ass from the back. As much as I wanted to tear her ass up, I couldn't, or I would have bust again. This girl had Satan in her pussy. Not wanting to look like a rookie, I got my shit together and started giving her all I got. That shit wasn't working, though. Every second, I had to convince my dick not to come yet.

"Baby, I'm about to come." Thanking the gods, I was happy as hell when she came all over my dick. As soon as she started shaking, I released my shit. Rolling over, I was about to get my ass back to sleep—until I looked at the clock.

"Fuck, baby, I'm sorry, but I have to go. You almost made me late. I'll be back, though, so be ready." Kissing her, I removed the condom from my dick and threw it in the trash. Washing up quickly, I kissed her again and headed out. Her brother and his friends were on the couch doing shit when I headed out the door. I thought to myself, *Lazy-ass-leaching-ass nigga*. As thoughts flooded my brain with the sex I just had with Drea, I didn't notice I was being followed as I drove to pick up the hooptie.

Chapter 14

Slick

"When this nigga leaves, we gon' follow his ass. That nigga gon' lead us to his house. I bet he got a safe there. We about to finally get paid around this motherfucker." Thinking about the lick we were about to hit, I was excited as fuck. My sister had a lottery ticket for all of us, and she didn't even know it. Yeah, I was gon' have to kill the nigga, but my sister just met him, so she would get over it.

"You sure, nigga? I'm tired of all these blank-ass missions." Pooh was really starting to work my nerves.

"Yeah, I'm sure."

Just as I was about to go off, *he* walked out the door. The nigga was walking different, so I could tell he just fucked my sister. As soon as he walked out, we jumped up and ran to Sleaze's car. Giving him enough distance, we started following him. When we ended up in this bullshit-ass neighborhood, the homies started going off.

"Nigga, ain't no way he lives here. You done sent our ass off." Pooh's ass was always complaining.

"Shut the fuck up, nigga. Let's just see what he gon' do."

He parked his vehicle and jumped into a raggedy-ass car. This nigga was about to be on some bullshit. I'm *definitely* following his ass now. Maybe we could just blackmail him with what we knew. Following him in the hooptie, he drove to a commercial area in front of some offices. Three other niggas came out dressed in all-black and got in.

"Nigga, we done came up. Fuck y'all's thought. I told y'all Slick knows what the fuck he be talking about." We ended up following them all the way up north to a bank. "These niggas about to rob a bank, and we about to rob they ass." Pulling out our guns, we watched only three of them go in.

"Hey, y'all go in, and I'm going to watch the nigga in the car. They not gon' see y'all coming.

Shoot all they ass." The homies jumped out of the car, and I watched them slip through the door. Once they did, the nigga in the car got out and went in behind them. Grabbing my AK-47, I got out and went in behind *his* ass. I could now hear voices.

"You niggas must not know who the fuck we are, but you gon' learn today." One of them was talking to my boys.

"Hold up, Quick, I want to know how the fuck they knew we were here before we send they ass to they Maker. How you know us?" Another guy spoke up. I could see they had their guns drawn on Pooh and Sleaze. "They not talking, so put they ass to sleep. We gotta get the fuck up out of here."

"Looks like y'all day done got worse. Put y'all's shit on the floor," I yelled, pointing at their ass. I could see Blaze looking at me crazy when it finally hit him.

"Nigga, that's Drea's brother. I'm gon' kill that bitch," Blaze finally spoke.

"Not before I kill you first."

Making the mistake of trying to grab the moneybags first, one of the other guys shot Pooh in the head. Leaving the bag so that I didn't get shot, I ran. Hearing the other single gunshot let me know that Sleaze was now dead as well. Saying fuck the car, I took off through the streets and jumped inside of a garbage can. Knowing I fucked up, I didn't know what I was going to do now. My bitch ass was on the run, but I won't be for long. They killed my niggas, and I wasn't gon' stop until they were gone too.

After hiding in the garbage can for about an hour, I finally climbed my ass out. Reaching for my phone, I dialed the one nigga I said I was done with. Hating to call him, I had no choice.

"Nigga, you must have some good shit to tell me if you're calling my phone."

"Tate, I fucked up. I need your help."

"What the fuck does that have to do with me?"

I swear, I hated this nigga, but I needed him. "Trust me; I know what you and your bitch into. Or have you forgotten? This will be worth your while."

"I'm listening." I knew I had the nigga's attention now. If I didn't have a choice, I would leave his bitch ass hanging.

"Me and my boys followed the Hoover Gang, and they were robbing a bank. Shit went south, and now my homies are dead. I know you can use the information to get what you want, but I need protection." There was silence on his end for about thirty seconds.

"Meet me at this address. I'm about to text it to you." Hanging up, I headed back to my car. I would have to reach out to my other homies to stay low as well. It was about to get ugly.

Chapter 15

Drea

"Ain't no nigga like the one I got, no one can fuck you betta." Feeling myself, I rapped the words to Jay Z's "Ain't No Nigga" loud as fuck. I was so in my zone, I didn't even realize my girls had walked in.

"Damn, bitch, what kind of dick he got? Shit must be laced in gold." Ash was standing there looking at me all crazy.

"If y'all would have seen that big motherfucker flopping around in them jogging pants earlier, you would know why this ho in here singing and shit." Laughing at Paris, I high-fived her ass because she was right.

"So, the nigga set you on fire, and you fuck him?"

Rolling my eyes, I walked past Panda. She was always trying to be our moral compass.

"Panda, some dick is worth getting burned for." Looking at me in disgust as she sat down, I laughed because I knew she really didn't find the joke funny.

"Dang, girl, loosen up. It was just a joke. He is so different, y'all. We sat and talked for hours last night. We didn't even go anywhere, and it was the best date I ever had." Smiling from ear to ear, I told them everything.

"Damn, now, that's new. Everybody knows Blaze only fucking. It sounds like you got his ass gone as well." Paris was over there actually looking shocked.

"Panda, can you hook my hair up while we sitting here? Oh, and I need y'all help. I want to do something nice for him since he keeps doing all this nice shit for me." I've been trying to think how I could repay him for all the nice stuff since he won't let me take him out.

"Come on, girl, but I don't have no ideas for your ass."

Laughing, I sat down to let her curl my hair. We laughed and talked about what's been going on with each of us and our niggas. Time flew by, and we were about to call it a night.

"I'm going to call y'all tomorrow, and we can come up with something good." As soon as I finished my sentence, the door to my house was knocked off the hinges. Blaze and his brothers came bursting in.

"Damn, bitch, you must got voodoo in your pussy. This nigga knocking the door in for it." Paris's ass was laughing, but looking at Blaze's face, it didn't look like a friendly visit. When he raised his gun, I knew that was not the case.

"What the fuck! Y'all on that kinky shit. Let me get the fuck up out of here." Ash was trying to leave, but his brothers raised their guns as well. "Quick, you gon' pull a gun on me?" He never even looked over at Ash. Their eyes stayed focused on me.

"Now, I may not be the smartest person in the room, but usually when you fuck a nigga and swallow his seeds, he don't come back to your house with guns drawn." I was starting to get pissed. Blaze walked over to me, and if I didn't know any better, I would think tears were in his eyes.

"Bitch, you set me up. You kept asking me who I was. You got your wish because you about to find out." The nigga started flicking his lighter, and I got scared.

"Hold up, bro, you can't burn this bitch. We need to find her pussy-ass brother first." Quick may have saved me from getting set on fire again, but I had no idea what they were talking about regarding my brother.

"My brother? What the fuck does he have to do with me?" Ignoring me, Blaze grabbed me and started shoving me to the door. He looked back at my girls and gave them a warning before we left.

"If I even think you told someone about this, I'm going to set your kids on fire and make you watch. If I even think you said my fucking name in your sleep, I'm going to cut your tongue out and burn that motherfucker. If I even think y'all even mentioned seeing me tonight, I will burn every piece of hair on your body and feed you to the fucking rats." When he snatched me out the door, I could hear them crying. I still didn't know who he was, but I knew he was someone I should be very afraid of.

Chapter 16

Shadow

After taking Drea to our hideout, I took my ass home to see my girl. Shirree still wasn't fucking with a nigga, but after this shit with Blaze and his girl, I knew I had to convince her to let a nigga back. She knew too much, and as my uncle always told us, it's cheaper to keep her. She could ruin me if she wanted to. My brothers would be pissed if they knew I told her everything. Not only could she fuck me over, but she could fuck them over as well. Even though this shit had me worried, I missed my girl. Ringing the bell, I wondered if she would answer. After five minutes had gone by, I was about to give up when I heard the locks moving.

"What the fuck do you want?" She looked like she had been crying. I thought after all this time she would have calmed down.

"Can I please come in so we can talk?" Moving out of the way, she allowed me to enter. A nigga was happy as hell. The last time I was here she had a gun held on me. Sitting down next to her on the couch, I could see she was still angry, but she missed me.

"A nigga fucked up, but I don't want to lose you. Me and my brothers were out drinking. You were stressing a nigga out, and every time I thought about it, I took another shot. The only thing I remember about that night is that I hurt you. That is no excuse, but just know I would never cheat on you."

"Nigga, you *did* cheat on me. What do you think that shit was?" She was getting upset again.

"I'm saying if I hadn't been that drunk, I would have never looked at another bitch. It was the alcohol mixed in with all the shit we had been going through. I'm sorry, I really am." Her facial expression started to soften up some.

"You hurt me, and that is nothing I could ever forget, but I will try to move past it." Feeling relieved, I tried to make sure she fully understood that I was sorry.

"We are supposed to be getting married. All the arguing and shit has to stop. You fucking with a nigga's mental, and that can't happen. When I'm out there handling business, I need a clear head. A nigga almost got shot tonight because I wasn't focused. Just know I don't want these bitches out here. All I want is you. Set the date. I don't want to wait anymore."

"I'll set the date, but you have to show me that you are all in. Where have you been staying?"

"At one of the houses in the city, but I'm ready to come back home."

"Not yet. You have to show me first, and then we can work on all the other stuff." Leaning down I kissed her. She felt so good against my lips.

"I'm sorry, and I am going to prove to you that you are all a nigga needs. I'm leaving now, but I'll be back." When she got up to walk me to the door, I noticed she had on this li'l-ass gown with nothing on underneath. My dick started rising.

"Gon', boy. You not getting none of this for a while." Smiling, I walked out the door feeling good. When I got in my car, my phone rang. It was Elise.

"What's up? Me and my girl gon' work on our shit, so I don't think you should call me anymore."

"Fuck all that. I'm pregnant, and you're the pappy."

"Bitch, what the fuck you mean I'm the daddy? You not about to convince me I'm the only nigga you fucking." This shit could *not* be happening. As soon as I convinced my girl to give me another chance, here this bitch come with this bullshit.

"It don't matter if you the only nigga I'm fucking. All that matters is every time I turned around, you were hitting this shit raw. Now, I'm not trying to bring no drama to your life, so if you want me to go away, there's always a way." I should have known this bitch was going to want some money.

"How much?"

She got quiet for a second and then knocked my wig back with her response. "One million."

"Bitch, you either on crack or dog food. Either way, you got me fucked up."

"Just think about it . . . You don't want to mess your perfect li'l family up, and I don't want this baby, but if you don't give me what I want, I'll push this motherfucker out like I'm taking a daily shit."

"I'll call you back." I can't believe I fucked up like this. I needed to talk to my brothers, but I didn't want to hear they shit. I was gon' have to figure this shit out on my own. A nigga don't even think it's my baby, but I was definitely hitting her ass raw. This shit was about to stress me the fuck out. Wondering how the fuck I could give her a million dollars without anybody

noticing, I got pissed at the fact I was gon' have
to pay this bitch off. My brothers would tell me
to kill her ass, but I wasn't that nigga. Knowing I
couldn't allow her to fuck up my life when I was
just getting it back, I decided I would have to pay
her. Heading to the city, I stopped at the liquor
store to grab me a bottle.

Chapter 17

Shirree

I know motherfuckers would say I'm a weak bitch, and I shouldn't have gone back. A month was too long to be away from my man, and he has suffered long enough. After I caught him with that bitch, I left. Anybody who knows me knows that I'm not a fighter. But a ho *will* get even. As soon as I put his ass out, I called the number this guy had given me a few days earlier. I had no intentions on ever cheating on my fiancé. I loved him, and he was all I needed, but some shit had to change. We had more than enough money, and he still was out here risking his life and freedom because he didn't know how to tell his brothers no. Even still, I could have dealt with that. Seeing him with another woman was too much. Knowing I had to get my revenge if I was going to even think about taking him back, I called the number.

***

"Hey, this is Shirree. Are you busy?"

"No, how have you been, sweetie? I thought I was never going to hear from your sexy ass."

"I need to get out of this house. Can I come over?"

"Yeah, I'll text you the address."

Hanging up the phone, I got dressed and headed out. When I got there, I was second-guessing myself. This was not me, but knowing I needed to do this for my own ego, I got out of the car. Knocking on the door, I was nervous as hell when he answered.

"Hey, damn, you looking good, girl."

"Thank you." Walking in, we sat down on the couch.

"You want something to drink?"

"Yes, please."

After he poured the Henny, and it started to take effect, I began loosening up. We were laughing and talking like old friends. After about three cups, I was feeling myself, and I was drunk as hell. Reaching over, I grabbed his dick, and he pulled it out, giving me a free go at it. It wasn't big, but I wasn't fucking him for keeps. This was for one night only, and I would have my revenge. Putting it in my mouth, I didn't have to suck long before he was ready to bust. Knowing I wouldn't feel the same satisfaction if I only gave him head, I stopped and told him to put it in. It felt good, but as soon as I started to enjoy it, he pulled out and nutted on my ass. Looking stupid, not that I had any idea what was supposed to happen next, I started talking. Once I started talking, the liquor took over, and I couldn't stop. Before I knew it, I had told him all about the Hoover Gang and how everybody thinks they so legit. How dumb they would look if I told the police they were bank robbers and had the biggest score ever coming up at the end of the month when they hit up Bank of America. I guess I was talking so much that he excused himself to go to the bathroom. Barely standing, I got up and looked around his place for the first time since I had been there. When I looked at the plaque on his mantel, I felt sick to my stomach. Right as he walked in the front room, I ran to the bathroom and threw up. After I rinsed my mouth out, I walked back in the front and to the door.

"This was really nice, but I have to get home now. I'll call you." Leaning down to kiss me, he didn't ask me to stay.

"Okay, do that."

All the way home I cried. How was I going to tell my fiancé that I just told his whole oper-

ation to the fucking police? Tate was a fucking cop, and I had just told him all about their next big robbery. I prayed he liked me enough to leave it alone, but something in my heart told me I had fucked up.

Nothing had happened, and the police hadn't come and kicked our door in, so I left it alone. Never mentioning anything to Shadow, I kept that secret to myself. If they were going to arrest him or take him in for questioning, they would have already done that. Knowing we were definitely even, I took my man back quick as hell. Praying he never found out what I did, I decided it was time to get my act together before I lost him. He was only out here doing what he thought was right for us. I have been fighting him every step of the way, but I was done. Looking at the calendar, I scanned it over to see when I wanted to set a date for our wedding. Nothing could come in between us now. We both got it out of our system, and it was time to move on.

Chapter 18

Baby Face

"I'm not trying to hear that shit, nigga. If her brother came to rob me, that bitch had to be in on the shit as well."

"Just calm down and talk to her. You don't know that, and the fact that you are this pissed is showing me you really like this girl." I was trying to talk some sense into my brother, but he wasn't listening.

"Fuck that bitch and her brother. These motherfuckers got me fucked up, and you do too if you think I'm letting this shit slide." We been going through this shit for hours. Shadow and Quick got tired of hearing it, so they left. My ass was about to do the same fucking thing. This nigga was bugging.

"Do what you gon' do then. I'm out. I taught you better than that, though. You thinking with emotions instead of using your head. Talk to the girl and see where her head is or what she has to say. If not, then kill the bitch. We not about to make this into some drawn-out-ass soap opera."

"Fuck you. Get your pretty ass out of here then. Looking like a fucking 10-year-old prince." Knowing it was useless to talk to him when he was like this, I left. Jumping in my whip, I called Juicy on Facetime.

"What you doing, girl?" She was looking sexy as hell. Her red hair was all over her head.

"About to lay it down."

Pausing for a minute, I decided to see what she would say. "Can I come over?" Giving her the best smile I could muster up, she nodded her head.

"Yea, I'll text you my address." Hanging up, I was happy as fuck. Damn near doing eighty miles per hour, I flew to her house. When I got there, I knocked on the door and waited for her to let me in.

"Hey, handsome." She leaned up to kiss me, and my dick got hard instantly. When she turned around to let me in, my dick almost burst out of my pants. She had on these little-ass booty shorts and a tank top. Being the creep that I was, I knew she didn't have on any panties or a bra. I didn't have any intentions of sleeping with her, but she was about to make this shit hard as fuck.

As she walked me to her bedroom, I tried my best to focus on something else. Once we lay in her bed, I refused to remove my clothes. Usually, I wouldn't lie in somebody's shit with my clothes on, but tonight, I needed some restraint. Laying her down beside me, I did something I hadn't done in a long time. I attempted to get to know her.

"Tell me something about yourself."

"I'm a counselor at the Westinghouse High School. I love working with kids, and I feel like they need somebody to help them. Too many people in this world don't care about our youth, but I want to be one of the people who does." Talking probably wasn't a good idea either. Her goals and aspirations had my dick even harder than it was before.

"Do you have any children?"

She looked sad for a second and then answered. "No, but I want one. The doctors say it will be hard for me to get pregnant or even carry one because I have a T-shaped cervix." I didn't know what that meant, but I felt bad for her. "Do you have any?"

"Naw, I don't want a baby mama. The girl I get pregnant, I want her to be my wife." She looked sad again, so I decided to change the subject.

"Do you have any siblings?"

"Naw, it's just me and my mama. She's all that I have in this world." No longer wanting to have sex with her, I wrapped my arms around her and hugged her.

"You have me. Now quit that sad shit and turn on Netflix. I got to pick the movie because we *not* watching no girl movies." She laughed for the first time since we started talking.

"What's a girl movie?"

"You know what the fuck a girl movie is, all that sad love shit." Surfing through the categories, I ended up picking *Brotherly Love.* Looking over at her, I knew she was going to be mine, but I wondered if she would stay once she found out who I really was. Halfway through the movie, she fell asleep. Holding her close to me, I decided to call it a night myself. Tomorrow was going to be hectic. I knew Blaze was feeling fucked up because he liked that girl. We were gon' have to get to the bottom of this shit and soon.

Waking up to the smell of breakfast had a nigga's stomach growling. Walking in the kitchen, she was in a different pair of li'l-ass shorts, and they were hugging the shit out of her ass. Not being able to help myself, I walked over and smacked that motherfucker.

"Good morning to you too, bae."

Why did her calling me bae make my dick hard? Down, Tsunami; now is not the time. I tried to talk to his ass, but he had a mind of his own.

"Morning. What are you in here burning?"

"I'm making your ass a steak omelet, and I know how to cook if I don't know how to do shit else." Sitting down, I was waiting to be the judge of that. I hated when a chick couldn't cook because I loved to eat.

"I meant to ask you last night, how old are you? Your ass look young as hell, and I'm not trying to go to jail dating a high school student. I work at the school, you know."

"It's a fine time for your ass to ask now. I almost fucked your ass to sleep yesterday. I'm 29." She turned around fast as hell to see if I was lying.

"That's how you got your nickname."

"Yeah, how old are you?"

"I'm 26." Setting my food down, she poured me some juice, and we continued to get to know each other. She walked over to me and kissed me. Her lips were soft as hell, and she was about to meet Tsunami when my phone rang. Seeing it was Blaze, I answered.

"Where the fuck is y'all at? This bitch won't stop crying, and I'm ready to cook this ho. If y'all trying to get some questions out of her ass, y'all better come on."

"I'm on the way now. I'm already in the city."

"You niggas went home to lie up with your chicks while I was stuck here suffering with my lying-ass girl?"

"We'll talk about this when I get there. I'm on the way." Hanging up, I actually felt sorry for his ass. I knew he liked her, and the first time he opened up to somebody, he feels she was flawed.

"I'll be back later. I have to go check on my brother." I kissed her and walked out the door. The fact that I explained to her where I was going, I knew I was feeling the shit out of her. Hoping I never had to go through what Blaze was going through right now, I allowed the smile to spread across my face. I got a girl. I can't believe it!

Chapter 19

Blaze

Waiting on my brothers to get there, I went into the room we were holding Drea and decided to let her know how I felt. I didn't want their asses laughing at me, so I got it out of the way now.

"I trusted you. How could you set me up?" She looked so confused, but I wasn't buying that shit.

"Blaze, I promise I don't know what your ass is talking about."

Ignoring her, I continued. "Do you know how hard it was for me to open up to you? A nigga thought you might be different, but you just like all the rest. You the worst kind, though. I can tell what them other bitches about from the jump, but your ass knows how to hide your bullshit."

"Blaze—"

I cut her ass off. "Shut the fuck up! I don't want to hear the shit. I was feeling you, and now,

I'm gon' have to kill your ass. Do you know what the fuck that's going to do to me?" She started crying again, and I didn't know whether to slap her ass or hug her. My feelings were all over the place. That's what was bothering me the most. If it had been anybody else, she would have already been dead. Then I heard the front door open.

"Blaze, where you at? I'm surprised this motherfucker ain't burnt to the ground." Quick tried to mumble the last part, but I heard him.

"Back here." They walked in the room, and I could tell they felt sorry for Drea. I wanted to yell fuck this bitch, what about me? This was my first heartbreak, and I didn't know how to deal with this shit.

"Drea, I am going to ask you some questions, and I need you to understand that your responses will determine whether you live or die. Okay?" She nodded her head as Baby Face continued to question her.

"Did you set my brother up to get robbed?"

She looked horrified. "No, I would never do that. Why would I do that?"

"*I'm* asking the questions; you just answer them, okay?" She nodded again. "How did your brother know where we were going to be?"

Now she went from confused to pissed. "My brother? What the fuck? I mean, I don't know."

"Where is your brother?"

She started crying again. "I don't know. He was gone, and I decided to have girls' night. That's when y'all kicked the door in."

Baby Face motioned for me to come out of the room. We left her in there crying and closed the door.

"Bro, I know you are pissed, but she didn't know." Watching her facial expressions as he questioned her, I already knew that. My trust issues are extreme, so I needed my brother to tell me. He knew how to read the shit out of people, and I trusted his word. Relieved, I started panicking because I had no idea how to do damage control.

"I can see what you thinking, Blaze, but you can't mess with her. That's her brother, and even though she didn't play a part in this shit, we *are* going to kill him." Quick snapped me from my thoughts.

"Y'all can leave. I'm going to talk to her."

"Let us know if you need us."

Nodding, I walked back in the room where she was. Untying her, I tried to think of a good way to tell her, but I said fuck it and went with the truth.

"Drea, I'm sorry for all of this, but I had to know that you didn't set me up."

"Set you up how? I don't understand." She was crying again, and I moved next to her and held her.

"What I'm about to tell you, I will kill you where you stand if you ever repeat it. Me and my brothers rob banks. That's our thing, and nobody knows this. When I left your house, that's where I was going. While we were in the bank, your brother and his crew busted in. They attempted to rob and kill us. You have to understand why I thought you were in on it. You don't have a job, and your brother is a petty hustler. The shit was fucking with my mental." She just looked at me.

"I will never repeat what you just told me. I want to go home now." Feeling defeated, I got up to take her home. The whole way there she didn't say a word. When we pulled up, she opened her door and then turned around to face me.

"Come in. I want to show you something." Getting out of my car, I followed her inside. Making a mental note to fix her door, I continued to her bedroom. Sitting on the bed, I watched her grab a crow bar and pull boards out of her floor. Grabbing some duffle bags out, she threw them at me. When I opened them, I realized there had to be at least two million dollars in there.

"Where the fuck did you get all of this?" She sat down and explained to me about her ex G

Money who was killed. I knew that nigga, and he was definitely paid. After explaining why she wasn't out here splurging, I wanted to kill her brother even more. She was penny-pinching so her bum-ass brother wouldn't rob her blind.

"I really am sorry, Drea, and I wish I could be with you, but I can't." She looked heartbroken, and I went on to tell her why.

"Your brother is dead as soon as we find him. How could I be with you knowing the kind of hurt I'm about to put in your heart? A nigga fucked up, but I ain't that fucked up. I like you, and I wouldn't be able to look at you while you mourn him knowing I killed him."

"My brother been out here wrong for a long time. I can't say that I won't be hurt because I would, but I understand what you have to do. His other friends aren't over here, so I know that he called and warned them. He didn't call my shit one time. He knew I would take the fall for this shit, and he didn't give a fuck. I love my brother, but I'm tired." She just gave me the okay in her own way to kill her brother. I was going to grant that wish.

Chapter 20

Quick

It seems like everything was coming together for my brothers and me. We went from being single, everybody except Shadow, to all of us in a relationship. After this last big score at Bank of America, we would be set. I planned to talk to my brothers about leaving this shit alone. Once we were done with this hit, we would never have to take shit again. Out of all the things going right, there was still one thing we hadn't been able to handle. We can't find that nigga, Slick. It's been damn near a month, and this nigga was hiding better than a roach when the lights came on. Knowing he was still out there, my family wasn't safe. My brothers and I were meeting up to go shake some shit up and see if we could find him. Pulling up to the office, I saw my brothers were already sitting in Blaze's truck waiting on me. Parking, I jumped out and got in the back.

"Do you always have to be late? Damn, I got a date with my girl, and your ass bullshitting." Shadow was back to his usual bullshit.

"It's good to see you're sober enough to tell the time now. Fuck out of here; I don't want to hear that bullshit."

"Both of you niggas shut the fuck up. Damn. Shadow, if you want to leave, you can go. Don't nobody wanna hear that shit all fucking day, and, Quick, you need to learn to be on time." Baby Face always thought he was running some shit because he was the oldest.

"Whatever, nigga." We drove the rest of the way in silence. When we hit the block, there was a group of niggas standing outside.

"Y'all get out and talk to them. I'm about to park down the street just in case shit go left. I don't want motherfuckers having my license plate." Blaze didn't have time to stop and get a hooptie. We never do our dirty work in one of our own cars.

We walked up to the crowd of niggas, and one of them started yelling like he knew us.

"Awwww, shit. Hoover Gang done graced us with their presence. What bring y'all down here with the common folks?" This JJ-looking-ass nigga was trying to be funny.

"You know us, nigga?" His demeanor was pissing me off.

"Who don't know you motherfuckers, but I know this ain't y'all block, so I'ma need y'all to move around." Before I could curse his lame ass out, Shadow walked up and knocked that nigga to the gods. Dude was literally on the ground asleep.

"Now that we got that out of the way, where that nigga Slick at?" These motherfuckers were trying us today, and I wasn't with it. His homies were laughing as I continued to question him.

"You don't hear me talking to you, nigga?" No answer. "You got five seconds to say something before you catch this fade." His friends were folded over from laughter. They thought I was playing, but I'm about to show their ass what it means to be a Hoover. I pulled my gun out so fast they didn't have a chance to respond. *Pow!* The bullet in his head sent him crashing down on top of his friend who was still asleep. Blaze ran up on me, snapping.

"The fuck you shoot him for?"

Getting aggravated, I went off. "Because I asked the nigga a question, and he ignored me like I'm some lame-ass nigga."

"Nigga, how the fuck he was gon' answer your ass? He a mute." Blaze was laughing, and I was lost.

"The fuck you talking about, nigga?"

"That nigga can't hear shit you saying or respond to your dumb ass." Now realizing what he was saying, I couldn't do shit but laugh.

"The nigga should have signed don't shoot then." Blaze was in tears, laughing.

"Nigga, how the fuck you don't remember Herb's ass?" Looking back at the ground, I moved him so I could see his face. It damn sure was Herb. Laughing, I remembered how the nigga became deaf.

Herb was one of my best friends when we were little. He stayed over almost every weekend, but Blaze couldn't stand his ass. He said I changed when he came around. One night, Blaze kept asking us questions, and we got pissed off.

"Go find you something to do. Damn. You talk too fucking much." Herb went off on Blaze's ass.

"A'ight. Bet." I knew my brother, so I made a mental note to keep an eye out on Herb. We went to sleep; later, I was awakened by Herb's screams. Blaze was sitting on top of Herb, making Herb hold his own hands over his ears.

"Nigga, what the fuck are you doing?" I tried to pull Blaze off, but he had a grip on Herb's ass.

When I finally got him off Herb, I saw smoke coming out of Herb's ears.

"Nigga, what the fuck did you do?"

"I made sure the nigga won't hear shit else since it gets on his fucking nerves." This sick *fuck had dropped matches in Herb's ears and held them while his shit caught fire. Nigga ain't heard shit since, and that nigga stayed far away from me as possible.*

"How the rest of you niggas wanna do this? I got all day." I was ready to shoot all they ass.

"We don't have all day. Where the fuck is Slick at?" Blaze interrupted me.

"He hasn't been around. We haven't seen him or his crew, and we been looking for his ass. He owes me money," a li'l nigga finally spoke up.

"If y'all see him, come holla at one of us at the club. Now, clean this shit up." We walked off down the street to the truck. Once we got in, Baby Face went off.

"I will *not* tolerate you motherfuckers doing stupid shit like that. I have worked too fucking hard to let you hotheaded motherfuckers fuck it up. After this last job, there are going to be some changes. The next motherfucker to do some stupid shit gon' have to see me." We all sat quietly. Usually, we would be cracking jokes and shit, but we knew when that nigga was serious. He was quiet and laid-back, but he was the craziest of us all. That silent killer is the worst. When we got back to the office, we jumped out of that motherfucker fast as hell. We didn't want that nigga to get pissed any more. Jumping into my car, I plugged my phone in. As soon as it charged, I had texts rolling through. Seeing it was Alaysia, I called her back.

"Hey, baby, what's up? I was handling some business, and my phone died."

"Can you come over? I want to run something by you." She said it all sweet and shit.

"You know I would go to the end of the world and back for you. I'm on the way." Smiling as I went to my baby's house, I made it there in fifteen minutes since I was already in the city. Knocking on the door, she opened it and was looking at me crazy.

"What's up, baby? What's wrong with you?" I leaned down to kiss her, but she walked away from the door and damn near let my lips kiss her ass. I was pissed, but I walked in anyway.

"Your ass better have a damn good reason why you treating me like I'm a nigga at pump seven asking for change."

"She is not going to kiss you in front of her nigga. Have a seat."

This girl had me slipping. I hadn't even noticed someone else was in the room. Reaching
for my gun, he stopped me when he showed me
his badge.

"You're in a room with two cops. I don't think
that's a smart move." Noticing it was only him
and her, I heard the message loud and clear.

"Alaysia, you set me up?" She turned her head
away from me, and I got pissed. "What the fuck
y'all want?"

"We want Bank of America." Looking confused,
I'm trying to figure out what the fuck was going
on. This nigga looked like he sang sweet jazz,
and he in here trying to punk me.

"The fuck is you talking about?"

"We already knew that you and your brothers
rob banks, but it just came to my attention that
you are about to hit your biggest score yet at
Bank of America. We want in."

"Nigga, you got me fucked up. I own clubs."

"You can come in now." Looking around to see
who he was calling, I almost passed out when
Slick walked in. "As I was saying, we already
know you rob banks. Now, you are going to rob
them for *us*. After you hit Bank of America, we
want 80 percent of the cut. Each bank you rob
after that, you will give us 60 percent."

"My brothers will never go for that."

"Well, you better make them go for it. If you don't do it, we have a third cop that is going to take all of the evidence and this eyewitness to our captain. Not only will you go down for bank robbery, but you will go down for two first-degree murders. How you wanna play this shit?" He already knew I would agree that he had us red-handed.

"It's a deal."

"Good, now don't try anything slick like coming back here to kill her. She won't be here. There will be eyes on you at all times, even if you don't see them. Stay free and do the right thing. We *will* be watching."

Getting up to leave, I wanted to spit in Alaysia's face, but I walked out. In due time, she will get hers. Jumping in my car, I needed to meet with my brothers. I couldn't tell them about Alaysia, but I needed to make sure they were on point and ready to continue robbing these banks. Knowing my brothers would never agree to this shit, I would just have to pay them out of my cut. Saying a silent prayer, I hope everything went how it was supposed to, and my brothers never found out. As I continued to drive, one thought consumed my mind. Who the fuck told them about Bank of America?

Chapter 21

Shadow

Everything had been going great between my fiancée and me. We had set the date, and we were going to have a spring wedding. Even though I ain't a soft-ass nigga, the shit had me excited. Once I paid Elise the million dollars, she said she went and got an abortion, and I haven't heard from her since. I was about to get ready for this meeting Quick called, and I'm happy as fuck my girl wasn't tripping any more.

"Baby, you seen my hoodie?"

"It's right here." I turned around, and she was standing in front of me with nothing on, but my hoodie. My dick damn near bust through my jeans.

"You know I have to leave. Why are you start-ing shit?" She licked her lips, and I damn near came on myself.

"What I do? I'm just telling you I had your hoodie."

Walking over to her, I removed my hoodie and leaned her against the wall. Lifting her hands above her head, I sucked softly on her neck. Making my way down to her breasts, I took them in one by one. She was trying to get her hands free, but I wouldn't let her. Holding them in place with one hand, I rubbed her all over her body with the other. Tonguing her down, I used my free hand to play with her nipples.

"Damn, daddy, stop playing and put it in."

Ignoring her, I slid my hand down to her pussy. I slid it in to get my fingers wet, then brought them back out to play windshield wiper with her clit. The more she moaned, the more I increased my speed.

"You gon' come for me, baby?" She nodded her head. With my lips so close they were brushing hers, I asked her again. "You gon' come for daddy?"

"Yes, daddy, I'm about to come. Fuck." Now going as fast as the fifth setting on a vibrator, I felt her body shaking. Once she was done, I slid my fingers inside and then pulled back out. Sticking them in my mouth, I sucked my fingers as she watched. Letting her go, I walked off.

"I'll be back. Be naked when I get home." When I turned the corner, I heard her mumble "Asshole." Laughing, I jumped in my truck and headed to the office.

When I arrived, everybody was there and on time.

"A nigga gets his bitch back, now he the one always late. I bet he ain't about to be talking about how time is important now." Quick wasted no time letting me have it. Knowing there was no win in that situation, I let it go.

"What's up? What's the meeting for?" I asked looking around.

"I think we should hold off on this robbery. Something don't feel right, and I ain't with it." Baby Face always went with his gut.

"It's cool with me; it's not like we hurting for money." I agreed with Blaze. Even though I just gave Elise a million dollars, I still was set.

"Y'all niggas bitching up? This is our biggest score yet. We would never have to do shit else in life. Don't go jinxing our shit now." I've never seen Quick this upset over a job.

"If you need some money, we got you."

He gave Baby Face the nastiest look he could find. "Nigga, do it look like I'm hurting for some money? This is what we do. We are the Hoover Gang, and you weak niggas need to start acting like it. We been robbing banks since bitches been selling pussy. Now, all of a sudden, we lying low." You can tell Blaze was thinking it over.

"Fucking right. I'm with you, bro. It ain't even about the money no more for me. It's the rush and the thrill, knowing we untouchable. If it's my time, then it is what it is. Just make sure y'all cremate my ass. If I'm going out, I wanna go in a blaze of fucking fire." This nigga Blaze done got worked up.

"Nigga, I ain't saying all that because I ain't ready to go, but I'm with it." I sided with Quick and Blaze.

"If y'all really wanna do it, fine, but after this one, I'm taking a break."

"This nigga finally gets a girl, and now it's fuck us. Bitch, we Hoover for life." I just knew Baby Face was about to lay into Quick's ass for that last comment, but he let it go. We stayed for another hour and went over the plan one last time. Then I headed home to my girl. I needed some pussy. Having to keep a clear mind, I couldn't fuck the day of a robbery. But I was definitely getting in them guts tonight.

Chapter 22

Baby Face

Normally, I wouldn't give in to my brothers when I had a gut feeling some shit wasn't right, but today, I did. Now was not the time to have the talk with them about me retiring. I knew that me walking away meant they had to walk away as well. It was always all or none with us. We had each other's back, and that was the reason we lasted so long. Nobody could fuck with us as long as we all stuck together. A nigga was damn near 30, though, and I was tired of this life. I just wanted to settle down and be a family man. So many nights, I wanted to tell Juicy what it is that I really do for a living, but I couldn't afford to risk the lives of my brothers. I was the oldest, and it was my job to protect them. Quick blowing up like that didn't sit right with me. There was a desperation in his voice. We would have to have a talk when this was all said and done.

Heading to the house, I pulled in the garage. I've never brought a girl to my real house, but there was Juicy upstairs waiting for me. We still hadn't had sex yet, and the shit was killing me. I couldn't tell my brothers, or they would clown my ass. This was the first girl I have dated that was worth waiting for, but this shit was hard as fuck. Literally. My dick stayed hard all the time. If she laughed, Tsunami was ready to tear some shit up.

After walking through this big-ass house, I realized she was in the bedroom. As soon as I saw her, I grunted. She had on some booty shorts, and all that ass was hanging from the bottom. She knew damn well she had too much ass to go in them li'l-ass shorts.

"Girl, you killing me. If you want me to honor your wishes, then you need to start putting on some clothes."

She turned over and smiled at me. "Boy, you seen a million chicks in booty shorts before. Stop it."

"Yeah, but they ass didn't look like *that*." Reaching in my drawer, I grabbed some jogging pants. "Put these on." Laughing, she slid them on, but I swear even the way she was doing that was sexy. "I'll be back." I went and jumped in the shower. Pissed, I poured some body wash in my hands. I was too damn old to be jacking my dick, and I damn sure was too damn fly for this shit. After I got my nut, I washed my ass and got out. This time, I was going to beat her at her own game. Rubbing some baby oil on Tsunami, I looked at my eleven inches and walked out of the room. This time, I was going to tease her ass and hoped she would give in.

When I walked in my room, I stood there, dick swinging and dripping oil for shit. She was knocked out. Walking over to the bed I started to slap her ass in the face with this big motherfucker. Lying down, I had an attitude like a motherfucker. She lucky I ain't a fucked-up nigga, or she would wake up with Tsunami touching her throat through her pussy.

Waking up, I dreaded going to the office, but we had to hit this bank, and I prayed everything went smooth. Dressing in all-black, I kissed Juicy and let her know I'd return.

"I'll be back in a few hours, baby. If you need something, there's keys to every car in the garage, I have a Black Card in the kitchen drawer, and I'll text you the alarm code if you leave."

"Boy, I ain't doing all that, but if I did, I have my own money and car. Gon' and handle your business."

Walking out the door, I jumped in my Range Rover and headed out. When I made it to the office, everyone was there and on time. Blaze already had the beater, and nothing else needed to be said. Jumping in, we headed to make the biggest hit in our lives. The ride was quiet until we got there.

"Y'all know what it is. We are in and out. Be safe and be smart." Shadow was with us this time because the bank was entirely too big. We needed the extra man. Even though I always told him he was left in the car for other reasons, it was really to protect him. He was the baby, and I had to look out for his ass. We pulled down our masks and headed in.

"Everybody get down on the motherfucking floor! Don't move or you won't live long enough to blink your eyes," Quick yelled as he jumped on top of the counters.

I headed to the vaults, and this time, Blaze was with me. That was the reason we needed Shadow. Since Blaze had a girl now, he wasn't fucking bitches to get the key. He had to open them on his own. Looking at the vault before us, this was not the one our informant told us. Blaze headed back out front and approached the manager. Bashing his head in, he snatched the key from around his neck. Running back toward me, we opened it and went to work. I could hear Quick yelling.

"We are over time! Hurry the fuck up." Trying our best to grab it all, we may have to fuck around and leave some. "Two minutes over time. Let's go." Right as we got damn near all of the money shots rang out.

"The fuck?" Blaze and I went running out of the vault.

Shadow was lying on the ground with blood everywhere. Quick had shot the security guard that laid Shadow's ass out. "Let's get the fuck out of here."

Grabbing the acid we carry for shit like this, I started pouring it where Shadow's blood was, making sure not to leave any DNA. We jumped in the hooptie and got the fuck out of there. I could hear Quick on the phone with the doctor telling him to meet us at the house. With tears in my eyes, I looked at my baby brother. He was barely hanging on, and I was blaming myself. If I had followed my gut, he wouldn't be here right now. We pulled up to the house and carried Shadow inside and laid him on the bed.

"Where the fuck is this doctor?" Blaze was yelling loud as fuck. Shadow was fading in and out, and we were all starting to panic.

"Somebody better tell me what the fuck happened. I didn't want to do this job, and now, my brother's in here fighting for his life. Quick, this was your dumb-ass plan. You care to shed some light on the situation?" I was going off, and my brothers and I were now looking at Quick for answers.

"Alaysia is a cop."

That was all he could get out when Blaze and I pulled our guns out. This nigga had us fucked up, and if he was on some snake shit, I was gon' have to kill my fucking brother. Looking at Blaze, I knew he felt the same way I did. This shit was all kinds of fucked up, but I would kill him where his ugly ass was leaking his Jheri curl juice before I let him cross us.

"Nigga, you better start explaining, or I promise, I'm gon' blow your bitch ass to the moon."

Chapter 23

Quick

Before I left the house for this hit, something told me it wouldn't go right. I was still trying to figure out how the fuck they knew about Bank of America. Only my brothers knew how we moved and what banks we were going to hit. Pulling up to the office, Blaze was already there. One look at his face, I knew he was feeling the same way as me.

"This shit don't feel right, bro. You know I don't give a fuck about no bank we hit. Shit ain't sitting right with me, Quick." Not knowing what to say, I just nodded my head.

"Nigga, say something. Fuck you looking all crazy for?"

"There's some shit on my mind. Me and Alaysia going through some shit, but I'll handle it." Not sure if he bought what I was saying, but we didn't get a chance to talk about it anymore.

Shadow's ass pulled up, and I couldn't have been happier. Right after, we got in the beater, and Baby Face pulled up. I guess everybody had their own shit on their mind. When we pulled up, Baby Face gave us our speech. We got out and headed in.

"Everybody, keep your fucking eyes on the floor. If I see a nigga move, I'm blowing his shit back. Come on, y'all, we got thirty seconds. It's time to move." Looking over my shoulder, I saw the security reach for his gun. I pointed my gun and fired on his bitch ass, but it was too late. He shot Shadow twice. Pissed off, I walked over to the guard and shot his ass five more times. "Shadow, are you straight, my nigga?"

"Hurry y'all asses up. He got me in the side. This shit hurts."

"It's time to move. Let's go." Baby Face had all of us carry Shadow to the car while he poured acid on the blood to make sure not to leave any DNA behind. Then he ran out the door and jumped in the car. He pulled off, and shit got crazy.

"Doc, I need you at the house right now." I called our personal doctor we had for times like this.

"What are the injuries?"

"Gunshot to the side and chest. Get the fuck there now." Hanging up, I looked over at my baby brother. He had to make it. I wouldn't be able to live with the guilt otherwise. All of this was my fault, and I don't know how I would explain this shit to my brothers.

Arriving at the house shit wasn't looking good for Shadow. I knew I would have to come clean. I just prayed he made it, and I didn't have to live with that guilt.

"Somebody better tell me what the fuck happened. I didn't want to do this job, and now my brother's in here fighting for his life. Quick, this was your dumb-ass plan. You care to shed some light on the situation?" Baby Face was going off, and my brothers were now looking at me for answers.

"Alaysia is a cop." That was all I could get out before my brothers all pulled their guns on me simultaneously.

"Nigga you better start explaining or I promise I'm gone blow your bitch ass to the moon."

"I didn't know she was a cop until the other day. The bitch played me, and I walked into a setup. Some nigga was in there waiting on me, and he said they both were cops. They knew we were going to hit Bank of America, and they want 80 percent of the cut and 60 each time after that. Then the nigga Slick walked in. He's working with they ass.

"He walked out talking shit, and they said there's another cop working with them. If anything happens to any one of them, the other cop takes the witness and the evidence to the captain. We get the murder charge and everything else." Dropping my head in my hands, I didn't want to look at their faces because I didn't want to see what they were thinking.

"Nigga, we gotta find a way to get that bitch. I will set that ho's pussy lips on fire." I knew Blaze was going to go off.

"I've been trying to think of a way to get out of this shit on my own, but I swear, I can't figure it out." The doorbell interrupted us. Rushing to let the doctor in, I ran to the foyer and opened the door. "He's in here. Please, you have to save him." The doctor came in and asked us to leave the room while he worked on him.

"This is why I been single for so long. In our line of work, who the fuck can you trust?" I started to break down, and my brothers comforted me.

"Nigga, you didn't have no control over this. You didn't know this ho was the enemy. We just have to work with them until we figure a way out of this." Baby Face was always the calm one.

"Yea, bro, look what the fuck I just went through with Drea. I almost gave my bitch a fade. This how this shit works. Motherfuckers gon' come at us from every angle, but we the Hoover Gang bitches. We can't get got. We gon' figure this shit out, and I swear when I catch that bitch, it's on. Now, who the fuck gon' tell Mama?" I was shocked Blaze didn't have something slick to say, but my brothers had my back. Now, I had to convince my mama of this shit.

"I'll tell her. As soon as I know how Shadow is doing, I'll go talk to her." He was shot because of me, so I would be the one to talk to her, no matter what happened.

We had been pacing the floor for three hours, and we were getting restless. This was the worst part of not being able to go to the hospital. We couldn't take him because he was shot at the bank. As soon as I was ready to snap, the door opened.

"It was a struggle getting the bullet out of his chest, but I was finally able to retrieve it. I have both bullets, and he is doing fine. I sedated him, so he is out of it, but he is just fine." I sighed from relief.

"A'ight, let me go tell y'all mama. Keep me updated."

"A'ight, bro, good luck." They laughed, and my ass was scared. She was crazy as fuck, but I would rather deal with her than have to look Shadow in the eyes. Jumping in one of the whips, I headed out to my mama's crib. I swear a nigga was sweating like I was working for the Chinese, making gym shoes for ten cents a pair. Grabbing my keys, I walked in.

"Ma, where you at?"

She came down the staircase looking at me like I was crazy.

"I don't see no bags in your hands, and that would tell me you're empty-handed. Now, I know that can't be the case, because that would mean you don't have my money. If you don't have my money, why the fuck is you here?" My mama, Debra Ann Hoover, was crazy as hell and didn't take no shit. From the outside looking in, you would swear my mama didn't like our ass, but she was like us. The same way my brothers and I fucked with each other, that's how she was. We had the best relationship ever.

"Come give me a hug, Ma. You know I got your shit. I'll bring it by later. What you trying to buy?" I really didn't care, but I was stalling for time.

"This pretty-ass Benz got my name on it. Where the hell is the rest of the crew? They done got them some steady pussy and don't know how to come visit."

"They at the main house. With Shadow." I said the last part low as hell hoping she didn't hear me.

"What the fuck you mean with Shadow? If all of them together, of course, they with him. What the hell is going on?"

Taking a deep breath, I told her what was going on. "Shadow was shot on our last job. In the chest and the stomach, but he okay."

Studying my face, she leaned in closer. "What the fuck *aren't* you telling me?" Ready to get it over with, I explained everything with Alaysia. Before I could read how she was feeling, she slapped slob out of my mouth.

"Ma." *Slap.* She hit me about three more times. "Ma, I didn't know."

"If something happens to my baby, I will kill you myself. You motherfuckers better tighten up. When did y'all start allowing the next nigga to one-up y'all? I didn't raise weak-ass niggas, and I'm not about to start having them now. Take me to my son before I beat your ass." Not saying another word, I walked her to the car. "Just so you know, I want double. You done got my baby shot and go come in here empty-handed. I would ask you who raised your ass, but I know

I'm legit. Had you brought her here to meet me, I could have told your ass she wasn't shit. You know I can read a bitch like she a book by A. J. Davidson."

"Ma, who the fuck is A. J. Davidson?"

She laughed. "I should have known your simple ass don't read. Don't worry about it."

Turning the music up, I drove to the house to check on Shadow. I'm glad he was okay, but I wondered if he was pissed at me. We needed a plan to figure this shit out—and fast.

Chapter 24

Shadow

I still can't believe my dumb ass got shot. My first time on the inside, and I got hit. My brothers were never gon' let me in again. While we waited on the doctor, I heard Quick telling what happened. It was time I came clean with my brothers as well. My situation didn't include them, but it was time to stop hiding shit.

The first thing I heard when I woke up was my mama. I knew she would act a fool.

"Y'all better move out of the way and let me see my baby before I beat all y'all's ass." She was threatening them, but we all knew she was harmless.

"You better go on somewhere. You know I keep a lighter on me, and that wig look new." Blaze knew my mama was still pissed about him setting her wig on fire after all these years.

"Try it if you want to. You got me fucked up. Shadow, wake your ass up." Turning toward her, I smiled.

"Mama, why are you making all this noise? A nigga can't get no rest even when I'm shot. Since I'm shot, I got a favor to ask you. Can you go in there and cook us dinner? We haven't had your food in a long time." I knew she wanted to go off, but she could never tell me no.

"Okay, I got you." Waiting until she walked away, I turned to my brothers. Knowing I needed to clear the air with Quick first, I started with him.

"Big bro, I know you wouldn't put me directly in harm's way. We have never crossed each other, and I know you was just trying to handle it yourself. We good." Looking at his face, I knew I lifted a burden off him. "Now, I got something to tell you all as well." They looked at me like I had fucked up too.

"Nothing like that, but we can't start keeping secrets from each other, cus shit like this happens. Elise got pregnant."

"Who the fuck is Elise?" Blaze was looking confused.

"Plus one, nigga; keep up." Quick laughed at him as he motioned for me to keep going.

"She called me asking me for a million dollars, or she would keep the baby and make my life hell. I paid her the money. I need to do a couple more banks to make sure I'm straight for life, but we have to figure out how to handle our problem, or we're fucked."

"Damn, nigga. Shirree gon' kill your ass. As far as the other shit goes, let me think on this. There has to be a way out, but in the meantime, we have to do what they are asking." I knew that was hard for Baby Face to say because he really wanted to stop doing this shit.

"Shirree ain't gon' find out. She had the abortion. Let's worry about this shit here and move forward. Now, somebody call her ass and tell her to get over here. She will definitely kill me if she found out I got shot and didn't tell her." Lying back down, I closed my eyes to get some rest. My girl and my brothers didn't quite get along, and this was going to be a long day.

Dinner with the family went well. Shirree was only worried about me and my well-being. She didn't care about anything else. We had been in a good space lately. We were leaving the doctor's office, and I could barely walk, but when I saw Elise approaching us, a nigga damn near took off running. I could feel Shirree's body stiffening up.

"Well, look at the happy couple. Shadow, why you walking like you have to take a shit?" Trying to ignore her, I kept walking.

"Oh, so you gon' keep walking like you don't see me standing here. I bet your ass see me in six months, clown." Knowing what she meant, I prayed Shirree didn't put me back out of the house. Shirree pulled me, and we kept walking. Once Elise was out of sight, my girl put her leg out and tripped my ass. I hit the ground, and I swear that shit hurt worse than getting shot.

"Baby, I'm sorry." As I was trying to get up off the ground, she started laughing.

"We good. Get your crippled ass in the car. Fuck that bitch." Shocked, I slowly got in the car. This bitch might try to poison me in my sleep. She was too calm about this shit. "Baby, after the shooting, I started looking at life differently. I could have lost you, and I'm not waiting to be married. The date is set for next month, and everything is already arranged. You and your brothers just have to be fitted. Buy your mom a dress, and have your ass waiting for me at the altar." Looking at her, I knew there would never be another bitch for me. She was my life, and I was going to make it up to her.

"I got you, baby. I'll be there with bells on. I love you." Leaning over, I kissed her with everything I had inside of me.

"You better handle that bitch, though. She better not step to me again."

"I got you, killer. You already shot at me; I don't need you around here shooting at bitches." Laughing, we pulled off. Even though I was smiling, I was pissed the fuck off. All this time, we had the city shook. Now, it seemed like everybody was trying us. I guess it's true what they say. "Mo' money, mo' problems." But I was the type of nigga that got rid of my problems. This ho had me fucked up. Either she was gon' give me my money back, or this bitch had to go.

Chapter 25

Blaze

A nigga had to get up out of there and go home. It seemed like everybody had some secrets, and this shit was beginning to be too much. Driving through the city, I rode around to clear my head. Too much was on my mind, and I wasn't ready to go home. I was so out of it that I never knew I was being followed. Pulling in the gas station, I got out to get some gas when a bag went over my head.

"What the fuck!" Snatched up, I was put in a van, and they drove off. Pissed, I was ready to kill everybody in that motherfucker. After what seemed like forever, the van finally came to a stop. The men grabbed me and dragged me inside a warehouse. Once they took the bag off, I was face-to-face with a nigga I thought I would never see again. He looked older, but he still looked the same.

"Hello, Blaze."

"Hey, Rico, or should I call you dad?" He could tell I was pissed. He didn't speak, so I took that as my chance to go off. "Where the fuck you been all these years? You had us thinking you was dead, and you were alive the whole time. What kind of sick, twisted shit is this?"

"I know you have a lot of questions, but right now, I can't give answers to you. The only reason I'm showing myself now is that you need me. We have been trying to locate the problem, and we need you all to lie low until we do."

"Nigga, who the fuck do you think you talking to? While you were somewhere fucking off, me and my brothers were out here making a name for ourselves. We got this, and we don't need your fucking help. You can go the fuck back where you came from. I won't mention this to my brothers because you gon' get the fuck on and not say shit to them. If you so much as even look their way, I will light up your ugly ass." Noticing his men didn't attempt to stop me, I walked out of the building. Fuck. They brought me here. Walking back in, I looked at them with a dumb look on my face.

"One of you bitches have to take me back to my car."

Laughing, Rico stood up and walked over to me. Handing me my car keys, he shook his head at me.

"Your car is in the back. We *will* meet again."

"I'm not playing, Rico. Stay the fuck away from us." Walking out the back, I jumped in my car and drove home. I felt like shit because now *I* was the one that was keeping a secret. This shit was getting ridiculous. Speeding all the way home, I got out and made my way to the bedroom. Not wanting to be bothered, I jumped in the shower and was ready to go to sleep. As soon as I walked out, my girl could tell something was wrong with me.

"Hey, you okay?" Nodding my head, I thought she would let it go. "Then why the fuck are you in here frowning like somebody killed your dog?"

"I'm OK. I don't want to talk about it." She sat up in the bed, and I knew if I didn't say something, I wouldn't be able to get any sleep. "Shadow was shot today."

"Oh my God, is he okay?" She had tears in her eyes, and I softened up.

"He good. I'm just not feeling the fact that now, all of a sudden, everybody trying us like they think shit sweet."

"You have to change up what you do. Once everyone knows where you are going to be or what you are going to do, they think they can chance it."

I appreciated what she was trying to say, but this wasn't the case. The Hoover Gang has never been predictable. We moved in silence, and it wasn't until we started dating all hell broke loose.

"I get you what you saying, baby. Thank you. Now get some sleep. I'm okay." She lay on my chest as she drifted off to sleep. As much as I wanted to join her, sleep didn't find my ass. Rico was fucking my head up. Why now? How did he even know where to find us? This nigga thought he could fake death and then come back twenty years later like shit was straight. A tear fell from my eye as I remembered the night he got murdered.

Quick and I wanted to follow our dad every-where. Our mother would tell him to leave us in the house and that we had no business with him, but we would cry, and she would give in. This night was no different. We begged and pleaded until he took us with him. Heading to the other buildings in Cabrini-Green Projects, he stopped and talked to a group of men. They all would give him money, and we would move on to the next building. When we got to the last one, only one guy was standing outside.

"Hey, Lee, where the fuck is these niggas at with my money?" My dad was pissed they weren't outside waiting on him like they should be.

"They in the hallway. I think they in there running a train on that junky Freda." My daddy started speaking in Spanish. He only did that when he was pissed off.

"I'll be right back. Y'all stay here with Lee."

We did as we were told, and two minutes later, gunshots went off in the building. Lee leaned down to us and grabbed our hand.

"Come on, let me take you home. Your dad ain't coming home tonight." Not understanding what was happening, we went with him. We were only 6 and 7. When we got to the door, and my mama saw us with Lee, she passed out, and her wig flew across the room. Walking over to the corner, I picked it up and tried handing it to my mama.

"Here, Mama, here go your wig."

She jumped up yelling at me. "Boy, I don't give a damn about this wig. Go to your room."

"You cared about it when it got caught on fire. I just didn't want you to think I did something." She snatched it away from me when I tried to put it on her head as tears fell from her eyes.

"I said go to your room, boy." As we walked off to our rooms, we didn't know our lives had changed at that moment.

Even though I hated keeping secrets from my brothers, I couldn't allow them to go through this hurt. We needed to be focused for the shit that was ahead of us. Rico's ass was gon' have to wait. He had twenty years to stop playing Houdini. That nigga could suck my balls while they were on fire. Fuck Rico.

Chapter 26

Baby Face

Man, I had to get the fuck up out of the main house. Between my mama and all of the secrets that were revealed, I needed some space. Wanting to leave this shit behind was going to be harder than I thought. My brothers needed me, and I will always be there for them. What I needed most was some pussy, though. Thinking about going to hit up a random, I thought better of it and drove my ass home. Juicy was driving a nigga crazy, but I liked her too much to cheat on her. Walking in the door, I got ready to take a shower. My grown ass was jacking off every day just to get a nut. When I got in the room, she was sitting there looking at me like I was crazy.

"What's wrong with you?"

"You have blood on your face." Damn, I changed my clothes, but I guess I didn't get all of the blood off.

"It's not mine. Shadow got shot today." She got up and jumped in my arms making Tsunami jump.

"Is he okay? What happened?"

Not really knowing what to say to her, I decided to tell her the truth. I was tired of the secrets. "He got hit in the bank."

She looked confused. "Somebody robbed a bank, and he got shot?"

Taking a deep breath, I answered. "No, he got shot while *we* were robbing the bank." Looking at her trying to see where her mind was at, I couldn't read her expression, so I just waited for her to talk.

"That's what y'all do? Or was this a one-time thing?"

"It's what we do. This was supposed to be the last one, but now we have to keep doing it for a little while longer."

"Why?" The shit came out in a whine, and I felt myself getting aggravated.

"Because my brothers need me. There's some shit going on, and I can't back out on them now. It's either all of us or none of us. We have a system." Nodding her head, she lay down and didn't say anything else.

Definitely not in the mood for her shit, I got up and went to shower. This shit was beginning to be too much. After washing my ass, I got out. A nigga couldn't even bring his self to jerk off tonight. Wrapping the towel around me, I walked out into the bedroom. All the lights were off, but candles were lit. She was in the middle of the bed in a black lace panty and bra set. She had her legs crossed in the air showing off her red pumps. Tsunami stood up so hard, he made my towel fall. Using her finger to call me to her, I walked over in a trance. Pushing me on the bed, she straddled me. Grabbing some oil, she started to massage me. I wanted to tell her bitch to ride this dick, but I let her do her thang. Once she started massaging Tsunami, I was ready to bust right then. She eased her way down and started placing soft kisses on the tip. Knowing how big Tsunami is, the tip was all she more than likely could get in her mouth. Letting spit fall from her mouth, she went down on it slowly. Before I knew it, she had all of him in there, and I was playing with her tonsils. No chick has ever been able to get him all the way in. Going up and down, she continued to make his ass disappear.

"Fuck, slow up. I'm not ready to come yet." She was about to make me bust, and that is not how I wanted my first time with her to go. I was trying to get myself together, and she started swallowing that motherfucker and moaning at the same time. As embarrassed as I was, I couldn't hold it any longer. My nut flew down her throat.

"I'm sorry, baby, but I asked your ass to stop." She just smirked at me and kept sucking. What the fuck was this girl trying to do to me? As soon as I felt Tsunami get hard again, I took control. Grabbing her, I was about to show her what this mouth do, but she straddled my ass. Sliding down on my dick, she groaned as she took me in inch by inch. It should be illegal for pussy to be this tight and wet at the same time. As soon as she got used to my size, she grabbed my hand and started working Tsunami's big ass. No matter how I tried to gain control, she wouldn't let me. She was fucking the shit out of me, and before I could stop it, she had me screaming like a bitch. Right there on my dick, she spun around on that motherfucker and started riding it from the back. All that ass was jiggling in my face now, and for the first time in my life, I wanted to eat ass. Holding on to whatever dignity I had left, I kept my tongue in my mouth. Her body started shaking, and she creamed all over my dick. What fucked me up the most was that she never slowed down. She kept right on riding that motherfucker.

"Fuck, baby, I'm about to come." A nigga couldn't hold it anymore, and I let my shit ride. When she turned around to kiss me, all I could do was say, "Damn, I love your ass." She looked me in the eyes and smiled.

"I love you too. Everything is going to be all right. You will come up with a plan, and you will win. Do what you have to for now, but make sure you figure out a way to come out on top. I'm here if you need me." That shit had me falling harder than I was. That's how the shit was supposed to be. A nigga come home from a stressful day in the streets, and instead of his girl bitching and complaining, she fucks the shit out his ass and helps his ass come up with a plan. My bitch was the shit, and I'm glad she's mine. Now I have to figure out a way to get us out of the shit Quick's ass got us in.

Chapter 27

Quick

My ass was stressed the fuck out, and Shadow and his simple-ass girl were planning a wedding. Too much was going on. My brothers were already waiting for me when I walked through the door.

"Nigga, fuck took you so long? It ain't like you got a bitch." This nigga Blaze ain't got no chill.

"Don't try to act like your bitch wasn't just two seconds away from catching a fade. We still don't know for sure if her ass was in on it." I knew that would piss him off.

"Fuck you, nigga, but have you heard anything? How is this shit supposed to go?" I didn't want to talk about this shit right now, but I could understand them wanting answers.

"I don't know. They said they would be in touch." I was glad when the seamstress called us to the back to fit us for our suits. The colors were cream and champagne. We were to wear cream, and the women would wear champagne.

"Who the fuck picked out these high school prom colors?" Baby Face must be feeling better; he was cracking jokes and shit.

"Shirree's ass, but she can have what she wants. Shut the fuck up and get the shit. Damn." Laughing, I wondered if he had heard from Elise.

"Have you seen Elise since that day?"

"Naw, I guess once she realized it didn't piss Shirree off, she moved around. I ain't never seen myself being a deadbeat, but this bitch makes me want to be one. How you gon' force me to be a father?"

"She didn't force you, nigga. Your dumb ass went in her raw every chance you got. The fuck is you saying? That baby ain't have shit to do with nothing, and you are going to do right." Baby Face was always the bigger person, but I didn't know if I could do that shit.

"Fuck what that nigga talking about. Issa dead beat. Bitch better move around." We laughed at Blaze as the lady measured us for our suits.

"Something is wrong with all you niggas." This was one time I didn't agree with Baby Face, though. The bitch only wanted to be pregnant to get some money.

"I need y'all to help me get my money back from her ass. She thinks shit sweet, and she can take my shit and still have this baby. She can't have it both ways." You could see that Shadow was pissed. He really fucked up with this bitch. We both did. I guess the apple don't fall too far from the tree.

"I ain't getting in that shit. If you would have called me, you wouldn't be in this situation. I would have told you not to give it to her." Usually, Baby Face would help, but that nigga wasn't budging.

"Nigga, you know that's Alaysia's cousin, so I can't get in the shit. I'm in enough bullshit with they ass." As much as I would love to help him, I couldn't. They already had us by the balls.

"I'm down. Pick me up tonight. Fuck that bitch." Laughing, I could only imagine what Blaze was about to do to get this money back. We continued to laugh and shoot the breeze when Alaysia walked in and kissed me.

"What the fuck is you doing?" I know this bitch didn't think we still had a thing going. Blaze was flicking his lighter, and Shadow was looking like he was ready to knock her ass out.

"We need to talk. Meet me outside."

"Let me see what this bitch wants. Don't leave." They let me know they would be there waiting on me as I walked out to see what the fuck she wanted. She climbed into a truck with tinted windows. I hesitated before getting in.

"Ain't nobody in here but me."

Climbing in the truck, I got right to it. "What the fuck you want?" She reached over and started rubbing on my dick. "Are you crazy? Get the fuck off me." My mouth was saying one thing, but my dick was saying another. The shit got so hard, it damn near bust through my pants. Unzipping me, she pulled it out. Knowing I needed to stop her, I didn't because I needed to bust. The shit I was going through with them had me stressed the fuck out. As soon as she put her mouth on it, I lay my head back and closed my eyes. Pissed at her for making me believe she was the one, I grabbed her by her head and started fucking her face. Slob was flying everywhere, and that shit only turned me on more.

"Fuck. Why did you have to go and fuck us up?" Knowing she couldn't answer, I just kept fucking her face. Feeling my nut rising, I started pumping harder. The whole time I thought I was punishing her, I wasn't. She started moaning, and I nutted all down her damn throat. I was so turned on that my dick didn't even go down. The shit stayed hard. Pulling her dress up, she tried to climb on top of me.

"Hold up, shorty. Y'all play games with kids. You got a condom?" She reached in her purse and pulled one out. Grabbing it, I inspected the wrapper making sure no holes were in it. After I realized it was good, I slid it down on my dick. She climbed on top and started bouncing up and down on that motherfucker. I ain't no bitch, and I ain't letting no chick fuck the shit out of me, so I grabbed her by her waist and started nailing her ass to the cross. She had me fucked up if she thought she was gon' blackmail me and fuck me like her name was Sweet Dick Willie. Biting her nipple through her dress, I continued to assault her pussy. Knowing I couldn't be in this shit long, I allowed my nut to rise. I didn't give a fuck if she got hers, I let my shit ride. Sliding her off me. I grabbed the condom off and held it in my hand. Blaze always told me, if you don't trust a bitch, don't leave the loaded condom with they ass, and I didn't trust this bitch as far as I could throw her. She fixed herself up and then turned to me.

"We want you all to rob Chase Bank on the Westside on April 3rd." Now, these motherfuckers thought they could tell us which banks to hit.

"Naw, that ain't gon' work. One, we always pick the banks, and two, that's Shadow's wedding."

"Aww, you thought we were asking? You no longer have a choice in this. I'll be at the wedding with you, and after it's over, y'all will handle your business." The authority in her voice had my dick getting hard again, but this bitch was out of her mind.

"Let me holla at my brothers. I'll get back to you." Getting out of the truck, I knew this shit was not about to go well. Walking back in the tux store, they were sitting by the front waiting on me.

"Nigga, you gon' have us waiting why you fucking a bitch that's blackmailing you?" This nigga Blaze do too much sometimes.

"How the fuck you figure I fucked a bitch?" These niggas was always guessing.

"Because your dumb ass still holding the condom." Looking down at my hand, I started to throw that motherfucker at Blaze like he did me since he won't shut up, but that nigga play all day, and I wasn't in the mood.

"Shut the fuck up and listen. These motherfuckers think they about to tell us what banks to hit and when. She wants us to hit up Chase out west after Shadow's wedding."

"I know I said I had your back in this shit, but this bitch's out of her mind. How the fuck I'm gon' leave my wedding? Count me out of this one. Y'all ain't about to have my ass getting put out again." Shadow was pissed, and I didn't blame him.

"Look, we have to call their bluff on the situation. I know we are all at risk, but we don't do business like this. We do this *our* way on *our* time. Tell them after Shadow gets back from his honeymoon, we will plan our next hit. Nobody, and I mean *nobody,* runs Hoover Gang." That was all I needed to hear. Baby Face laid down the plan, and that's what it is. They had us fucked up. We dabbed it up and went our separate ways. I grabbed my phone to tell Alaysia the plan. They just had to deal with it. Fuck they thought this was.

Chapter 28

Tate

My plan was coming together perfectly. Everybody was on board, and these niggas was about to help my ass retire. It was time for Alaysia to get off her high horse and fuck Quick. She didn't realize her ass was dispensable as well. She was becoming a liability, and if her ass couldn't even get this nigga to act right, she had to go as well. If she wouldn't fuck him, the bitch had to go. Walking in her door, I hoped she went along with the plan. I liked her, but not enough to let her fuck with my paper. Her ho-ass sister was already interfering in our shit.

"Baby, where you at?" I called out to her.

"I'm in the room." Walking in the room, I was ready to fuck her, but I needed her to go fuck that nigga. She was lying in bed naked reading on her Kindle.

"What you reading, baby?"

"I just finished reading this book called *Where I Want to Be* by Manda P. I'm looking for *Cherished by a Boss 2* by A. J. Davidson, but the shit don't come out until the 26th. Guess I'll read *Giving You My Love With No Limits* by KB Cole." She was going on and on about some damn books like I really gave a fuck. I hate I even asked. She was about to start back talking, so I cut her off.

"Look, Quick and his brothers on their way to the tux shop to get fitted. I need you to go up there and run the plan by him. You gon' have to sweeten him up by fucking him, though, baby. That's the day of the wedding, and they not gon' be too happy about it, but my person on the inside said it has to be that day. We can clear the vault out if we do it on that day. You need to make sure they understand that they don't have a choice."

"You think he still gon' want to have sex with me after all of this? What if they do something to me?"

"They not. If they were, they would have already done it. Damn. If you want some of the money, you have to do your part. I can't be the only one out here trying to get this shit. No nigga is going to turn down some pussy." She was pissing me off with all this whining shit. If she didn't do her part, her ass had to go as well. I would never go to my captain with this shit. We don't even work in robbery. I would have to explain how the fuck I even know all of this shit, and Slick's ass is not a reliable witness. But, Alaysia and the Hoover Gang didn't need to know that. All they need to know is I would do anything to make them know I'm not playing with they ass.

"Now get your ass up and go meet him. I'll be here waiting for you when you get back." She groaned as she got out of bed, but she threw on a dress and headed out the door. This bitch better come through or she was going to pay with them.

An hour later she walked back in the door looking all refreshed and shit, humming to herself and smiling, I almost smacked piss out of her ass. Knowing I didn't have the right to be jealous, because I'm the one who told her to fuck him, but, damn. She didn't have to be so happy about it.

"I don't recall you singing and shit after fucking me." I was an asshole, I can admit it.

"Shut up. My song was on the radio. You the one told me to fuck him."

"Whatever. Did you tell them the plan?"

"Yeah, and he was pissed, but I told him they didn't have a choice." Her phone rang, and she put her finger to her mouth. It must be his ass. She put it on speaker.

"What's up?" The bitch started smiling and didn't even realize it.

"Look, this how this shit gon' go. We always pick our own banks, and that shit has worked for us. We will call you with the plan once Shadow gets back from his honeymoon. If your nigga don't like it, he can kick rocks."

"You niggas think y'all running this shit? You do it how we say you do it."

I couldn't hold back any longer. "Nigga, you can't even fuck your bitch right. How you giving orders? Try to fuck her. I bet your li'l-ass dick keep slipping out. Now, if you want us to do this, no problem, but it goes how the fuck *we* say it goes. Oh, and stick to eating her pussy. I'll make sure she gets dicked down."

The clown hung up before I got a chance to respond. Walking up to Alaysia, I started choking her ass.

"Bitch, what the fuck you tell him about me?" I could hear her trying to say something, but she couldn't talk. "Bitch, if you don't get him to change his mind, all of you motherfuckers is going to pay." Releasing her, I walked out of her house. This bitch was playing both sides of the fence, and I was gon' teach her ass what it meant to cross me. I wasn't with the shits, and they had to learn who the fuck was in control. Grabbing my phone, I called Slick.

"What up, Tate?" Nigga sounded like he was getting some pussy.

"Change of plans. The bank job is off, but I have another idea. They gon' listen one way or another."

"A'ight. Bet. I'm down." I hung up the phone and realized everybody was getting laid but me. Grabbing my phone, I dialed a number.

"I asked you not to call me anymore."

I laughed. "People ask for a lot of shit, but that don't mean they get it. I need some pussy, and I decided it's going to be yours."

"I'm not fucking you again."

"If you don't want your fiancé to see this video, you will."

"I'm on the way."

Hanging up the phone, I smiled at the irony. Quick was fucking my bitch, but I was fucking Shadow's.

Chapter 29

Shirree

After I got the phone call from Tate, I cried all the way to his house. When I pulled up, I cleaned my face. He would never get the satisfaction of seeing me break down. He was a sucker-ass nigga, and I couldn't believe I got myself involved with his ass. Getting out of my car, I knocked on the door. This nigga walked outside and didn't let me in. Getting happy, I thought the nigga was just fucking with me and didn't really want none.

"Take your clothes off."

I looked at him like he lost his fucking mind. "I'm not doing that shit out here. Are you crazy?"

"The choice is yours. Are you willing to take that risk?"

Not being able to hold it, tears welled up in my eyes. I slowly started taking my clothes off. Once I was naked, I stood there looking dumb.

"Get on your knees." Looking at the concrete, I wanted to pass out. That ground was gon' tear my knees up. There was no way I could explain that shit to Shadow. Grabbing my clothes, I folded them as much as I could and placed my knees on top of them. He dropped his pants and kneeled behind me. As soon as he slammed it in, the tears started rolling down my face. He fucked me like I was a ho on the street. The only good thing about it is that his dick was little. If he had a big dick, my insides would be split the way he was ramming his shit inside of me. If it weren't for the shame, I wouldn't have any emotion coming out of me. He must have got pissed because he was doing all of that, and I still wasn't making any noise.

"Bitch, you better scream and moan my name, or I'm going in your ass." Even though I didn't think that would hurt since his dick was so small, I decided to do what he asked. Not wanting to be violated anymore, I started moaning.

"This dick good, ain't it?"

"Yes, this dick is so good." Rolling my eyes, I continued to play the role. "Fuck me, baby. Yes, just like that." My plan was working because his speed increased, and he started grunting. I knew he was about to come. Right as he was about to nut, he pulled out and ran to the front of me.

This clown-ass nigga nutted all over my face. After he pulled his pants up, he walked toward his door.

"Get the fuck off my porch." He walked into the house and slammed the door.

Getting up, I quickly got dressed. To someone looking from the outside, you would swear I did something to this nigga. Running to my car, I grabbed a towel and tried to wipe his semen off the best I could. I cried all the way to the dress boutique. I had nobody to blame but myself. Knowing I wasn't about this life, I should have kept my pussy to myself and just stayed mad at Shadow's ass, but a bitch had to get even and fucked around and picked a psycho cop. Getting out of my car, I went inside.

"Hey, Paris, I'm ready for my last fitting."

"OK, boo, I'm ready." We walked in the back room, and I slid on my dress. I started crying as soon as I put it on.

"Aww, don't cry. Save that shit for your day." That wasn't the reason I was crying. I felt so much guilt, knowing what Shadow did to me was the only thing keeping me from breaking down and cancelling the wedding.

"I'm okay. Let's get this shit over with." She walked in front of me and started pinning the dress. Suddenly, she stopped in her tracks.

"Bitch, is this nut in your hair?" Embarrassed, I ran to the mirror to see what she was talking about. Fuck! It *was* nut all in my flat wrap. I'm glad she caught it, and I didn't go home like that.

"You know how it is, bitch. I guess I didn't catch it all." She laughed and kept pinning my dress. This shit was gon' be the death of me. This couldn't keep going on. The next time he calls, I'm going to threaten to go to his captain. He was not about to make me lose my fiancé over this stupid shit. Fixing my face, I realized *I* was the one in control. If he had a tape, we would deal with that shit if it happened, but I was gon' have to call his bluff. Deciding not to wait until he called again, I grabbed my phone and texted him.

Me: If you ever call me again or try to threaten me, I will go to your superior. Lose my number.

Tate: See you soon.

Not knowing what he meant by that, the shit made me shiver. I hope Shadow was as understanding as I was.

Chapter 30

Rico

Watching my son's fiancée fuck another nigga in broad daylight had me laughing my ass off. These niggas swear they don't need my help when they bitches are running amuck. I wanted to get out and put a bullet in her head right then and there, but I decided against it.

"Boss, you want us to go kill that nigga?" One of my men wanted to take out the officer.

"Naw, let that nigga be great. I want to see where this lead." After telling my niggas to drive off, I started going over everything I learned so far. My sons owned two clubs that were successful as hell, but they were out here robbing banks. Blaze was set up by his girl's brother, Shadow has a baby on the way by another woman, and his bitch was fucking the officer that was blackmailing him. This shit was all over the place. I offered my help in hopes they would, in turn, help me, but I see that's not going to happen. I was Rico Hoover, a drug dealer to my core. Some shit went left, and I had to fake my death. Leaving Chicago was the best thing a nigga could have done. Going back to Puerto Rico, I ended up being the man. Bitches threw pussy at me left and right. I was living the life. Not caring who I crossed to get to the top, I was now the head nigga in charge. But I crossed the wrong nigga, and I had to pay my debt or all of it would come to an end. Once I learned that my sons were paid out of they ass, I came here hoping they would take me in with open arms. Now that I know that's not the case, I had to come up with another plan. Looking over to one of my workers, I nodded my head giving him the okay.

"Make the call." I leaned back in my seat. This shit would be easy. I would be back in Puerto Rico in no time.

Chapter 31

Baby Face

We were at the main house having the rehearsal dinner for the wedding. Everybody was here, and we were having a good time. The fellas were in the den because we had shit to discuss. Shadow and Blaze were telling us what happened the night they went to get the money back from Elise.

"Nigga, I'm telling y'all she got this nigga Shadow spooked. When we pulled up, he was talking about maybe we should leave and forget the money. You know I ignored his soft ass and went in. The bitch was in there knocked out like she didn't have a care in the world. I walked up to her bed and flicked my Bic."

"Nigga, you set her on fire?" I don't know why Quick sounded shocked. He knew how this nigga was.

"Naw, I didn't; well, I did, but not like how y'all niggas thinking. Just let me finish. Damn. Where was I at? Oh yeah, so I walked up with my lighter, and this bitch had on some big-ass eyelashes. Them motherfuckers looked like duck feathers. I put my Bic up to them motherfuckers and cooked that damn goose. She didn't wake up until I threw the water on her to put the lashes out. She was like what the fuck are you doing? I told the bitch if you don't want to lose all the other hair on your body, give up the money. She thought I was playing until I lit the other lash. She told us where she had it stashed, and Shadow went and got it." We were laughing our ass off. This nigga crazy as fuck. I loved the shit out my brothers, even though they got on my fucking nerves.

"Nigga, I couldn't stop laughing. This nigga went to walk out the door and told her ass, you could have just gave up the money. Now, your dumb ass in here looking like Caillou." Shadow was laughing so hard that he could barely tell the story. "When I looked back at that bitch, and her shit was burnt and bristled up on her eyelids, the nigga had to drag me out of there." Shadow's ass could barely stand up now telling the story. Now, I was mad I didn't go with them niggas.

"Hey, Shadow, didn't Paris make Shirree's dress? Tell her ass to bring Ash and them to the wedding." Shaking my head at this fool, I told him no.

"Nigga, she got a man. Sit your janky ass down. You better keep fucking Alaysia's ass. I mean, the bitch is blackmailing you, so you might as well get the pussy."

"Fuck you, nigga. She caught me slipping one time."

"You a one-time lie. I saw y'all text messages, and y'all been fucking since that day. Lie again if you want to." Blaze started flicking his Bic like he was daring him to lie.

"Her pussy good as hell." We all started laughing at his ass.

"Nigga, you a sucka. That bitch couldn't blow on my shit. Snake-ass ho." We all know how Blaze felt about loyalty. He already hated bitches. I'm glad he had Drea. That nigga was happy, and I was even happier for him.

"Why the fuck y'all got me out there with y'all chicks? I ain't no fucking babysitter. Y'all got me fucked up." My mama's ass was always going off.

"We coming, Ma. Damn. We had business to discuss." We stood up to walk out of the room.

"Business, my ass. Y'all was in here talking about Blaze setting a girl's hair on fire. Nigga, you better break out of that shit. Somebody gon' beat your ass." She started fixing her wig, and we couldn't do shit but laugh. She was still pissed after all these years about Blaze setting her wig on fire.

"Ma, you need to let that shit go, for real," Blaze said as he flicked his Bic. Pushing him in the head, we went upstairs to join everybody else. My mama threw down as usual, and we all had a good time. Then we all headed out because we had to be up early for the wedding.

Once Juicy and I made it home, I started taking her clothes off.

"Let me find out your ass sprung." Laughing, she ran away from me. Chasing her up the stairs, I caught her ass and pulled her into a kiss.

"You know you gon' be a Hoover one day, don't you?" Tilting her head up, she looked in my eyes to make sure I was serious.

"How you know you won't be a Johnson? Especially since *I'm* the one laying it down in the bedroom. You might change *your* name." That was it. I was about to fuck her ass to sleep. Throwing her on the bed, I pulled her arms up over her head. Using my free hand, I unbuttoned her jeans. Sliding my hand in, I found my way to her clit and started massaging it.

"Damn, baby, that feels good."

Kissing her while I played in her wet spot, I
was finally ready to taste it. Pulling her jeans
all the way off, I made my way down and slid
my tongue up and down her slit. The taste had
me mesmerized. I could eat this shit all day.
Done playing with her ass, I placed her clit in
my mouth and started sucking on it. I sucked
that motherfucker until she came in my mouth.
Still not done, I started swirling my tongue all
around that motherfucker until she couldn't
take it anymore. Knowing her shit was sensitive,
I kept flicking my tongue on it. Going back up
to kiss her, I slid Tsunami in, and the shit was
wet as fuck. Staying focused, I leaned up and
grabbed her feet. Spreading her legs apart, I
damn near had them in a split. Slamming my
dick in and out, I showed her why his name was
Tsunami. Flipping her legs back over her head, I
pushed all the way down until her ass was in the
air. Standing on my feet, I went balls deep in her
shit.

"Face, okay; that's enough. You won."

"I what?"

"You won." Knowing she couldn't take this
position, I went harder. By the time I let her up,
she had come twice. Still not done, I flipped her
over. Pulling her ass to me, I entered her again.
Looking at her pussy lips, I could tell they were
swollen.

"Who lay it down?"

"You do, baby, I'm sorry." *Slap*. Watching her ass jiggle, I knew I didn't have long before I came, so I went to work on her ass. Grabbing her ass cheeks, I pulled them apart so I could see my dick going in and out. That made her pussy noises even louder.

"Fuck, I'm about to come." Knowing I couldn't hold it any longer, I came with her ass. Rolling over, I pulled her to me. Her li'l kitty kat was throbbing. That motherfucker had a heartbeat. Laughing at her, I got cocky.

"I bet your ass won't talk shit no more."

"Fuck you."

Kissing her on her lips, I knew I was blessed to have her in my life. Tsunami started waking up and pressing against her ass.

"I'll cut that motherfucker off if you put him back in me tonight. Don't make no sense for one man to have a dick that big."

Laughing, I drifted off to sleep. This was where she belonged.

Chapter 32

Shadow

I can't believe this day is finally here. Knowing how bad I fucked up, I felt like the happiest nigga in the world. My girl and I were finally in a good place, and I couldn't believe she was about to be my wife.

"Nigga, you sure you want to go through with this? Last chance. I'll sneak you out the back, and we can get gone." Laughing at Blaze, I continued to get dressed.

"I ain't never leaving that girl, and your ass ain't going nowhere without Drea with your sprung ass. How the fuck you gon' get me out of here?"

"Who said I was leaving her? You know damn well I'm gon' need some pussy on the road." This nigga was always late, yet his ass was on time today. The best part of it all was I can marry my girl guilt free. She knew all of my dirt, and even though she didn't know it, I knew all of hers too. I went by the shop the same day she did her last fitting to pay for her dress.

"Hey, Shadow, with your nasty ass." Ash was smiling at me all crazy and shit.

"What the hell you talking about, girl?" I was lost as hell.

"You know what she talking about. Y'all too old to be having quickies and shit. Get a damn room." Now, Panda's ass done got started, and I still didn't know what they were talking about.

"Is anyone going to let me in on what the fuck y'all ugly asses talking about?"

"They being messy, that's what they ass is doing. Gah, didn't I tell y'all not to say shit?" Paris's ass was always going off, but it took her forever to get to the point.

"Say shit about what, Paris? You better say it, or your ass ain't getting paid."

"Your fiancée just left here. Her simple ass came in here to get fitted after y'all fucked, and her nasty ass damn near got nut all over the wedding dress. She had nut all in her hair." Panda and Ash started laughing.

"Nigga, you better learn how to aim. It's good to know I'm not the only bitch that don't swallow."

I didn't need to know all of that about Ash.

"Y'all crazy. Here, take this money." I paid Paris and left the shop feeling free. In another situation, I would have killed her ass, but I had fucked up big time. We were even now, and I didn't have to keep struggling with the guilt. I didn't even say shit to her ass when she got home, but I wouldn't kiss her until I saw her brush her teeth. Bitch wasn't about to have another nigga all on her breath, then put her mouth on me.

That's why this day was special to me. I know I fucked up, but she got even, and we can be happy now.

"Nigga, what the fuck are you smiling about?"

"You wouldn't even understand."

He was about to say something smart when Quick and Baby Face walked in.

"I'm proud of you." Once Baby Face said that, they all walked over and hugged me. We had been through a lot, but we always had each other's back.

"Stay y'all ugly asses like that and let me get a picture." My mama was always cutting up. We took the pic like she asked.

"Blaze, can I see you for a minute?"

He walked out, and I continued to get ready for a day I would never forget.

Chapter 33

Blaze

Releasing my brothers from our embrace, I was about to talk shit to my mom when my girl walked in.

"Blaze, can I see you for a minute?"

Following behind her, I wondered if she was okay. I knew weddings made chicks all sentimental and shit.

"You okay? What's wrong?"

She didn't say anything; she just kept walking. Now, my antennas were raised. In that very moment, I realized I still had some doubt when it came to her brother. Was she about to set me up now? Was he here? Remembering I didn't have my gun on me, I started to get pissed. We turned the corner and walked in a door that said PASTOR'S STUDY. When we got inside, she closed the door and locked it. Grabbing my suit, she undid my pants. My ass standing here thinking she was trying to set me up and her horny ass in here trying to get this dick.

"Your nasty ass just gon' fuck in the church? You don't even care that we in the pastor's room?"

She answered me by wrapping her lips around my dick.

"I guess not. Suck that motherfucker then." Leaning against the desk, I dropped my pants all the way to the floor so that I didn't get nut on it. Grabbing her by her head, I guided her up and down on my dick. I was trying to speed up the process. I didn't want to be caught assed out in church. My mama would beat my ass, and my brothers would never let me live it down. Once I started hearing the slurping noises, I didn't give a fuck anymore. Grabbing her up, I leaned her against the desk and pulled the dress up to her waist.

"This what you want?"

She nodded her head.

"Is this what you want, Drea?" I wanted to hear her say it.

"Yes, I need to feel him."

Sliding my dick up and down her slit, I played up against her clit for a second before I slid it in.

"Fuck, I love the way you feel." Her muscles always gripped my dick just right. Not being able to control my moans, I started going to work. Gripping her ass the best I could, I slid in and out of her like it was my last time in some pussy.

"Yes, Blaze, fuck me, baby. Fuck me."

"Girl, calm down before we get caught." She ignored everything I said once she was ready to come.

"I'm about to come, baby. Yes, fuck me, baby. Yesssss."

As soon as she started shaking, I couldn't control myself any longer. Feeling my nut rise, I realized we didn't have on a condom, and I couldn't pull out, or I would mess up her dress. Knowing this was my Karma for fucking in the church, I said oh well and shot my nut in her. My body jerked, and I swear that's when I realized I was in love with this girl. She was my kind of girl. She was not like the other bitches I fucked with. She was mine.

"I love you, Drea. Let's get married." She looked shocked as she tried to wipe herself off with the tissues on the pastor's desk.

"When? Today? Are you serious?"

"Not today. This is my brother's day, but soon. Will you?"

"Yes, I will." Crying she ran to me, and we had a long, passionate kiss when my phone went off.

"Nigga, where you at? They ready for us."

"I have to go, baby, but I will see you after." After giving her one last kiss, I walked out. My brothers were going to clown the shit out of me when they found out about this. Today would definitely be a day we would always remember.

Chapter 34

Shirree

"Gah, if you get makeup on this dress, I'm gon' beat your ass. This dress is white as the fuck, and your ass crying and shit." Paris was going off as usual, but I couldn't help it. My ass was getting married today, and I was emotional.

"Who the hell says 'as the fuck'? Is that supposed to be some type of slang?" Ash was looking confused, and Panda laughed as she did the finishing touches on my hair.

"You know that's that Louisiana bullsh— Excuse me, Lord." I laughed as Panda stopped herself from cursing in the church.

"I didn't even realize I was cursing in church. Paris, you about to get all of us sent to hell." We laughed as Ash made fun of the way Paris talked.

"Forget, all of y'all. How 'bout dat?" I was so happy they were here to cheer me up.

"Thank you, Drea, for introducing me to them. I appreciate it. I look absolutely stunning." Looking at myself in the mirror, I couldn't be happier with the result.

"Well, I ain't do nothing, but if y'all have some kids, you can send them to my day care." We laughed at Ash, and I walked to the door ready for the next chapter of my life.

Looking over at Alaysia, her vibe was rubbing me all wrong. I didn't know her, but Quick begged me to allow her in the wedding. She sat back here with the rest of the bridal party quiet as fuck.

"Alaysia, are you okay? You looking like you don't want to be here."

She gave me a weak smile. "I'm sorry, weddings always get to me. Thank you for allowing me to be a part of your big day."

"You're welcome. You're with Quick, so you're family." She turned her head away when I said that. When I looked up at her, I realized where I knew her from. She was in the picture at Tate's house. What the fuck! Did she know who I was? Was she here to bust my ass out? I got nervous again and almost ran out of the church. Knowing I couldn't hurt Shadow like that, I stayed, and if my secrets came to life, all I could do is pray he forgave me like I forgave him. But after this wedding, I was going to see what her angle was.

"We'll see you outside. You really do look beautiful."

All the girls agreed with Panda as they walked out the door. My parents were deceased, and I didn't have anyone to walk me down the aisle. That thought alone almost made me cry again. Suddenly, someone knocked at the door, and I went to answer it.

"Baby Face, what are you doing in here?" Hugging him, I was curious to know what he wanted.

"I came to walk the lovely bride down the aisle if you will have me." Trying not to cry, I grabbed my tissue and dabbed at my eyes.

"Don't cry. We can't have you big faced and ugly on your day. Come on; it's almost your turn to walk in." Standing at the door, he looped his arm through mine, and I was so grateful to him at this moment. I heard the music turn on, and he looked at me.

"You ready?" Nodding my head, he told them to open the doors.

I walked down the aisle crying as "With You" by Tony Terry played. Shadow was standing up top with his brothers and the girls. He was looking so handsome. The moment I got close, he started crying with me. At this time, no one else in the room mattered. All I saw was him. After the preacher asked who was giving me away, Baby Face took his place next to his brothers. After saying our vows, the preacher moved on to the next part.

"If there is anyone here who feels these two should not be married, speak now or forever hold your peace."

Not expecting anyone to stand, I continued to look into Shadow's eyes . . . until I heard gasps. Slowly turning my head, there stood the bitch Elise, and she was walking toward the altar. I wasn't confrontational, but she had me fucked up. I was about to beat her ass all over this church—or die trying. As soon as I got ready to turn this bitch ratchet, the doors opened, and Tate walked in. I was fucked.

Chapter 35

Quick

When Shirree came through that door, I don't think there was a dry eye in the room. And that was including me. She had the perfect song, and my brother walked her down the aisle knowing she didn't have anybody. Seeing shit like this makes you want to take that leap. Thankful there was no one in my life, I didn't have to worry about that shit. Looking across the stage to Alaysia, I wondered how things would be if she weren't a lying, conniving bitch. I was falling for that girl, and she didn't give a fuck about my ass. The whole thing was a setup. Turning away from Alaysia, I focused back on the preacher.

"If there is anyone here that feels these two should not be married, speak now or forever hold your peace."

Out of the corner of my eye, I saw Elise stand up, and my heart dropped. This bitch was walk-

ing toward the front of the church. I could see
death in Shirree's eyes, and I knew what was
about to happen. Running toward her, I tried
to stop her before anything happened. Then the
doors burst open and in walked Officer Tate.
Looking back at Alaysia, I was ready to spit in
her face. This bitch had set us up once again.
Looking at my brothers to see what they wanted
to do, Blaze had a look of shock on his face.
When I turned back around and saw Slick standing beside Officer Tate, I knew this was not about
to end well. It was like everything happened in
slow motion. I jumped and pulled Shirree and
Shadow down with me because they were the
closest. As soon as the gunshots started, I looked
over at Blaze and Baby Face. At that moment, I
knew how much Blaze loved Drea. He was trying his best to get to her and protect her. When
the first bullet hit him, it was like everything
stopped. I could hear Baby Face screaming.

"Blaaazzzeeee!"

The second bullet hit him, but he kept running
toward Drea. Once everything stopped going in
slow motion, and I was able to come out of
shock, the bullets hit Blaze nonstop. The shots
finally stopped, and Tate and Slick were gone
just like that. I stood up to walk to my brother
when the screams stopped me. Looking behind

me, Alaysia and Elise were also hit. I couldn't worry about them. I started back to my brother.

"Oh God, not Blaze. You can't take my baby. God, please don't take my baby." My mother was screaming, and all we could do was sit down beside her.

"Somebody call an ambulance."

Shadow was screaming, and I couldn't make out shit he was saying. I don't even know how long we stood over Blaze crying before the paramedics asked us to step back so that could check him.

"He has a pulse, but it's faint. We have to get him out of here."

We walked behind them as they loaded him in the truck.

"He's coding. Let's go, people." The last thing I saw was his body jerking as they closed the door and drove him away.

"Quick, you need to snap out of it. Let's go. We have to go be there for Blaze."

We jumped in the car and sped off. So many thoughts were in my mind, and I couldn't help but allow the guilt to creep up. All of this was my fault, and there was nothing I could do about it. As if my mother could read my thoughts, she started smacking me over and over.

"This is your fault. I hate you. How could you do this to him? How could you?" I didn't even attempt to stop her. Every smack she gave me, I took it.

"Ma, it's not his fault. Don't put that guilt on him. We have to stick together right now."

No matter what they said this time, I would always believe it was my fault. Once we got into the hospital, my mother continued her assault.

"Where the fuck is my son? Where is he?"

"Ma'am, what is your son's name?"

"Zayn Hoover."

"He's in surgery. You all can sit in the waiting room. The doctor will come and talk to you once they know something."

We all took our seats, and I knew this was going to be the longest wait of our lives. My mother started going off again, as usual, causing a big-ass scene. Right in the middle of the argument, a group of men walked our way, and I prayed they weren't Tate and Slick because I didn't have my gun. Once they got closer, I couldn't believe my eyes. What the fuck!

Chapter 36

Baby Face

Watching the bullets hit Blaze's body did something to me. I was supposed to protect him. I ran toward him, and his body dropped. I was too late. The entire time, I kept screaming his name.

"Blaaazzzeeee." But the nigga wouldn't stop running. He was trying to protect Drea. I respect him for that, but at the same time, I was angry at his ass. Once we got in the car to go to the hospital, I wanted to beat my mama's ass for the first time in my life. She was knocking the shit out of Quick and telling him it was all his fault. Knowing my brother, he was already beating his own ass and blaming himself. He didn't need her shit as well. Once the nurse told us we had to wait for the doctor to talk to us, we sat down, and our mama started again.

"All of you are some fuckups. How the fuck could you allow this to happen?"

"Ma, can you stop attacking people? We all are hurt just like you, if not more. We were with him every day, not you." I was getting fed up with her bullshit. It was time for her to shut up.

"You can shut the fuck up because *I'm* the one that pushed him out—*not* you. And you are supposed to be the oldest. You were supposed to protect him. How the fuck did you let this happen?"

"Don't tell me what the fuck I should have done. You weren't there with us. All you did was reap the benefits. We risked our lives every fucking day, and we came home and brought the money to you. We never asked you for shit, but I'm asking you now. Stop this shit. We don't need this."

"Nigga, I ain't never asked you for a fucking dime, but I deserved it. I was the one breaking my back making sure you all were okay. Don't sit here and act like I didn't handle my business."

"Ma, you want a fucking award for being a parent? Everything you did, you were *supposed* to do, and right now, you are supposed to be comforting your kids—not attacking us. We know you are hurting, but we are hurting too." I know she was pissed, but she heard me.

"Your ass talk to me like that again, I'm gon' beat your ass."

Before I could respond, a group of men walked up on us. I knew my eyes had to be playing tricks on me.

"Either my ass is losing my mind, or this nigga is back from the dead."

My mama turned to see who I was talking about.

"What the fuck?" She took the words right out of my mouth.

"Hello to you too, Debra." My dad who was supposed to be dead was standing here smirking at us like the shit was cool.

"Nigga, I thought you were dead. You telling me I struggled for twenty years and grieved your ass the whole way, and your bitch ass was still alive?"

"You already know how I get down, Debra. Watch your mouth. I let your son get away with it, but I won't let that shit slide twice."

I was confused, but I wasn't gon' let him disrespect my mama.

"Nigga, you got life fucked up, and you must be ready to die for real this time."

Shadow and Quick stood up with me.

"And what brother is you talking about?" Quick asked the question I was wondering. That only left Shadow and Blaze.

"Blaze. I met with him a few weeks ago offering my help, and he turned me down. Looks like he should have accepted it instead of calling me all types of bitches."

He was a disrespectful motherfucker. And anybody that knows me knows I hate a disre-spectful motherfucker. This clown-ass nigga had us fucked up.

"Nigga, you got one more time, and I promise you gon' catch this fade. You supposed to be our father. We cried so many nights because you were gone, and you bring your ass here after twenty years, talking shit. Nigga, you got us fucked up."

"Listen, you li'l punk-ass motherfucker. I came back because I wanted you to be a part of my life. I was finally able to come back for my kids, and you niggas talking to me like I ain't shit. You call yourselves Hoover Gang, but, bitch, whose blood running through you? Mine. I gave you the Hoover name, and you are going to respect me—or else."

Grabbing my gun from my waist, I pointed it at him. "Or else *what*, nigga? Don't let this suit fool you. My heart don't pump pussy; it pumps blood. If you want to be a part of our lives, you went about this shit the wrong way, my nigga."

"You think—" He was cut off by the doctor approaching us.

Lowering my gun, I was going to wait until he walked past us. I didn't want him to call the police and put us out before we found out what happened to our brother, but he stopped right in front of us. With a solemn look on his face, he finally spoke.

"Family of Zayn Hoover?"

Chapter 37

Quick

COME CELEBRATE THE LIFE
OF ZAYN BLAZE HOOVER

BORN INTO LIFE ON JULY 12, 1991
RECEIVED HIS WINGS ON APRIL 3, 2017
ZAYN LEAVES BEHIND HIS MOTHER, DEBRA
HOOVER. THREE BROTHERS, ZAIRE BABY
FACE HOOVER, ZAVIER QUICK HOOVER, AND
ZAVIEN SHADOW HOOVER. HE LEAVES BE-
HIND LOTS OF LAUGHS AND UNFORGETTABLE
MOMENTS. COME JOIN US AS WE CELEBRATE
HIS LIFE AND THE MEMORIES WE SHARED
WITH HIM. MEET US AT GARFIELD PARK TO
SHARE IN THIS MEMORIAL SERVICE.

I had read the flyer a million times, and I still couldn't believe it. How the fuck did we end up here is all I could keep asking myself. Laying my phone down, I looked at the clothes I had laid out for Blaze's memorial service, and for the umpteenth time today, I broke down. Trying my best to get my shit together, I sat down on the bed and tried to take a breath. I hadn't spoken to my brothers since the night at the hospital. I kept telling myself, there was no way I could go and face everyone at this memorial service, but I would really feel like shit if I didn't. We aren't having a regular funeral because he wanted to be cremated.

Everyone was invited to come eat, drink, and celebrate his life. Baby Face sent me a text of the flyer, but I told him I wouldn't be in attendance. Walking to the shower, I got in so I could get dressed and pay my last respects to my brother. As the water ran over my face and the tears ran down my eyes, I thought back to the worst day of my life.

It seemed like it took the doctor forever to speak. It was so quiet, you could hear a bitch blink. No one was moving. All eyes were focused on him.

"I'm sorry, but there is nothing else we can do. Zayn was pronounced dead at 8:52 p.m."

Suddenly, screams came from every direction in the room.

"No, not my Blaze. There has to be something else you all can do. Please." My mother was begging the doctor to go back inside and work on him.

"We have money. It doesn't matter what it costs. Please just go save my brother. My brother can't die. Doc, I'll pay whatever; just go back in there and try."

The look on the doctor's face told me there wasn't any amount of money Baby Face could give him that would help my brother live.

"Naw, bro. You have to wake up Blaze. Please, Doc, you have to save him. Please."

All the pleading we were doing fell on deaf ears. All around the room, the only thing you heard was "No, not Blaze. He has to make it. He can't die."

There wasn't a dry eye in the room, and I felt like shit. "There is a chapel here in the hospital, and we can have the priest come and speak to you if you need it. This is a time for your family to come together, not everyone fighting. We have a family room for you if you all want to go in one by one and view the body. We will have to get him cleaned up first, and then you will be allowed to go back. Is there a funeral director of your choice you would like us to contact?"

I knew he was talking, but I completely zoned out after he said my brother didn't make it. My brother and my mother arguing snapped me back to reality.

"Yes, I have a funeral home in mind."

Before she could finish, Baby face cut her off. "Are you out of your fucking mind? My brother wanted to be cremated, and his wishes won't be ignored."

"How the fuck is you going to tell me what I can't do with my son?"

"Ma, I swear if you don't get the fuck out of my face, I will knock your wig in your purse."

My brother was about to snap off some more when Drea and Shirree walked in. The shooting was just a couple of hours ago, but Drea looked like she hadn't been to sleep in months.

"How is he?"

Dropping my head, the tears I was trying to hold back began to fall. Baby Face walked over to Drea and wrapped his arms around her neck. When the tears started falling from his face to hers, she lost it. "Oh God, please, no. This can't be happening. He just proposed to me. He can't leave me now." The way she fell to the floor screaming made everyone else break down. We were trying to hold it together, but the moment we saw how bad off she was, the floodgates opened.

"*Drea, listen to me. He wouldn't want this. We have to stay strong. Some way, we have to pull it together. He wasn't a sad person, and he wouldn't want us doing this. Actually, he would want us to set the hospital on fire. You know my brother. He was strong, so we have to be strong. Okay?*"

I know that he was trying to make her feel better, but none of us believed that shit. For the first time since we arrived, Shadow spoke up.

"*Get the fuck out.*" *We all turned around to see who he was talking to. He was approaching Drea, and I was confused. He grabbed her by her hair and started dragging her toward the door.*

"*My brother got shot trying to save you. If he hadn't met you, my brother would still be here. Get the fuck out!*"

She was trying her best to get loose, but this nigga had a grip on her. We ran over to them and tried to break it up. Even though I agreed with him, I didn't agree with him putting his hands on a woman.

"*You can get the fuck out too. It's your fault just as much as it is hers.*" *My mother started screaming at me and fighting me.*

"*This some dumb-ass shit.*" *As soon as Rico opened his mouth, Baby Face let Shadow go and ran up to him. He didn't even say shit. He swung and knocked the old nigga out. His friends looked like they were about to jump in it when Baby Face pulled his gun again.*

"I'm sorry, I know you all are grieving, but I'm going to ask all of you to leave. This is a hospital, and we have sick patients in here fighting for their lives." The doctor looked at us like he was disgusted. We all grabbed our things and headed out to the parking lot. My body was moving, but I have no idea how I was walking.

"Quick, can you hear me?"

I could hear Shadow, but I couldn't respond.

"Nigga, are you okay?"

As soon as my body hit the ground, I knew some shit was wrong.

"Take them home. I'll stay here with Quick. They not gon' let us all back in there."

I was trying to tell Baby Face that I was okay, but I couldn't. He picked me up and carried me back inside.

"I need a doctor. He just passed out."

I was thrown on a stretcher, while the doctor looked into my eyes with a flashlight.

"It looks like he has gone into shock. We're going to take care of him. It's going to be OK. Oh, we never agreed on what actions to take with Zayn."

"He wanted to be cremated, Doc."

"Okay, you still have to choose a funeral home, and they will do the cremation. You can pick up his remains from them. Now, let me go and take care of this brother. Again, I'm sorry for your loss."

They rushed off with me, and as soon as I made it in the room, everything went black.

That was five days ago, and I hadn't spoken to anyone since. I checked myself out of the hospital, and I have been drunk as a skunk ever since. Alaysia had been steadily calling me, and I wouldn't answer. The shit only pissed me off more. She made it and was alive, but my brother was dead.

Feeling myself getting weak, I got out of the shower and grabbed my clothes. Everyone was asked to wear black and red. Wanting to be simple, I wore my all-black Gucci tee shirt, my all-black Gucci jeans, and my all-red Giuseppe gym shoes. Grabbing my strap, I was ready to go. Jumping in my all-black G-Wagon, I headed to the memorial. When I pulled up, tears started flowing from my eyes. They had his red and black G-Wagon lined up with my other brothers'.

You would think we had talked to one another
because everybody was in theirs today. I pulled
behind Blaze's, and we all got out. They either
knew me very well, or they prayed I would come.
I told them I wasn't coming, and they still waited
in the line for me. Once we got out, everybody
started screaming at us. The DJ got on the mic
and announced us.

"The Hoover Gang has arrived to celebrate the
home going of a fellow Hoover. This one goes
out to you, Blaze."

We walked toward the memorial set up for
Blaze as the song began to play. There wasn't a
dry eye in the crowd as the DJ played "Gangsta
Lean" by D.R.S. Trying to be strong for each
other and not break down, we wrapped our arms
around each other and tried our best to make it
through the crowds.

When we finally reached the memorial, pictures of Blaze were all across the stage. A fire was
blazing in front of the stage just like he would
want it. Drea and my momma were already
standing there, and we just walked up and stood
next to them. This had to be the hardest thing
any of us ever had to do. The DJ walked over to
where we were standing.

"Would any of you like to say something?"
None of us responded except my mama. She

grabbed the mic and walked around toward the stairs. She went on stage and kissed each of Blaze's pictures.

"I want to thank all of you for coming to celebrate with us as we say our final goodbyes to my son, Zayn. Many of you may know him as just Blaze. My firebug. He played with lighters and matches for as long as I can remember. Hell, a lot of us learned firsthand how he got his name. He may have used fire in a way that we will never understand, but he used those same flames to melt away at our hearts.

"My heart will never be the same without him. No mother should ever have to endure the pain of losing a child." She broke down crying, and I felt like shit, knowing I would never be able to console her. I just stood there and cried. Out of nowhere, Rico's ass walked on the stage and hugged her.

"What the fuck is he doing here?" Baby Face had murder in his eyes.

"Not today, bro. Fuck him." Acting like the nigga was never there, we shook hands and talked to people who knew and loved our brother. Everybody ate, drank, and laughed at the memories they shared with him. While they laughed, we continued to shed tears. Tomorrow, they would go on about their everyday lives, and after today, our lives would never be the same. Baby Face went and grabbed the mic from the DJ.

"I would like to thank all of you for coming out and sharing this moment with us. Blaze was no ordinary nigga, so we didn't have an ordinary home going. Usually, at a burial, we throw stuff in the grave with our loved ones to keep with them in eternity.

"Of course, we don't have a body to drop down in the ground, so we are going to do something different. Everybody can come up and throw something in the fire as we say our final good-byes. We gon' light it up one last time for Blaze." He then handed the mic back to the DJ as he played the last song for our brother.

As "When I See You Again" by Wiz Khalifa played over the speakers, everyone came and dropped something in the fire. After everyone was done, my brothers and I stepped forward. We all reached in our pockets and pulled out a lighter.

"I'm sorry I didn't protect you, baby brother, but I promise I'm going to send you some company. I love you always." Baby Face threw his lighter into the flames.

"I'm going to miss you, and I know you are watching down over us from up there. Keep us safe, big bro, and don't give them too much hell." Shadow threw his lighter into the flames.

"I'm sorry. I don't know what else to say, but I'm sorry. Please forgive me, bro, please. I didn't mean for none of this to happen. I need you; please, don't leave me." I didn't even realize I had gotten that loud or started breaking down until my brothers grabbed me to hold me up. Wiping my face, I let out a deep breath and threw my lighter into the flames. Drea couldn't even hold herself together to throw her item into the fire. Paris, Ash, and Panda had to hold her up. They all tossed in a flower and said their goodbyes. My mama walked up with Rico on her arm.

"Baby, you have been trying for years to set your mama's wig on fire. From the first time that fire hit it, you been after it ever since. Here you go, baby. I love you." We all looked in shock as my mama took off her good wig and threw it into the flames. "Come on, let's go. My ass out here looking like baked chicken."

I guess she didn't think it all the way through when she threw the wig. Baby Face handed Blaze's keys to Paris.

"Drive her back to the main house. We'll meet you all there."

"OK, we got her. Y'all be careful." Panda hugged us like she wasn't about to see us in a few minutes.

"Quick, do you mind if I ride with you?" I didn't really want to be bothered, but I nodded and let Ash in my car.

Seeing Juicy jumping in her own car, I wondered why she didn't ride with my brother. We stood at our G-Wagons looking back at Blaze one last time. This would be the last time we did the brother line. It just wouldn't be right without him.

Getting in my whip, I headed to the main house. Looking over at Ash, I wondered what she wanted to talk about. She was quiet, and I found myself staring at her longer than I intended. In another lifetime, she would have been the perfect girl for me. If Ash and I had stayed together, none of this would have happened. Just that quick, I got mad at her ass, and I wanted to put her out of my truck. If she hadn't left and got in a relationship, we would have been together, Blaze would still be alive, and I wouldn't be feeling like my life was over. Yeah, this bitch definitely needed to stay the fuck away from me.

Chapter 38

Baby Face

Leaving my brother's memorial, it felt like I left a piece of me behind. I knew that after today, my life would change drastically. Juicy and I were already into it left and right. She didn't understand why I had to be the one to find my brother's killer. If she thought I was going to let that shit slide, she had me fucked up and may as well leave now. There is nothing anyone could do to stop me from finding Tate and that punk-ass nigga Slick. For some reason, I had a feeling I was gon' have to add my daddy to that list as well. This nigga disappeared for twenty years and then just pops back up, and that's what he has been doing since he's been back, just popping up. There was something about this nigga, and I was going to find out what it was. I hoped Quick came to the main house. We had not seen him since the hospital. He was taking this shit hard and feeling at fault for Blaze's death. I needed to talk to them and let them know what happened at the hospital when Quick passed out. I wanted to get past the memorial service first, though.

As I drove to the main house, I thought back to the night that would change our lives forever.

"I'm sorry, but there is nothing else we can do. Zayn was pronounced dead at 8:52 p.m."

I couldn't get the doctor's words out of my head as I sat around and waited for them to give me news on Quick. I don't remember crying this hard in my life. When our dad faked dying, I had to be strong for my mother and my brothers. The shit hurt, but not like this. I was supposed to protect him, and I failed. I was standing right next to him. With each hit, his blood flew on me. I tried to grab him, but he was trying to get to Drea. Everybody was blaming each other, but the truth is, this is on me. I'm the older brother, and I should have protected him. Just when I thought I was able to leave this life behind, I was pulled back in. If a motherfucker thought this shit was over, they got me fucked up. Everybody involved has to pay.

"*Excuse me, your brother is fine. He went into shock and had a panic attack. He asked that you leave and not be let back. I just wanted you to know he was OK. We are going to keep him for a few days, but he is good.*" Nodding my head, I wiped my face and stood to leave.

"*Quick question. Do you know the women who were shot at the church as well?*"

"*Yeah.*"

"*Nobody has come forward about them, and we need someone to give us information regarding them. One of them was pregnant, and we have her on a breathing machine. We couldn't save the baby, though. The other one is sedated from the surgery. Someone will need to be here when she wakes up. She is paralyzed. It may help if she has family here with her.*"

"*My brother that you have in the back now is the boyfriend of the paralyzed one. Her name is Alaysia. The pregnant one is my other brother's baby mama. Her name is Elise. Can I go back to see them?*"

"*You can see Elise, but Alaysia is sedated. You can come back and see her tomorrow.*"

I followed him to Elise's room, and he left and gave us a minute. Thoughts of her walking toward that altar flashed into my mind. I wouldn't allow anyone else to hurt my brothers. I walked over to her heart monitor and unplugged it so that the doctors couldn't hear her flatline. Reaching for her breathing tube, I bent it. I stood there with tears falling down my eyes. After about twenty minutes, I released the tube. After I plugged the machine in, I ran to the other side of her bed. The machine started going off, and I screamed for the doctors. They came rushing in to work on her.

"You have to leave. We need to work on her." I stood outside her door praying they weren't able to revive her. The doctor walked out ten minutes later with the same look he had about announcing my brother's death.

"I am sorry I have to keep bringing you bad news. She didn't make it."

While I allowed the tears to fall, the doctor patted me on my back. He thought I was mourning her, but I was having a moment with Blaze. I was going to avenge him, and I wouldn't stop until everyone was dead.

"Thank you, Doctor. I have to go and inform my brother about this."

I never told them, but I would once we were together. They may be pissed I made a decision without them, but I couldn't let the opportunity pass me by. The bitch had to go. Pulling up to the house, I grabbed my phone and called Juicy.

"Hey, baby, are you coming over to the main house?"

"I'm surprised I'm invited." This sarcastic shit was getting on my nerves.

"You were invited to the memorial, but I needed to ride by myself. Why don't you understand that?" There has never been someone in the car with us when my brothers and I do the line. I was not about to fuck up his memory doing it now. It wasn't for everyone else. It's a brother thing.

"I'll be there." She hung up, and I got out of the car. When I walked into the house, I realized I was the first to arrive. Going into the kitchen, I made sure the cook had all the food prepared. We would have our personal repast. No outsiders, just us. By the time I walked back in the front, Quick and Ash walked in. Looking at him broke my heart. I knew there was nothing I could do to convince him that it wasn't his fault. Hell, I still blamed myself. Shadow, Shirree, Paris, Panda, and Drea walked in together. The only person we were waiting on was my mom. When she walked in the door, I was pissed.

"You gon' keep trying me, Ma? I don't know what the fuck has gotten into you lately, but you this close to getting your ass knocked out." She had walked in the door with Rico.

"You better watch how you speak to your mama. I don't give a fuck what you say or do to me, but you won't disrespect her." This nigga had me all kinds of fucked up. Pulling out my gun, I walked up to him.

"This is the last time I'm going to say this. You are not welcome here. Not today, not tomorrow, not even on Christmas to shovel my fucking snow. Get the fuck out of my house." He had death in his eyes, and that alone told me I was right not to trust him. This nigga trying to force his way into our lives, and there was a reason for it.

"Son, as long as my name is on the lease with yours, he is welcome here. Now, get the fuck out of the way."

Putting my gun away, I decided to drop it for now, but my mama and I would definitely talk later.

"Look, I wanted you all to come here so we could have a repast of our own and grieve in peace. Also, I wanted to speak about Blaze's assets and how they would be dished out." We all walked in the den and sat down.

"Let's get this out of the way. Drea, do you want to continue to live in Blaze's house?" She looked up, and I swear, I don't know who looked worse, her or Quick.

"No. There's too many memories, and I can't deal with it." She dropped her head back down. I know she was going through it, but her ass acting like she died with him. She damn sure looked like it.

"We'll sell the house and give all the money to Drea." I was about to keep going when she cut me off.

"No, I don't want it. Just split it amongst y'all. I'm good." If I didn't know it before, I knew then that she genuinely loved my brother. Any other bitch would have jumped at the money.

"OK, the clubs and the real estate will be split between the brothers. Ma, we will cover what Blaze gave you every week on top of ours. Everybody good?"

"No, the fuck we not. Where is *my* cut? You all brothers this and brothers that. I'm his *mother*. How dare you leave me out." She was pissed, but I didn't give a fuck.

"You just said that you gon' have this nigga around. As long as he's around, you will never get a cut. You are well taken care of and always will be." She sat down pissed, and I could tell Rico was as well.

"I have something for all of you. After Blaze was . . ." The words got caught in my throat. "I went by and had his ashes put in specialty urns. I had them made into keepsakes. The brothers have ashes that are inside of a Bic lighter, Drea and Ma have a necklace, and then we have one where we will go by the lakefront and spread the ashes in the lake."

"This is moving too fast for me. It's like you trying to erase any memories of him. Fuck that. And why the fuck do we have to sell his house right now? Everything can stay as it is, and we'll handle it later if we need to." Quick was going off, but I understood.

"Bro, I know this hurts, but he's gone, and we can't act like he isn't."

"You think I don't know my brother is fucking dead? I know he's gone, but that don't mean we have to erase all things Blaze right now. I'm not going to do that."

Nodding my head, I decided to give him time. "Okay, bro, we won't sell the house, and we will leave this last urn in the main house until you're ready. Paris, you think you can decorate the mantel and shit and make it like a shrine to Blaze?"

"Don't play with me. You know I can do anything somebody asks me the fuck." We laughed at her ass, but she didn't bust a smile. She was trying to see what was funny.

"A'ight, I'll hit you up when I'm ready. Let's go eat." I passed out the keepsake urns, and we went into the dining area to eat. Juicy walked in the door, and I could tell she was pissed.

"Damn, you couldn't wait on me?" Standing up to pull out her chair, I leaned down and kissed her on the cheek.

"You didn't sound as if you were coming. I'm sorry." She rolled her eyes, but I ignored it. I had enough shit on my plate, and none of it was food. The last thing I wanted to do was fight with my girl, but she was on her way to being single if she thought I was gon' let her come in between my brothers and me. That shit would never happen.

"Can somebody pass me the rolls?" Juicy must be a mind reader and could tell what I was thinking. She grabbed the rolls and tossed one at my ass.

"Fuck you and these rolls." When that hard-ass roll hit me in the lip, only one thought popped into my mind.

This ho ain't got no manners.

Chapter 39

Juicy

I've been sitting in my car, wondering if I want to go inside for the last hour. Deana Banks is what my mama named me, but everyone calls me Juicy. All my life I considered myself to be fat because of my big ass and hips. It wasn't until I became grown that I realized men loved that shit. When I first met Baby Face, things were great, and I loved everything about him. Lately, though, we can barely stand to be around each other. The night Blaze was killed, something in him changed. He would lie there at night just staring into space. He acted as if everything was good, but would curse me out if I made the bed wrong. Shit just wasn't the same, and he tried to turn the shit on me. Yeah, I wanted him to leave that life behind, but instead of him doing that, he dived deeper into it. The night of the shooting, the nigga had the nerve to come home and not say shit. I didn't even find out until the next morning. Even after the way he has been treating me, I tried to comfort him and be by his side. Instead of it drawing me closer to him, he's pushing me away. The memorial was the last straw for me. I woke up this morning wanting to be there for him, and he acted as if I were the scum on the bottom of his Red Bottoms.

"Morning, baby. I made you breakfast. I know it's going to be a long day, so I wanted you to eat something."

"I'm good, thank you, though."

Trying to act as if my feelings weren't hurt, I kept trying to make small talk. "What time are we going?"

"I'm going in a few. I have to take Drea the keys to Blaze's G-Wagon so that it can be in the line."

"Are you going to come back and pick me up?"
He looked at me as if I was getting on his nerves.

"No, you're going to meet me there."

"OK, how about I leave with you now, and I can drive Blaze's truck to the line?"

"What the fuck, Juicy! Just drive your own car, and I'll see you at the memorial. Is that too hard to do? Damn."

With tears running down my face, I tried my best to talk to him. "You don't have to talk to me like that. I'm just trying to be here for you. I'll drive my car."

"If you want to be here for me, quit nagging all the fucking time. That is not what I need." Grabbing his keys, he was out the door. When I made it to the memorial, he hadn't even noticed I was there. He didn't say one word to me, nor was I allowed to come to the front with the rest of the family. When he called me to come to the main house, it was as if he just remembered that I existed. This nigga tried to put on a front like everything was good between us. That's why I hit his ass with them hard-ass rolls.

After I threw them dog biscuits at his ass, I jumped up and ran to my car. What hurt me the most was that he didn't even try to stop me. Not wanting to go to his house, I drove to my mom's. When I walked in, she was in the kitchen cooking.

"Girl, you scared me. What are you doing here?"

I sat down at the counter, and the tears started to flow. "You remember the guy I told you I'm dating? Me and him been going through it lately.

His brother died, and now he's treating me like shit. I don't know what to do."

"Your first mistake was being up under that man all day. Go home and give him some space. People grieve differently. You're trying to be there for him, but he doesn't want that."

"I get that, Ma, but he doesn't have to talk to me the way that he does. The shit hurts, and he don't even give a fuck."

"Do you hear yourself? He just lost his *brother*. He needs time to deal with it and come to terms. Even if he seems to be OK, he isn't. Give him some space and some time. He'll come around." Knowing she was right, I decided to give him time and stay at my place for a while. Kissing my mom, I headed out to grab some of my stuff.

I couldn't believe how much stuff I had accumulated at Baby Face's place. I would just have to come back. Putting as much stuff as I could in my duffle bag, I threw it over my shoulder and turned to walk out the door. He was standing there looking at me with tears in his eyes.

"You gon' leave without saying anything?"

Tears now fell down my face. I tried to get around him. "I didn't think you would care. Just let me leave, please." Why did I have to look up into his eyes? As soon as I did, the bag seemed to drop off my shoulder on its own. He grabbed me and cradled me around my waist. With my legs wrapped around him, he lay his head against mine. We sat there for a moment just lost in our own thoughts. Then he walked me over to the bed and laid me down. Pulling my jeans down, he started to rub his fingers up and down my slit. Looking me in my eyes, he spoke and sent chills down my body.

"Please, don't leave me. I need you. I'm sorry, baby. Please don't leave me." Then his mouth covered mine. Everything I was feeling went out the window when his tongue went in my mouth. Tsunami was poking a hole in my leg, trying to get free. Sliding down, he began making love to my wet spot with his tongue. As mad as I wanted to be with him, I couldn't.

"Damn, baby, right there. Don't stop."

His tongue started going in a whirlwind against my clit, and my body began to shudder. My juices laced his face as I came all over the fucking place. Standing up, he removed his pants and snatched mine all the way off. Grabbing me by my feet, he placed them on his chest as he slid inside of me. Then he started stroking me and began sucking on my toes. The shit was feeling so good that I made a mental note to slap his mama. Winding my hips against him, I tried to pick up the pace, but he wouldn't let me. He continued to slow stroke me. Grabbing me by my feet again, he spread my legs apart. I was damn near in a Chinese split as he went as far as he could inside of me. When he started pulling all the way out, my clit was pulsating so hard I thought it would bust. He was making his tip rub against my clit. I couldn't take it anymore. He was teasing me, and I needed him to stop.

"Come on, Tsunami."

I wanted to tell him I wouldn't be able to come like this, but my body betrayed me at the sound of his voice. As soon as I started shaking, he increased his pace. By the time I creamed all on his dick, he had stopped taking it out and put it all the way in. He was now going full speed.

"Fuck, baby, I'm about to come." His body started jerking, and then he fell on top of me. We lay there in silence for a while, and then he spoke.

"I know I haven't been easy to get along with lately, but I need time to heal. Just stick with a nigga." Never responding, I just kissed him on his forehead and closed my eyes. This man had my heart, but I couldn't stand by and allow him to treat me like shit. I would stay for now, but this shit had to get better. I *needed* it to get better. As much as I wanted to be with him, I would leave him if I had to for my own sanity.

"I love you, Juicy."

"I love you too, Face." Those four words tore down the walls I was trying so hard to build up. As I rubbed his head, I prayed things got better for us. This nigga was everything I had dreamed of, and he had that dope dick. A bitch was sprung, and I wanted him in the worst way. What scared me was that sometimes what you need and what you wanted didn't always go well together. Closing my eyes, it felt like I had the weight of the world on my shoulders. As I continued to massage his head, I hoped sleep found me soon.

Chapter 40

Shadow

After the ladies left our personal repast, Baby Face sat down and talked with us.

"When Quick was in the hospital, the doctors told me Elise and Alaysia were there. He said that Alaysia was paralyzed, and Elise was on a breathing machine. I convinced him to let me in the back to see Elise, and that bitch will no longer be a problem for you, baby bro."

"What you mean? I already paid her off, and the bitch still tried to step to me. That ho not gon' go away. I fucked up." I wasn't getting what he was saying.

"Nigga, you so damn smart you dumb. He telling your ass he cancelled that bitch like Nino." Quick used our favorite line from New Jack City.

"Good looking, my nigga. If you hadn't, Shirree's ass was damn sure going to try." I was relieved as fuck, but a part of me would miss her. This was definitely for the best because that bitch's pussy had voodoo in it.

"Why the fuck didn't you kill Alaysia?" I know that Quick is hurt right now, but that wouldn't be a smart move on our part.

"Because they still have evidence, my nigga. If we kill that bitch, all of us go down. We have to figure out a plan. The first part of that plan is to kill Slick's ass. He is their eyewitness." Nodding our heads in agreement, we looked over at Quick.

"You know you gon' have to go see her, right?" He was playing the blame game, but we needed to know what they ass was up to.

"I'm not going to see that bitch. If I do, her ass gon' be at the crossroads with Uncle Charles's ass." Laughing at this nigga, I decided to leave it alone. He would come around.

"A'ight, y'all, I'm out. I have to go and check on my fiancée."

We dapped it up and headed out.

That was two hours ago, and her ass still ain't home. I called her phone a million times, but she didn't answer. This bitch had me fucked up if she thought she was going to continue to cheat. I let the shit slide once because it made us even, but she had me fucked up if she thought she was going to carry on with this shit. As soon as I heard the door open, I went the fuck off.

"Where the fuck have you been, Shirree?"

She looked at me like I lost my mind. "Damn, I didn't know I had a curfew. I'm *not* the one that got caught cheating—*you* are." She had me fucked up, and it was time to knock the grin off her Peter Pan-looking ass.

"You didn't get caught, but you definitely got even." She looked like a nigga trapped in the closet with his dick out. "Yeah, I know, and I figured we were even, but the shit ends."

"How do I know that you aren't still fucking that bitch?"

"Because the ho is as dead as your edges. I'm not going to tell you again, the shit ends today." She got happy as hell.

"I'm not cheating on you, Shadow. I did that one time, but that's it. I promise. Me and the girls went to check on Drea." Feeling like shit, I walked over to her and hugged her.

"My bad, baby. I kept calling you, and your ass wasn't answering. There's too much shit happening. You can't be disappearing like that."

"Okay, I'm sorry. It won't happen again."

Grabbing her, I pulled her in to me. Now I know on days she don't shave she can look a little manly, but I know this bitch ain't started wearing men's cologne.

"Shirree, I know damn well Drea's ass ain't wearing no Gucci Guilty. I'm not gon' ask you again to dead whatever you have going on."

For a brief second, she had fear in her eyes. At least, that's what it looked like to me, and then she started laughing. "Shadow, I told you there is no one else. The girl sprayed your brother's cologne all over her house. She said she wanted to feel as if he were there. Quit looking for something that is not there. If you don't mind, I would like to get your brother's scent off me. The shit is creepy."

"My bad, baby. When you get out of the shower, stay naked. I wanna lay this dick up in you." She laughed, and I smacked her ass when she walked off. Walking into my room, I started removing my clothes. I had to stop thinking Shirree's ass was up to something if I wanted this shit to work out. They say a guilty motherfucker stays accusing the next person to hide their guilt. That shit was as real as it gets. I know she wanted to set another date for our wedding, but there was no way I would ever step foot in another church. Blaze's death had me fucked up in the head. I hadn't been getting any sleep, and I was thinking maybe busting a nut would help. Also, knowing that Elise's bitch ass was not a factor helped ease my mind. Looking at Shirree step out of the shower, I realized my brother's death was affecting something else. My damn dick was softer than baby shit. Willing my dick to stand up, this motherfucker just lay there like a Ramen noodle. This shit was about to go left quick.

Chapter 41

Shirree

Leaving the repast, I knew I didn't have long to get back to the house. Tate had been blowing me up, and I couldn't wait to get out of there. Jumping in my car, I headed over to his place. I can tell he was used to bitches doing what the fuck he wanted, but I told his ass not to contact me anymore. As soon as I got there, I was going to call his fucking captain and tell his ass what the fuck was going on. I don't take kindly to threats. Pulling up to his house, I stepped out of the car and knocked on the door. Pissed that he was taking his time, I started banging on the motherfucker. He snatched it open and had the nerve to have an attitude.

"Quit hitting my fucking door like that." Grabbing me by my arm, he snatched me in the house. Grabbing my phone out of my purse, I let him know what the fuck was about to happen.

"I see you don't believe fat meat is greasy. Didn't I tell you what would happen if you called me again? I don't take kindly to threats, and this shit ends today." As I unlocked my phone, I heard him cock his gun back.

"I will blow your fucking brains out all over this coffee table. Don't play with me, bitch. You think I'm that stupid? If I go down, so does your man and his brothers."

"I don't have shit to do with their business. Just let me go, and I won't say anything." He laughed all crazy like.

"Bitch, you not gon' say shit no way. Matter fact, you talk too much any-fucking-way. Open your mouth. I bet I know how to shut your ass up." When he placed the gun to my temple, I knew I had no choice but to do what he asked. He unzipped his pants and pulled out his dick. I opened my mouth and let him have his way. As he damn near tore my mouth apart, he never moved his gun. My jaws were in pain, and I could feel the sides of my mouth splitting. Slob was shooting everywhere, and his body finally started shaking.

"Ah, fuck, damn, girl." After two minutes, he was shooting his sperm down my throat. As soon as he pulled away, I heard another voice in the room.

"Damn, girl. I'm gon' start calling your ass the Joker. Your shit should be split all the way to your ears the way he fucked your face." Turning around, I looked in the face of the man I had seen at the memorial.

"Let me formally introduce myself. I'm Rico, Shadow's father and your soon-to-be father-in-law." He smiled as he watched me mentally shit on myself, and I'm not talking about no big-ass turds either. In my mind, I had that runny-ass flu diarrhea shit running all up and through my thongs.

"What do you all want from me?" I now realized I should never have come here. I should have gone straight to the police station.

"Well, first, I want to see what your pussy feels like since I had to watch you in action from the porch. I haven't had any black pussy in years. Then, you are going to bring me $10 million, courtesy of my son, and he will never find out about any of this."

"I can't get $10 million from him at one time without him noticing. I'm not even sure we have that much." Tears started to fall down my face.

"Then you will figure out a way to bring me as much as you can until you have paid it off. If you try to tell him, know that my son *will* kill you. If he doesn't, one of the brothers will. If you go to the police, I will kill him and make you watch before I kill your ass. Do I make myself clear?" Nodding my head, I cried. I fucked up, and there was nothing I could do about it.

"Now, take off those clothes and let me see what my son is so crazy about." Pulling my pants down, I damn near passed out when I saw Tate pulling his dick out again with Rico. As my fiancé's father pulled me on top of him to ride his dick, Tate started massaging his shit. Rico guided me up and down on top of him.

"Ride this dick or I will kill your ass right now." Looking into Rico's eyes, I knew he wasn't playing. Grinding my hips slowly at first, I started picking up the pace. The shit wasn't easy to do because his old ass had a big-ass dick. Finally catching a rhythm, I started bouncing my ass up and down on his dick like it belonged to me. Rico grabbed me and pulled me down to him. As soon as he did that, I felt Tate rubbing his dick against my asshole. I tensed up as I prepared for him to enter me. As soon as he shoved it in, I screamed out in pain. For his dick to be so little, it still was ripping my ass open. When he started pumping harder, I could feel my ass getting wet. The situation I was in was fucked up, but I would lie if I said this shit didn't feel good. My juices were running all down Rico's dick. Moans started escaping my mouth, and I couldn't control it. Once Rico realized I was into it, he slid his tongue in my mouth as he massaged my breast. Sucking his tongue, I continued to ride that motherfucker until I felt my body start to shake.

"That's right, baby, come on daddy's dick." Leaning forward, I slid my breast in his mouth as I bounced my ass against Tate's dick. He started shaking; then I felt him go limp. Once he pulled out, he lay on the floor and just watched the rest of the show. Rico spread my ass cheeks apart and started slamming me up and down against his dick. Right when I thought he was going to come, he lifted me and pulled me to his mouth. This old-ass nigga had a tongue like no other. He sucked another nut out of me in two minutes. Right after he sucked my soul out, he slammed me back on his dick. Gripping my muscles, I knew he wouldn't last much longer. His body started to shake; then he released inside of me. Lying back moaning, I started winding my hips against him. Yeah, I knew the shit was wrong, but the deed was already done. I kept winding my hips against him until I felt his dick getting hard again. As soon as his shit rose up, he flipped me over and slid back in. Once he started hitting me from the back, I damn near fell in love. Holding on to my breasts as he slammed inside of me, I moaned at the pleasure I was feeling. Tate crawled over to us and slid under me. He started sucking on my clit as Rico kept hitting me from the back. I wondered if Rico's balls were hitting him in the forehead and damn near laughed. Leaning down, I started sucking on Tate's dick. I almost forgot that I was getting fucked; I started sucking his dick so hard. The nut that was rising brought me back to what was going on.

"Fuck, I'm about to come again," I moaned to no one in particular. When Rico's pace picked up, I knew he was about to come as well. All you heard were the sound of his balls slapping my ass and the slurping from Tate and me. Out of nowhere, everyone started moaning and screaming at the same time. My body started shaking first, and then I felt Tate's nut shoot down my throat. He slid from under me, but Rico was still pumping his nut out.

"Fuck. Shit. I'm coming. Fuck!" Rico screamed, and his body started shaking. Once he shot his nut inside me, we collapsed to the floor. Don't get me wrong, Shadow's sex is off the chain. He was the best I ever had . . . until I fucked his daddy. The thought of what just went down almost had me creaming again. I was feeling so good and relaxed that I damn near could have gone for another round.

"Now, get the fuck out and go get me some money." Rico snatched my ass back to reality, and I remembered why I was here in the first place. Getting up to put my clothes on, I couldn't wait to steal some money so I could come back over here. As long as I had to be blackmailed, I might as well enjoy it.

When I left, I stopped by Drea's house to check on her. As soon as I walked in the door, I was ready to leave. She was spraying cologne everywhere, and my ass damn near choked to death.

"What are you doing?"

She looked crazed. "I need to feel like he's here. This was his favorite cologne, and the scent was leaving my bed. If it leaves, then he leaves. He can't leave." She sat on the floor and started crying. Getting down there with her, I just held her. I didn't know what to say in a situation like this. Then someone knocked on the door. I got up to open it. Panda, Ash, and Paris walked in.

"Gah, why does it smell like car air fresheners and incense in here?" I didn't want to laugh at Paris, but the shit was funny as hell.

"Drea, are you in here trying to have a séance and shit? You know that shit fake, and you can't talk to the dead, right?" Ash was looking like she really hoped that wasn't what she was trying to do.

"Ash, a séance *is* real. Don't make fun of people's culture." Everybody looked at Panda like she lost her mind.

"Gah, sit down. You sound crazy as the fuck. How in the hell is talking to dead people a culture?" Everyone laughed but Panda. Gathering my things, I laughed at Paris's slang. Who says "as the fuck"?

"I'm glad you all made it. I'm about to head home and check on Shadow. I'll call you tomorrow, Drea." Jumping in my car, I headed to my house. I made it there damn near an hour later. Shadow's truck was there, and I knew he was going to question me on where I had been. Happy that I stopped at Drea's house, I now had an alibi.

Just as I thought, he was going off and asking me a million questions. After I convinced him that nothing was going on, I jumped in the shower to wash the shame and betrayal off me. Not to mention, his father's nut from all inside of my coochie cat. When I walked out of the bathroom, I really didn't want to have sex, but I have never turned my man down. He would know something was up if I did. Praying my coochie cat could get wet one more time today, I headed over to the bed. After trying a million things and sucking for ten minutes, his dick still wouldn't get hard. He tried to apologize to me over and over, but I kissed him passionately, letting him know it was OK. Lying down with a smile on my face, I was happy to have dodged a bullet.

Chapter 42

Rico

When I first came back to the States, I intended to get close to my sons and ask them for help. A nigga saw they were in trouble, and I would help them. Blaze changed all of that. Him getting shot had me having to reveal myself sooner than I wanted. Even then, their ass wasn't trying to welcome a nigga back.

Getting back in with Debra, I just knew these niggas would give her a lump sum of their money. Imagine my surprise when Baby Face told her they wouldn't give her a dime because of me. A nigga started to panic, and I knew I could never return to Puerto Rico without the money I owed or I was a dead man. Using my head, I thought back to the day I saw Shirree fucking Tate. I had my way in, and I didn't have to kiss my sons' asses to do it. I showed up at Tate's house, and the nigga was pissed and wanted to know who I was.

"Who the fuck are you, and why are you at my house?" He had his gun raised, and I chuckled and walked past him.

"I'm someone you need to know. You and I have a mutual problem, and I think I can help you."

"I don't need your help; you can leave."

"It's funny how people feel they always covered their tracks when they fuck up. You just shot up a church, and my son was killed. I have been following you for a while, and I have it on tape. You can either help me, or I tell my sons where they can find you."

"What the fuck am I getting out of the deal?"

"You get what you wanted from the beginning. Money. Shirree is the key to all of this. She is in it up to her neck, and she has no choice but to comply. If my sons found out what she has done, they will kill her and wouldn't think twice about it."

"What do you need me to do?"

"Call her."

When she came over, I didn't expect her to give in so fast, and I damn sure didn't have intentions on fucking her again. What I didn't expect was for Shirree's pussy to be this fucking good. She was throwing that shit back, and I was turned on like a motherfucker. It would be hard to kill her when this was all over, but she had to go. She knew too much, and the bitch was easily broken. Now all I had to do was start laying this good dick in Debra's ass, and I know she will hold a nigga down. They didn't give her Blaze's money, but they still took care of her. I need all the money I can get—and fast. My original plan didn't exactly go the way I wanted it, but my sons would all feel my wrath. Fuck them.

Chapter 43

Debra

Leaving the main house, I was pissed. Baby Face done lost his damn mind. That was my son, and I pushed him out of my pussy. How the fuck was he going to tell me I couldn't get a dime of his money. True enough, I didn't want for anything, but I didn't like how he did that shit. He's been talking to me reckless too. He knew not to play with me. I wasn't that mother that allowed disrespect, and I wasn't about to start tolerating that shit today. We are all dealing with Blaze's death in our own way. Another thing I didn't understand was their hatred toward their father. I'm pissed as well, but I don't hate the nigga. He's been sniffing up and around this good shit lately, but before I open my legs and my heart up to this man, I needed answers.

Jumping in the shower, I freshened up and threw on some pajamas because he was coming over. Going into my closet, I grabbed a wig and threw it on. My dumb-ass sons stood there and let me toss my hair in that damn fire, knowing my ass was as bald as a crackhead's mouth. As soon as I adjusted it on my head, the bell rang. Walking down the stairs, I realized my hips had some extra swish in them. I laughed to myself. Mama still got it. Then I swung the door open.

"Damn, baby, you looking good." Rico walked in the door on good bullshit.

"Nigga, I always look good. Fuck you, though. Bring your ass in here. Sugar ain't good for my diabetes, so quit trying to sweet-talk me." Making sure I swished a little harder, we walked into the front room and sat down on the couch. "Rico, all jokes aside, where the fuck have you been?" He took a deep breath and went on to explain what happened.

"The night I got shot, they took me to the hospital, and I didn't die. Franco walked in and told me I would be transferred to his estate to get better, and no one would know where I was. Once I knew I was okay, I tried to leave, but he told me I had to do one more run first. If I did, I could go back to my family safe, and no one would bother us again. I had to meet with the connect in Mexico and do one last exchange. When I did, the police came in and arrested me.

The nigga set me up, and I been in jail ever since. Baby, I just got out, and I came straight here."

I don't know if it was old feelings that came back rushing over me, or if it was because I had been lonely all this time, but I wanted him in the worst way.

"I'm sorry you went through all of that. My sons needed a father, but we did all right, and they came out great. I just wish I had known where you were all this time. Me and them niggas would have been eating tortillas and corn all day and drinking Coronas because I would have moved to Mexico."

"You would have done that for me, baby? I didn't write or anything because I didn't want you to give up your life because mine was gone."

"I gave it up anyway. I haven't been with another man since you. It was always you, Rico." He leaned over and kissed me, and the juices I thought had turned to powdered milk came flowing down my legs. We headed to the bedroom, and I knew this was going to be a night to remember.

"Must be love on the brain that's got me feeling this way. It beats me black and blue, but it fucks me so good, and I can't get enough. Must be love on the brain." I sang Rihanna's "Love on the Brain" to the top of my lungs. That sex from last night had me feeling good. I was walking through the house, cleaning and singing. Rico had left to get his stuff. He was going to move in, and I couldn't be happier.

As "Fire and Desire" by Rick James came on, I really got in my groove. That was . . . until I hit a part in the song that shook me to my core. "Then I kissed your lips, and you turned on my fire, baby . . . And you burned me up within your flame." As soon as I sang that, I started thinking about Blaze. How the fuck could he leave me? I didn't have favorites, but he always clung to me more. We had a special bond, and now he was gone. As the tears rolled down my face, I went from sad to pissed and from pissed to crazed. Thinking about all of our memories, I couldn't remember a single time he didn't threaten to set my wig on fire. Jumping up off the floor, I ran to the closet. I snatched each wig off my rack. I didn't want to see another wig ever in life. That shit brought back too many memories. Fuck this shit, fuck these wigs. Fuck the bastard that took my baby. Every time I thought of a different thing I could say fuck it to, I threw a wig into the trash. This shit wasn't fair, and I was pissed. The harder I cried, the madder I became. I grabbed my lighter and threw it in the trash can. Fuck him and fuck them wigs. Sitting on the floor, I cried. A piece of me was never coming back, and I didn't know how to deal with it. This shit was hard, and I was glad Rico would be here to help me through it. Looking through the fire, I could see Blaze. What the fuck is going on?

Chapter 44

Quick

"Stop calling my fucking phone." Hanging up for the umpteenth time today, I powered my phone off. Alaysia wouldn't stop calling me. My brothers were getting on my nerves as well because they wanted me to talk to her. Fuck that bitch. If they want to make sure she doesn't talk, then they can fuck with her ass. The only person that has been helping me through this situation was Ash. When she got in my car leaving the memorial, I was about to put her ass out. I just didn't want to deal with anybody right then.

"Quick, I get it. Nobody understands what you are feeling, but I get it. When I was a teenager, a girl stabbed my cousin in the throat. I was taking up medical at the time, and I knew what to do in a situation like that, but I did nothing. I just stood there stuck.

"The blood had me frozen in place. By the time I was finally able to move, I ran home instead of helping him. I went and got help, but I didn't help him. When he got to the hospital and died, they said it was from blood loss. All I had to do was put something to his neck to stop the bleeding, but I didn't. I stood there frozen. Nobody understands that kind of guilt. It's like you will always feel if you did this differently, they would have made it. Everyone around you telling you it's not your fault, but nothing they say eases the guilt in your heart. It's almost ten years later, and I still feel that guilt.

"I learned to get through it, but it wasn't easy. All I want is to help you get through it. I didn't have anybody helping me." I looked at her and the tears flowing from her eyes, and my heart melted. She was the only person who understood what I was feeling.

"Thank you, Ash. That means a lot to me." She leaned over and kissed me on the cheek.

It was going to be a long road, but I was glad I had someone to go through this with me who knew what I was feeling. She had been texting me all day checking on me, and I appreciated it. She was stopping by the house later to bring me some food. I would have let her come now, but I had a stop to make first. I needed to see my mom. The way she was acting toward me and treating me was eating me up. I was kicking my own ass, and I didn't need her to do it as well. Besides, as long as she was going at me, Baby Face and she would be into it, and I didn't want that.

I pulled up to her house, and my heart started racing. The upstairs room was on fire. "Blaze!" I screamed. Jumping out of my car, I took off toward the house. He was the only person in our family that had an infatuation with fire. Running in mom's door, I took off up the stairs. Once I burst through the door, my mama was sitting on the floor while the flames rose from a garbage can. It had already busted the windows out and was now spreading throughout the room. I ran out the door and back down the stairs. Grabbing the fire extinguisher, I headed back to my mama's bedroom, spraying until the fire was out. I couldn't figure out for the life of me why she was just letting it burn. As if she knew what I was thinking, she answered me.

"It was like I could see him in the fire. He was there. I could see him. I knew if I put the fire out, he would leave. I didn't want him to leave me." Sitting down next to her, I put my arms around her. For the first time since Blaze died, she let me touch her. "Why did he have to leave us?"

"I ask myself that question every day, Ma. I'm so sorry. Just tell me what I have to do to make this right." Now I was crying with her. She looked at me and pulled away.

"Son, I was hurting. I know it's not your fault, but I needed someone to take my anger out on. I'm sorry for making you feel like that." We hugged again and cried for what seemed like hours. "Son, can you do me a favor?"

Leaning back to look at her, I answered. "Yeah, Ma, anything."

"Can you take me to the beauty shop to get my hair done? Fucking with that nigga, he finally won. I done set all my damn wigs on fire." Leaning back, I laughed hard as hell. I needed that shit to. A nigga was tired of crying.

"I was wondering why you were in here looking like a slave off Django."

"Fuck you, nigga. Let's go."

"I'm just saying, every time I looked at you, I heard 'give us free.'" She slapped me as we laughed down the stairs. Just like that, we were back to normal. Knowing I was going to be a little longer than expected, I texted Ash.

Me: I'm going to be a little longer. You can let yourself in, and I'll be there as soon as I'm done with my mom.

Ash: We can do it another time if you want.

Me: It's cool, I haven't eaten in a week. The code is 0712. Punch it in the garage pad, and you can go in the house that way.

Ash: OK.

I looked at my mom and laughed again. I couldn't believe she burned all her damn wigs.

It took her two hours, but she was finally done, and I must say, she looked good as hell. I have never seen my mama wear her real hair. I don't know if she was already bald, or if she had them cut it, but she was rocking it in some type of low cut with spikes. It looked good on her. She got out of the car when I dropped her off at home.

"Ma, I'm going to send somebody over here to fix your windows. Make sure you open the door and call me when they leave."

"Okay, baby." She walked off, and I drove home. I called the window repairman, and they said they would send someone right away. As soon as I pulled in the garage, I received a text.

Ma: They here, and he ugly as shit. At least you could have sent a fine nigga.

Me: Ma, he there to fix the windows, not be your man.

Ma: Who said anything about being my man? I just wanna see what that mouth do.

Me: Bye, Ma. Let me know when he leaves.

I got out of my car and punched in my code. When I walked in the door, my house was smelling good as fuck. My shit has never smelled like a home cooked anything—not even breakfast. Walking in the kitchen, Ash was singing and throwing down.

"Ash, what you cooking, girl? The shit smell good as fuck." She jumped when I said her name.

"Boy, you scared me. I'm making lasagna, salad, and garlic bread."

"You remembered after all this time that lasagna was my favorite food?"

"I remember everything about you, Quick." She turned her head and continued making the salad. I felt my dick getting hard, but I didn't need that complication in my life right now. She fixed our plates, and we ate in silence. I had so much to say but couldn't bring myself to say anything at all. Deciding to leave well enough alone, I ate my food and wrestled with my thoughts. After we were done, I didn't want her to leave just yet. It felt good to have someone here. If it was just me, all I would think about was Blaze.

"You want to watch a movie with me?"

She laughed. "Nigga, don't be trying to Netflix and chill. I know what that shit means."

"No, seriously. Just a movie."

She came and sat beside me on the couch.
When she lay her head in the crook of my neck,
I wrapped my arms around her and played the
movie. Ten minutes into the movie, I fell asleep.
When I woke up, it was morning, and Ash was
gone. That was the first time in days I had been
able to get some sleep. I'm gon' have to find a
way to get her ass over here every day. Looking
at my phone, I saw a text from my mom.

Ma: They gone.

Ma: Nigga, you not gon' respond?

Ma: The fuck did you tell me to text for if your
ugly ass wasn't gon' say shit?

This lady is bat-shit crazy, I swear.

Chapter 45

Ashanti aka Ash

Being there with Quick was bringing back so many memories. At one point in my life, you couldn't have paid me to think we wouldn't be together. Sitting here watching him eat, you could tell there was a lot he wanted to say. I wasn't going to force him because I know he needed time. When he asked me to watch a movie with him, I knew I needed to go home. Having a man, I couldn't just walk in the house at any time of the night. But one look into Quick's eyes, I knew I couldn't say no.

There was so much sadness there, and he was looking to me to help him. When I snuggled up against him, everything felt right . . . but it was wrong. Ten minutes later, he was snoring. I gave him another ten minutes to make sure he was all the way asleep; then I slid out. As soon as I got in my car, I cried. I had met Quick when I was 18.

He was in love with me, Ashanti Smith. We went everywhere and did everything together. He was my first everything. He gave me anything I wanted, even bought me a BMW truck before I knew how to drive. All the hoes hated me, but he didn't see anybody but me. He was the love of my life, and it was supposed to be him and me forever, but he changed all of that in one night.

I had just found out that I was pregnant. I jumped in my car so that I could tell him the good news. I never thought he would be upset or not want the baby because we were so in love with each other. Using my key, I let myself in his house. The farther up the stairs I got, I knew he wasn't alone. Nothing was out of place, but the feeling that came over me almost made me run back down the stairs and out the door.

His bedroom door was open, and I didn't even get the chance to walk all the way in the room. He was laid back on the bed, and my best friend had his dick down her throat. Her head bobbed and weaved as she moaned from enjoyment. I eased down the hall and took off down the stairs. I never told him why I broke up with him. All he would do was try to convince me of how sorry he was.

Never speaking to that bitch again, the only people in my life that I knew I could trust were Drea, Paris, and Panda. Fuck a new friend. Half these hoes are only your friends to get close enough to see what you got. Once they see what you have, they plotting on a way to get what you got. Motherfuckers could have that shit.

Pulling into my driveway, I noticed my boyfriend Jason's car was there. Wiping my face, I got out of the car and made my way inside.

"Mommy, where have you been? I missed you."

Grabbing my son, I picked him up in my arms.

"Yeah, where the fuck have you been?"

Ignoring Jason, I responded to my son. "Zavi, I told you that TT Drea is sick right now, and she is going to need Mommy to help her feel better. I'll take you with me next time. Now, why aren't you in bed?"

"Daddy told me I could stay wake and wait for you."

Cutting my eyes at Jason, I got Zavi ready for bed. After having him potty and brush his teeth, I laid him down. Kissing him, I turned the light off and walked out of his room. As soon as I rounded the corner, I was knocked off my feet.

"Bitch, you think I'm stupid. You smell just like another nigga. You ain't been with Drea."

Crying, I stood to my feet. "You are *not* going to keep hitting me. You promised the last time was it. Besides, you just hit me for nothing. I *was* with Drea. Her entire house smell like Blaze because she wants it that way to be close to him. If you took your ass in there, you would come out smelling like another man too."

"Then you should have said that when I asked you. Don't play with me, and I won't have to beat your ass."

"If you hit me again, I will take our son, and you will never see him again."

"Bitch, that threat don't mean shit to me. Your ungrateful ass keeps forgetting that he *ain't* my son. Fuck out of here. Now you keep talking, I *will* leave your ass with nothing. What nigga gon' want you with a baby and nothing else?"

I walked away from him, locked myself in the bathroom, and cried.

Quick would kill me if he knew I kept his son from him all these years. When I left his house that night, I promised I would never look back. He had hurt me to my soul, and I wanted to do the same to him. Two weeks later, at my lowest moment, I met Jason. Being the girlfriend of Quick, I never had to work because I didn't want for anything. There I was in Walgreens because I needed a ginger ale and some crackers. I didn't have enough money, and I slid down to the floor, crying. Jason walked up to me with my stuff in a bag. He helped me up off the ground, and I looked at him. He was fine as hell.

Not as fine as Quick but still fine, nonetheless. His caramel complexion was so smooth, and his dreads were nice and neat. He was on the big boy side, but not in a flabby kind of way. Walking me outside to my truck, he looked confused.

"How the hell you got a BMW truck, but can't pay for a soda?" Standing in Walgreens parking lot, I broke down again telling him my story. "Come on, you staying with me tonight." I left with him and have been there ever since. He was willing to step in and be the father to my child under one condition. I could never tell anyone that he wasn't the daddy. I agreed and thought he was my savior, but he was far from that.

He has torn me down to the lowest he possibly could. He constantly reminds me of what he does for me and how he took in my son. I hate his ass with a passion, but I have nowhere else to go. I hate I even put myself in this position. He supported me all through school and when I opened my day care. I thought shit was finally going well until he made me close it down. He told me he wanted to work on having a child and the stress from the center would cause complications.

I listened, and the nigga never had any intentions of giving me a baby. Every time I talked about starting the day care back, he would go off on me and said I wasn't taking my family seriously. It was all a control thing. He made sure there was no way I could ever leave him. A bitch cried herself to sleep every night, especially since we barely sleep in the same room.

I knew this shit was unhealthy, but what the fuck was I supposed to do? Until I was able to get away from him, I was stuck with his fat, funky ass. I refused to keep raising my son in this environment, but I needed a plan first. I could stay with Drea, but I would have to make sure Quick never saw his son. He was the splitting image of his ass. I know that going around Quick is like playing with fire, but he needs me, and I plan on being there for him. My dumb ass just has to figure out a way to keep all of my skeletons in the closet. The shit was getting complicated, and I knew I would have to tell him, but I wasn't ready to die, and I knew that nigga was going to kill me—if his brothers didn't kill me first. This was the only baby out of them, and no one but my girls knew he existed.

Chapter 46

Drea

"Boy, I need you bad as my heartbeat. Bad like the food I eat, bad as the air I breathe."

I cried as I screamed out the lyrics to "I Need You" by Jazmine Sullivan. It seemed like everybody was moving on with their life, and my ass was sitting here stuck. It's been two months since Blaze has been gone, and my ass is still going crazy. Every day, I would spray my house with his cologne so that I could be close to him. People still came to visit, but not as frequently as before. Ash was the only one that stopped over all the time, but that was only because she was using me as an alibi. She thought I was crazy, but I knew better. When the next song came on, I damn near lost it. Seems like Pandora was trying to put me on suicide watch.

"Some people want it all, but I don't want nothing at all if it ain't you, baby . . ." Alicia Keys had me singing my soul out. The tears were flowing, and my nose was running.

"Okay, bitch, I can't take this sad shit no more." Paris had scared the fuck out of me. I didn't realize she, Ash, and Panda had walked in.

"What the fuck I'm supposed to do? Walk around happy and shit like I'm sucking dick every night like your ass? My man gone. What the fuck am I happy about?" Everybody was starting to piss me off. They wanted me to pick up the pieces and shit, but I couldn't. I don't think I will ever be the same.

"For starters, you can take your ass to the doctor and get some prenatal vitamins." I looked at Ash like she had lost her mind.

"The fuck I need those for?"

"Gah, if we don't know shit else, we know a pregnant ho." Paris's ass was gon' make me smack her.

"What Paris is trying to say is that's the reason you can't pick up the pieces and get your life back on track. Your hormones are all over the place." Even though I was shocked at what they were saying, at least Panda said it better.

"Have you even looked at your stomach, sis? Your shit has always been flat as a Chinese booty, but you got a pudge and shit. I know you haven't been eating much, so what else could be the reason?"

I heard what Ash was saying, and I thought back to the last time I had my period. It has been a couple of months, and the only time I had sex with Blaze without a condom was in the church . . . the night he died.

"God has a sick way of bringing Karma to my door." The girls looked at me like I was crazy. "The only time me and Blaze didn't use a condom was at the wedding. We dipped off for a quickie." Dropping my head in shame, I felt like this was God's punishment for disrespecting his house.

"Bitch, have you lost your mind? What would possess you to fuck in a church?"

Rolling my eyes at Panda, I got up off the floor and went into my room to throw some clothes on. I didn't have time for her righteous-ass ways today. If I was carrying Blaze's baby, I would be so happy. A piece of him would still be here with me, and that would make shit worth living for. Walking back into the front with the others, they looked at me like I was crazy.

"Where the fuck you going, gah? You got company, and you just gon' jump your depressed ass up and leave?"

I shook my head at Paris. "Girl, I'm about to go to the doctor, and y'all ugly asses coming with me."

"Hell yea, I'm going for this tea. Let's go, bitch."

I knew Ash's ass was only gon' tell Quick. That's why she wanted to go. We jumped in Panda's truck and headed to the doctor. As soon as I walked in, I got irritated. The shit was packed, and a bunch of kids were in there. Why were so many kids in the doctor's office in July? I filled out my paperwork and waited to be called. Ash got up and started playing with the kids.

"This girl thinks that everywhere she goes is her day care. Why won't she open it back up?" I asked Panda and Paris.

"Jason won't let her. He said he don't want her to work."

Sounded like some controlling shit to me, but I kept my mouth closed. This was what she loved, and I couldn't imagine someone telling me I couldn't work if I wanted to.

After waiting an hour, they finally called me to the back where a nurse took my vitals. Then I pissed in a cup, and we all waited for the doctor to come back to see me. The room was quiet, and I started thinking I should have made them wait out there and found out on my own first, but the doctor walked in and sat down at that moment.

"I see you have a lot of love and support. Let's do an ultrasound." I lay on the table, and the doctor rubbed gel on my belly. As soon as the monitor hit my stomach, you could hear the heartbeat. Tears immediately fell from my eyes. When I looked over at my girls, they were crying as well.

"Why is everyone crying? This is supposed to be a happy occasion."

"The father of my child was just killed three months ago."

"I'm sorry to hear that, and now I can understand why the weight is so low. This little one needs you to eat and give it proper nutrition, okay? Come back in a month, so I can see where you are, and make sure that your weight is picking up. I'm going to prescribe you some prenatal vitamins, and I want you to make sure you don't stress." She left the room, and the girls ran over to me and hugged me.

"I'm so happy for you, Drea. At least you will always have a part of him."

Hugging Panda, I thanked her.

"Bitch, now that you know you pregnant, you need to get your shit together. Your ass can't be sitting around talking to the dead and shit anymore."

I swear Paris's ass just didn't know when to stop.

"I know. Now, let's go. I need to grab something to eat. Blaze Jr. needs some food."

"Bitch, no, you will *not* name that baby Blaze Jr."

Everybody laughed at Ash, but I was going to think of a name that would incorporate Blaze. As soon as I found out the sex, I would go from there. We left the office, and I was glad things were finally looking up. I just wish he were here to share this moment with me. As I walked back to Panda's truck, the breeze was blowing all over me. Any other time, it would have just felt like wind, but right now, at this moment, it felt like Blaze was wrapping his arms around me.

"Hey, let's go to Chilis."

They all groaned in unison. I'm sure they were tired of that place. It was my favorite spot, and I dragged their ass with me every time I went.

"Bitch, I hope the baby starts craving something else. A ho can only eat a fajita so many times. Damn."

I closed my eyes and thought about my baby. I couldn't wait for it to get here.

Chapter 47

Quick

"Didn't I say I wasn't ready yet? Damn. Give a nigga some time." My brothers were pissing me off because they were ready to spread Blaze's remains in the lake, and I still wasn't. You would think they would understand. We were at the main house having a heated discussion.

"Nigga, I'm giving your ass one more month, and then we gon' do the shit with or without you."

I was getting real sick of Baby Face's ass. "Nigga, who the fuck put you in charge of everything? He was our brother just like he was yours. You can try that shit with Mama, but I'm telling you now, I will shoot the shit out of your ass if you keep playing with me."

"You heard what the fuck I said. Have you spoken to Alaysia? I'm trying to find these niggas, and their ass done disappeared like a bitch's edges after wearing micros." We laughed.

"I haven't seen that bitch. Fuck her."

"You already fucked her, but you can't do that shit, Quick. You putting all of us at risk. You need her on your side until we can figure this shit out. Hell, at least until we find that nigga Tate and Slick."

I knew Shadow was right, but I didn't want to look at that bitch. "I hear what y'all saying, but I need time."

"*You* talk to this nigga. He gon' make me fuck him up. He acting like a real bitch right now." Baby Face walked out the door.

"Fuck him."

"Naw, Quick, you saying fuck all of us. This was *your* mess, and now *you* have to live with it until we can figure out how to clean the shit up. You gon' have to man up and take one for the team, my nigga. Get your shit together." With that, Shadow got up and walked out the door as well.

I walked over to the shrine that Paris made of Blaze and just stared at it. She really did a great job. She had someone come in and paint the whole wall with a picture of him, and she had gold tables set up all around it. On each table was something of Blaze's, including the urn with his ashes in it.

"Bro, I need you to tell me what to do. They asking me to do something I don't think I can do. I need your guidance right now." I stood there for another ten minutes, then finally decided to leave. He didn't want to talk to my ass, and I didn't blame him.

Grabbing my keys, I walked out and locked up. Jumping in my whip, I headed to the house. As I drove home, I hoped that Ash would stop by. Since she has been coming around, I have been able to deal with my guilt, and I could sleep. The days she didn't come, I tossed and turned all night. Pulling into my driveway, I looked at this big-ass house and wondered why I had it. I didn't have any kids or a girl to share it with. Nigga was just in this big motherfucker like a li'l-dick nigga floating in a pussy with no walls.

Walking in the door, I sat on the couch and tried to get comfortable. The doorbell suddenly rang, and I got happy as hell. I wonder why she was coming to the front door instead of using the key. Opening the door, I was ready to hug Ash—but I was thrown off at who was standing at my door.

"What the fuck you doing at my house, and how the fuck you know where I live?"

This bitch Alaysia was on my doorstep in this ugly-ass wheelchair. You would think all the money they were scamming from niggas, the bitch should have at least been able to get a Hoveround.

"Quick, we need to talk."

"Bitch, if I wanted to talk, I would have answered when you called. Get the fuck off my doorstep." She was looking at me with tears in her eyes, but I didn't give a fuck. "Roll, bitch." She looked at the nurse that had brought her here.

"It's fine. You can leave."

"I didn't know your ass was deaf too. You're not staying here. Your arms about to be strong as shit." I went to close my door, but she stopped me.

"Don't make me turn you in, Quick. I don't want to do that, but I can't allow you to force me away. I wouldn't help Tate, and *that's* the reason I got shot as well. We can take him down together, but I need you. If you say no, then I have no other choice but to turn you and your brothers in."

"How the fuck you gon' blackmail a nigga to be with you? That's some pathetic shit." Moving out of the way, I walked back into the house, but I left the door open for her to come in.

"I love you, Quick. Please don't be this way."

"If you loved me, you wouldn't be here black-mailing a nigga. You are going to help us find Tate, and then your ass have to go." I looked at this bitch roll over to me on the couch so she could look me in my eyes.

"Nobody wants him as much as I do. Just don't shut me out. I know we met on fucked-up terms, but we were getting past that."

Yeah, she and I were sneaking around having sex, but that's all it was for me.

"I'm not the nigga you want, Alaysia. You just need me right now. We can help each other, and I won't treat you like shit, but I won't go out of my way either." Getting off the couch, I headed upstairs.

"You gon' leave me down here?"

Laughing, I looked back at her. "I told you at the door, your arms about to be strong as shit around here. I'm not a fucking nurse."

Seeing the tears in her eyes did something to me. That let me know, I liked her a little more than I let on. "There's a bedroom down there. The shit is already made up. A bathroom is in the room as well. Just go through the kitchen." I went to my room and thought about the shit I got us all in. I wondered if Ash would be upset once she found out Alaysia was here. I jumped in the shower and washed my ass. The pressure from the water running over me had my dick hard. At least, that's what I told myself. Truth is, every time I thought about Ash, my shit was on brick. Massaging it, I wondered if I could get a quick nut and be good. The more I stroked it, the harder it got, but my nut wouldn't come up. Fuck.

Grabbing a towel, I went downstairs to see what Alaysia was doing. I'm sure she was happy I had a walk-in shower because she was rolling her chair out of it. She was asshole naked, and her breasts were sitting up so damn pretty and perky. She caught me staring at her and decided to capitalize off my weak moment. She rolled back into the bedroom and grabbed her lotion. Then she slowly started massaging her body with it as she stared me in my eyes. Grabbing her legs, she lifted one on top of the chair. When she started playing in her pussy, I knew I was about to do something I was going to regret. Walking over to her chair, I dropped my towel and slapped her lips with my dick. She opened her mouth and swallowed me whole.

"Fuck." I leaned my head back and allowed her to go to work. Her mouth was so wet that she had slob running down my balls. Grabbing her by her head, I started fucking her face. I wasn't trying to make love to her or enjoy this shit. I just wanted my nut. No matter what I did, the shit wouldn't come. Getting frustrated, I pulled my dick out of her mouth and lifted her out of the chair. Placing her in the bed, I grabbed her legs and pushed them back all the way over her head. Right as I was about to slide my dick in, I thought about that shit.

"Hold up." I ran out of the room and upstairs. Grabbing a condom, I came back down, and she was lying there playing in her pussy again. Putting the condom on, I threw her back in the position I had her in. Sliding my dick in, I went to work. This was the shit that had me sneaking and fucking her ass the last time. This bitch had some good-ass pussy. Slamming my dick as hard as I could, I tried to work my nut up.

"Baby, I'm about to come. Fuck, don't stop, Quick. Go deeper."

I knew the bitch's legs were dead, but, damn, was her pussy paralyzed as well? I had all my shit so far in her, she should have tasted it. Gripping her hips, I used them as leverage and slammed as hard as I could. Her body started shaking, and she cried out. Finally, I could feel my nut rising, and I kept slamming until the shit shot out of me. I lay on top of her as my body shook, and she tried to kiss me. Getting up, I walked out and closed the door. I could use her ass for a nut, but that's it. A nigga was trying to get back with Ash, and I couldn't be in no relationship with Alaysia's ass. Not to mention, I didn't want to. I cared about her ass a little, but I could never be with that ho. *She* was the reason I was going through all of this shit. I opened up to her, and the bitch blackmailed me. She already walked all over my heart. I wasn't about to let her roll over that motherfucker as well.

Chapter 48

Baby Face

"Wait, so the bitch just got dropped off on your doorstep?" My brothers and I were riding around looking for this nigga Slick.

"Yea, nigga. She wouldn't tell me how she knew where I lived, but I'm guessing since she the fucking police, it ain't that hard. Now she blackmailing me to stay with her."

I felt bad for my baby brother.

"This shit is crazy, but at least she's ready to help us get Tate. That's all I give a fuck about."

I agreed with Shadow. Right now, we need her ass.

"All I'm trying to figure out is how the fuck she gon' help us? Who the fuck gon' be rolling her ass around during a shoot-out?" The visual alone had me laughing harder than I meant to.

"You, nigga. That's your bitch."

"Shut the fuck up. Y'all niggas play all day. Her ass was sitting at the bottom of the stairs like I was gon' carry her ass up. She got me fucked up. I ain't no fucking caregiver."

Quick was going off, but I knew my brother.

"You fucked her, didn't you?"

Quick was trying to look disgusted, but Shadow and I started laughing.

"Nigga, you fucked up. How you fucking the disabled? Can't you go to jail for that shit?" Shadow was dead serious, but I couldn't stop laughing.

"Fuck y'all. This nigga hiding in a cave some-damn-where like Bin Laden. Y'all may as well roll with me over to Mama's house. I have to take her some money." I chuckled to myself as I envisioned Alaysia trying to be sexy with her dead legs. That shit was funny as fuck to me.

We pulled up to my mama's house. I was glad he needed to come over here. I've been meaning to check on her after Quick told me what happened. It seemed like all of our asses was losing it one way or another. Grabbing my key, I unlocked the door, and we walked in. Music was playing, but we couldn't tell where she was. Smelling food, I decided to look in the kitchen. When I walked in, I threw up all over my Red Bottoms.

"Ma, what the fuck!" Rico's punk ass had her lying on the table, legs spread, and eating her shit like it was a sundae covered in chocolate syrup.

"Aw, hell naw. Why the fuck would you ask me to come over, knowing this nigga was in here eating powdered eggs?"

"Fuck y'all. This my house, and if I want to get my pussy ate, I can. Where the fuck is my money so I can get back to this love session?"

"Y'all nasty as hell, and, Rico, your ass gon' have a throat full of sweet hair. Sitting there sucking on all that wolf pussy. Ma, you oughta be ashamed all of that damn hair." I turned to leave before I threw up again.

"Nigga, don't disrespect your mama like that. Show some damn respect." I swung around so quick I damn near slid on some chocolate.

"Fuck you say to me, nigga? Respect *what?* Two old motherfuckers in here acting like some nasty-ass kids. I'm trying to let you be great, but I promise you trying me, and the shit ain't gon' end well for your ass."

"Bro, let's go. This ain't the time. Your slow-ass mama still standing here with her coochie screaming 'I'm Rick James's bitch.' She ain't even tried to cover up, and I ain't trying to be in here fighting with Mama's juices all over the fucking place."

Shaking my head, I turned to walk out the door.

"Where's my money?"

I turned around, and she was standing there with one hand on her hip and the other stuck out, coochie hair still sweeping the floor. I walked out without responding. I would come back later after she was decent and give her the money. Juicy was gon' have to do me a favor and take my mama with her to get waxed. That shit don't make no damn sense. We climbed in the car, and Quick threw the money in my trunk. I was really trying to figure out Rico's angle.

"Fuck is this nigga around for now? Everywhere I turn, this nigga is there. I'm so close to ending that nigga's life it's ridiculous."

"Why you hate him so much, bro? He was a great dad before he fake died. Maybe we should hear him out."

I looked at Shadow like he lost his fucking mind. "Nigga, he's been gone twenty fucking years. He couldn't come check on us once? Fuck that nigga. He up to something, and there's a reason he around. Stay the fuck away from him until I figure out what the fuck it is."

"Nigga, you don't have to tell me. Fuck him. I wonder what he said to make Mama go back that easy, though. She usually can smell bullshit a mile away."

Quick was in deep thought about it.

"Big bro, people can always see somebody else's shit, but when it's their heart, they become blind as a motherfucker."

I couldn't agree more with Shadow. When I pulled up to the main house, I let them out because I had somewhere else to go. When I got ready to pull off, Quick yelled through my window.

"Hey, nigga, take your mama to handle that. She got more hair on her coochie than she got on her wig."

I laughed at his clown ass and drove off. I wanted to check on Drea. I know the girls always go by and check on her, but our brother would be disappointed to know we didn't look out for his girl. Parking in front of her house, I got out and rang the bell. When she opened the door, I knew she wasn't expecting it to be me. She was asshole naked and out of breath. Pushing her out of the way, I forced my way into her house. I know I didn't have the right to be mad but wasn't no nigga about to fuck my brother's bitch, and he hadn't been gone but three months. Checking each room, I noticed she was here by herself.

When I walked back in the front, she was walking past me to go in the back. I couldn't help but look at her. I told myself don't look at her in that way, but my dick didn't listen. Her body was perfect, and her skin was smooth as hell. My dick was trying to bust out of my pants, and I knew I couldn't be in here long. When she came back out of the room, she had a robe on, but the shit was still hugging her body.

"Who did you think was at the door?"

She rolled her eyes at me. "Paris and them. They coming over here so we can go out to eat. I just got out of the shower. Why are you here?" She had an attitude, and I didn't know why.

"I was just coming to check on you. Are you straight? Do you need anything? You still our sis, so if you need something, we got you." My mouth was saying sis, but my dick was saying blow her back out.

"I'm okay, and I appreciate you checking on me, but since you here, I can tell you. You're going to be an uncle. I'm three months' pregnant."

I couldn't express the feeling that came over me. I was so fucking happy that tears welled up in my eyes. Before I knew it, they started falling down my face. To know that I would have a piece of my brother did something to me.

"It's gon' be okay, Face. He's watching down over us." The only person that calls me Face is Juicy. She walked over and hugged me. I didn't even realize the tears were still falling down my

face until she wiped them. "It's going to be okay."
My ass didn't even realize I was still hugging her
until my dick got brick hard again.

She didn't pull back when she felt it, but
she looked up in my eyes, and I knew why my
brother was so in love with her. She was pretty
as fuck, and her lips alone would make your
dick jump. Tsunami was begging me to let him
out, and I was begging him to lie down. We had
been in a stare off for about thirty seconds when
I couldn't take it anymore. I leaned down and
kissed her. When she kissed me back, I knew
I had to do it now before I came to my senses.
Taking her robe off, I picked her up around my
waist. Kissing her again, I cuffed her ass, and
I swear I almost came right then and there.
Laying her on the couch, I took her nipple in my
mouth while I massaged the other one. Making
my way down, I took her clit in my mouth. As
soon as I got one lick, she jumped up.

"I'm sorry, Face, but I can't do this. I'm lonely
and losing my mind, but I can't fuck my fiancé's
brother. This shit is so wrong." I heard what she
said, and I felt like shit. Looking at her, I knew
she was saying it, but she wanted me as badly
as I wanted her. Picking her robe up, I placed
it back on her, allowing my fingers to graze her
nipples as I closed it.

She was right. I think we were only having this attraction because we both were missing my brother. I'm glad she had sense enough to stop me because I would have held so many regrets. Kissing her on her lips one more time, I headed toward the door.

"I'm sorry. Please don't hold this against me."

"I won't. We are both grieving and don't know how to deal with it. I'm not mad at you." When she hugged me as I stood in the door, all common sense went out the window.

"Fuck this. You just gon' have to hate me." I kicked the door closed and picked her up. Walking her to the bed, I lay her down and kissed her with my whole being. I wanted her to know that I needed her. Even though it was wrong, right now, she was what I needed to feel closer to my brother. Sucking her breasts this time, I eased my pants down without her noticing. I wouldn't give her a chance to stop me again.

Coming back up to kiss her, I could feel her getting ready to protest and stop me. Before she could get it out, Tsunami was sliding inside of her. Her pussy was so tight against my dick that I had to tell him not to come yet. Grabbing one of her legs, I slid in and out of her slowly to let her get adjusted to my size. As I continued to stroke her, I kept kissing her, never allowing her the chance to ask me to stop.

Once she was grinding back on me, I knew she would finish, and we would have to deal with the consequences and guilt tomorrow. Sliding out of her, I went back to do what I initially wanted, and that was to suck her soul out. Sliding my tongue up and down her ass, I sucked all of her juices. I have no idea why I did that. I hadn't even licked Juicy's ass. Using my tongue to find my way to her clit, I sucked and swirled until her body was shaking under me.

When I felt her creaming all in my mouth, I got back up and slid my dick back in. I sat down on my ass and pulled her to me. Once she cradled me, I held her tightly as I felt the tears fall down her face. Gripping her ass, I guided her up and down on my dick. Looking at her fine ass cry, I leaned in and kissed her. Feeling my nut rising, I pulled her farther in the kiss as I shot my nut inside her. As soon as my body was done shaking, the guilt came over me like a rush of wind.

"I'm so sorry. Fuck. I can't believe I just did this shit." With tears now rolling down my face, she climbed off me. Wiping my tears, she looked at me.

"It's okay. I shouldn't have allowed you to do it. We are both wrong, but it was something we both needed. On tomorrow, we will never speak of tonight again, and it will never happen again. Is that clear?" I nodded my head as my dumb ass continued to cry. I was ready to leave and go beat myself up some more . . . until I felt her mouth on Tsunami. This was only for tonight. I kept telling myself that. Just for tonight. When I felt her deep throat me, I knew that was gon' be easier said than done.

"Suck that motherfucker then." As her jaws tightened around Tsunami, my veins started bulging, and I knew it wouldn't be long. She must have known it too because she let it go and slid down on it. Once she started riding, it was over. She was doing tricks I had never seen before.

"Fuck. I'm about to come again." I knew it was quick, but I couldn't hold it. She tightened her muscles and gripped my nut right on out. I'm glad she was already pregnant, or we would have a problem. When she slid off me this time, I headed to her shower. There was no way I was going home to Juicy smelling like Drea's pussy.

When she climbed in with me, I knew I had to hurry up and get out. This girl was about to have me sprung, and that couldn't be. It was just for tonight, and tomorrow, we would forget it happened. As I told myself that again, I found myself with her clit back in my mouth. This shit is fucked up.

I finally made it out the door, and I swear I wanted to run my car off the road. A nigga ain't never cried this much in his life, but here I was again with tears falling down my face. If it's true what they say, and Blaze was looking down on us, I prayed he would forgive me.

Not wanting to go home and face Juicy, I decided to swing by my mama's house. I still had the bag of money in the trunk for her. When I pulled up, I grabbed the money, but this time I knocked on the door. After about five minutes, my mom finally opened it.

"Damn, Ma, what the fuck was you doing?"

"Why you didn't use your key?"

Looking at her like she was crazy, I snapped. "You know damn well why I didn't use my key." Laughing, she walked away from the door and sat on the couch. I passed her the bag of money, and she smiled.

"Thank you, baby. The next round I'm gon' fly to the car lot to get my Benz."

"Ma, there's more than enough money in there for you to get your car, and you don't have to wait for drop-off days for some money. You know any one of us will give you anything."

"Yeah, I know, but the drop-off days be having a bitch feeling like she the Queen Pen and y'all paying me what you owe me." I swear this lady was crazy. "Besides, I'll get the car the next time because I have to give Rico some money."

Pissed wasn't even the word to describe how I was feeling. "Why the fuck is you giving that nigga money? I'm not about to give him shit." She grabbed my hand and pulled me back to the couch.

"You not giving him anything. You are giving it to your *mother*. Once I have it, it's mine to do with as I please. Now, me and your father is back together, and the only thing I know how to be is a ride or die. That shit won't ever change. He trying to open up shop again, and I'm going to help him." I get what she was saying, and I loved that my mother was a down-ass chick, but I wasn't with him using her.

"Why the fuck he don't have his own money? Fuck did this nigga come from anyway?"

"Calm down, son. You are so angry at your father, and it's not healthy. You just lost your brother. You don't need to be harboring all of these feelings around. He just got out of jail. He been there the entire time. In Mexico, Franco fucked him over in more ways than one."

"What you mean by that, Ma?"

"That don't matter, son. All that matters is, he is back, and I need you to find a way to forgive him for me."

"I will be cordial for you, but I'm still not fucking with that nigga." She nodded, and I decided to change the subject. "You about to be a grandma."

"Oh my God, son, I'm so excited. Congratulations. Just don't let the baby call me granny or no shit like that. I'm too fly for all of that."

"Ma, Juicy is not pregnant. It's Drea." The hurt came over her face, but I could tell she was still happy.

"I knew my son wouldn't leave me. He left a piece of him with us. That will help." Knowing what she meant, I nodded in agreement; then I stood up to leave. Time to take my ass home.

"Ma, where that nigga at anyway?"

"I don't know, and he got me fucked up. That's what took me so long to answer the door. I was cutting his clothes up." Laughing, I opened the door.

"You too old for that shit."

She kissed me, and I walked out the door. Jumping in my car, I had so much on my mind. Juicy was only trying to be there for me, and I pushed her away, but I opened up to Drea being there. I was foul as fuck, and I was gon' make it up to my girl.

She needed me as much as I needed her. Drea was only for one night; Juicy was my lifetime. It was time I showed her. When I got home, I got in bed and just hugged my girl. As I drifted off to sleep, all I could hear was Shirley Murdock: *We forgot about all the pain we'd cause as we slept the night away. As we lay.*

Chapter 49

Shadow

I know men have double standards and shit, but I will kill Shirree where she stands if she is still out here cheating. Don't get me wrong, I know I fucked up, but I have been straight ever since I went back to my girl. This ho started leaving in the middle of the night and all hours of the day. I have never been the type to follow a bitch or go through her shit to see what she's doing, but I'm damn near tempted to do all of the above. She keeps saying she's with Drea and helping her since she's depressed. I've talked to my brothers, and they chicks be over there a lot too. Some shit just seems off, though. Maybe she thinks I'm cheating since my dick still ain't working. I don't know what the fuck is going on, but my shit been flaccid ever since Blaze died. The shit was weird as fuck to me. I tried numerous times, but nothing she does gets him to stand up. That nigga be dead-ass asleep like it worked a twelve-hour shift. Tonight, I was determined to get this motherfucker up and running. I would be damned if my bitch be out here cheating on me because my dick ain't working.

Grabbing my MacBook, I pulled up Pornhub and started watching videos. Grabbing my dick out of my jogging pants, I started slowly stroking it. By the time the chick had deep throated the nigga, my dick was at full attention. Reaching in my nightstand, I grabbed some oil and rubbed it on. Shirree told me she was on her way home, and I was determined to keep this motherfucker hard until she got here. Making sure I didn't bring my nut up, I slow stroked it as I watched two bitches eating each other out. My dick was brick hard, and I couldn't wait for Shirree to walk her ass through the door.

"Is this why you can't fuck me? You only get turned on by bitches on the internet?"

Trying to stay focused, I kept stroking. "No, I was trying to make sure I was hard for you when you got here. I need to feel my pussy, and I don't know why my brother's death made my shit stop working, but I'm ready now, baby. Come get this dick." The look on her face almost looked like she didn't want to, but she came over and got in bed.

Laying my laptop to the side, I made sure it was still playing, just in case the shit tried to go limp again. As soon as she put her mouth on it, I felt my shit going soft. Fuck. Looking back at the screen, I tried to focus on the threesome that was taking place. They were going at it, but it was a lost cause. My shit had shriveled up so badly, the nigga was damn near invisible. She immediately caught an attitude.

"Don't ask me to do this no more unless you sure the shit is gon' work."

"I'm sorry, baby. I don't know what's wrong." I prayed she didn't think it was because of Elise. That ho was a nonfactor. All I wanted to do was fuck my fiancée.

"Did you ever think how it makes me feel? That my man can't even get his dick hard no matter what I do? The shit hurts, and I'm not putting myself through that anymore unless I know for a fact it's back to normal." I couldn't be mad at her, and I knew how the shit was making her feel, but shit, it ain't like I didn't want some pussy. Needing a drink, I got up to go to the store.

"I'm about to head to the liquor store. You want something?" She shook her head and headed to the shower. Feeling like shit, I got in my G-Wagon and drove off. As soon as I pulled up, this girl was getting out of her car, and I swear that my dick jumped at just the sight of her. She had on some booty shorts that stopped midcheek, and half of her ass was hanging out. As she walked in front of me, I was so focused on her ass that I didn't even realize she stopped. I ran right into her.

"Damn, nigga, your dick hard as hell. Let me find out."

"What you gon' do about it if you find out?" She smiled as I got in line. I don't even know why I was talking shit, because as soon as I would pull it out, the motherfucker wouldn't work. I laughed at my damn self. All this money a nigga got, but his dick can't get hard.

She walked over to the back, and I ordered my drink. Paying for my shit, I walked out. A nigga was not trying to get in any more trouble. When I got outside, I walked in the back of my truck and pulled my dick out to piss. Halfway through, I felt a hand wrap around my shit.

"Let me hold it for you." This chick was bold as hell, and I was starting to realize I was a ho magnet.

"It's all good; I'm almost done." She didn't release my dick, and I didn't move her hand. When the piss stopped, she actually shook my shit. When she did that, my dick became brick hard. She started massaging that motherfucker, and I wanted to tell her so badly to stop. A nigga couldn't take the embarrassment more than twice in one night, but the more she stroked, the harder it got. I know I needed to get my ass home to my girl, but a nigga needed an ego boost.

"Get in my truck." I climbed in, and she got in the passenger side. As soon as the door closed, her mouth was on my shit. Her head wasn't all that, but a nigga was happy that his shit was staying hard. Leaning my seat back, I grabbed her head and forced it all the way down on my shit. Instead of getting mad, she started moaning. That caused a nigga to lose his mind.

"I'm about to come. You gon' catch it?"

Her response was to go deeper on my shit and tighten her jaws. I shot my nut down her throat, and my body started shaking like a stripper. She kissed it and sat up.

"Thank you. Man, you don't know how badly I needed that shit." My body was still shaking, and I was trying to gather myself. Reaching in my pocket, I grabbed out ten one hundred-dollar bills. A nigga can't fuck with her, but I can thank her for her services. I handed it to her, and she thanked me.

"Thank you, and I know you don't want me in that way, but take my number. Maybe I can help you out from time to time."

Thinking about what she said, I stored her number in my phone and told her I would hit her up. Driving back home, I couldn't wait. My dick was back working, and I would just surprise Shirree. I knew she would be asleep, but I was gon' wake her up with this good dick. When I walked in the door, I headed straight for the shower. Rubbing it a little as the water ran over me, my shit got brick hard. I got out and went into the bedroom, but as soon as I got in the bed and got near Shirree, my dick went soft.

What the fuck is going on? Maybe it ain't my brother's death after all. It may be the guilt from Elise, or, hell, maybe I'm grieving Elise. Whatever it is, I hope the shit goes back to normal soon. I didn't even catch the girl's name from the store, but I guess I *will* be calling her. A nigga need a nut. This shit was really fucking with my mental. I needed to figure out what the fuck was going on. I didn't even open my liquor after releasing that nut today. A nigga went straight to sleep.

Chapter 50

Quick

"How your nigga feel about you hanging out with me?" Ash had been meeting up with me damn near every day. Since Alaysia been at my house, I been doing pretty good about keeping Ash away. I didn't want her to pop up over there and see her. Knowing I needed to tell her, I tried to build my way up to it.

"He doesn't know. I tell him I'm with Drea." She continued to eat like it was no big deal.

"I don't want to cause problems in your house, ma. A nigga love you being around but not if it's gon' cause friction."

"You can't cause something that's already there."

Realizing there was something deeper going on with Ash had me feeling like shit. All this time she's been over here helping me, but I didn't know shit about what was going on with her.

"I have something I need to tell you." Looking her in her eyes, I decided to go on and say it before I lost the nerve. "I have a chick staying with me now." Something in her eyes changed, but it was fast as hell.

"It's all good. Look, I should get going. Jason gon' have a fit if dinner is not ready." I wasn't letting her off the hook that fast. I knew she was only leaving because of what I told her. Grabbing her hand, I saw the tears forming in her eyes.

"She blackmailing me, Ash." Knowing I didn't want to hurt her, I told her everything from the beginning. She knew I blamed myself for Blaze's murder, but she didn't know why until now.

"Quick, that's so fucked up, and I understand. Until you can find a way out, you have to do what you can to keep her happy." Wanting to lighten the mood, I looked at her and grabbed a handful of my mashed potatoes.

"You better not. Quick, I'm not playing your ass—better not—"

Before she could finish her sentence, I threw them in her face. The shit was all in her hair like I released my nut sack on her shit. Laughing, I jumped up from my seat. She took her whole plate and threw it at me. Standing there with gravy dripping off me, I knew I had to get her back. Taking the pitcher of wine she was drinking, I poured it on her ass and dashed out the door. Jumping in my car, I started it up. She came flying out the door chasing me with a cup of something. When she opened my door, I stopped her ass.

"Ashanti, your ass better not throw that shit in my Maybach." She didn't listen and threw it anyway. Laughing, I put the car in drive.

"Your ass better come on before they lock you up." Realizing I just had her skip out on the bill, she jumped in the car fast as hell. I pulled off, and I couldn't quit laughing because of the look on her face.

"Why would you do that?"

"I knew you wouldn't do it if I told you to. A nigga had to trick your ass." I knew the owner, and I would pay his ass tomorrow, I just wanted to see her have fun for once. It felt good as fuck to laugh. Knowing she needed to shower and change before she went home, I stopped in Walmart since the mall was closed. Any other bitch would have looked at me like I was crazy, but Ash was different. That's why she could get anything I had.

We walked around the store holding hands as she picked out something to throw on. Settling on some leggings and a tank top, we headed to the register. After I paid for it, we jumped in my car and headed to my house. I knew Alaysia would have an attitude, but I needed Ash to know that it wasn't like that. When we walked in the door, she slapped me and took off running.

Chasing her trying to get her back, I fell up the last four steps.

Laughing at me, she did a victory dance and went into the room. Limping in behind her, I sat on the bed. She was undressing in front of me, and I was trying to be a gentleman. I know I had seen every inch of her body, and I was her first everything, but she was more filled out now. She was thick as hell and had a grown woman's body.

Leaning forward, I tried to hide my dick so she wouldn't see that I was hard. She walked in the bathroom and got in the shower. Trying my best to sit there, I lost that battle and followed her in the bathroom. Opening the shower door, I stood there and looked at her. When she looked into my eyes, all the feelings I had for her came flooding back.

"Ash, why did you leave me?" The question caught her off guard, and I could tell she was about to lie. "The truth, Ash. Keep it real with a nigga." She took a deep breath and told me how she came home and saw me getting head from her best friend. All these years, I never knew that was the reason she left. I didn't even know she saw me. She never said a word.

"Ash, I was young and stupid, but know I didn't intentionally hurt you. When I got out of the shower, I climbed in my bed. I didn't even know she was in the room until her mouth was on my dick. A young nigga like me getting money wasn't equipped to turn down some shit like that.

"Fucked up part is, the shit wasn't even that good. I lay there thinking about you and how you were going to kill me when I told you, but you never came back. I didn't even fuck her. Now, I know that doesn't change what happened, but I swear I loved you so much, and I didn't mean to hurt you." Looking at her now, I could see how much I hurt her. She was crying tears, and I just wanted her pain to go away.

Coming out of my clothes, I stepped in the shower with her. Hugging her, I tried to let her know how sorry I was. Since she wouldn't stop crying, I kissed her. Thinking she would turn me away, I was surprised when she returned the kiss. Grabbing the soap, I lathered up the sponge and started to wash her up. She grabbed the sponge and did the same to me. I wanted to fuck her right there, but I needed to wash my hair first. Leaning my head back, I grabbed the shampoo and washed all the food out of my shit. She did the same, and her hair curled up. It was the way she used to wear it when we were together. Picking her up, I put her around my waist and walked out of the shower.

"You better not drop me."

I didn't even respond because I was concentrating on not slipping. Laying her on the bed, I kissed all over her body. When I got to her breasts, I sucked harder than I meant to, leaving a hickey. I was so turned on, a nigga wasn't thinking about her nigga and started putting them all over her body.

When I got to her clit, I sucked on that motherfucker too. Her body still knew my touch, and I still knew what she wanted. Licking her softly, I moved my tongue up and down as I gently sucked on her clit. After doing that shit about six times, I pushed her legs back and went crazy. Flicking my tongue as fast as it could go, her body shook like crazy.

Slapping her on her ass, I was giving her my best. It's been years since I been this turned on. My dick was about to explode just from rubbing against the bed. When I felt her come all over my tongue, I was happy as fuck. Standing up, I knew I should have gone over to the dresser and got a condom, but I didn't. My ass wanted her to get pregnant so she could come back to me.

Bitches do it all the time, so why the fuck a nigga can't trap a chick? Laughing to myself, I knew she would run out of here if she knew what I was thinking. I rubbed my dick against her clit to create friction. Replacing my dick with my thumb, I slid in her. A nigga could barely get it in her shit was so tight.

"Damn, ma, when is the last time you had sex?" She dropped her head in shame when she responded.

"Almost a year. He won't touch me. He acts like I disgust him." I don't know what the fuck was wrong with her nigga, but I'm glad he dropped the ball. Now I could drop my balls in her and know I'm the only one going in her. Leaving my tip sitting there for a minute, I knew I was going to hurt her. Deciding to just push it all in so she could get past the hurt, I rammed it in.

"Fuuccckkk! It's so damn big." Letting it rest against her walls, I gave her a few moments to get used to the size again. I started stroking her slowly until I felt the juices running down her legs. Lying down on top of her, I kissed her as I worked my entire dick inside. Lifting one of her legs, I knew my dick would go all the way in using this position. Sucking her breasts, I picked up the pace. Sitting up, I placed her legs against my chest, grabbed her by her hips, and I started slamming my dick in and out of her.

"Tell me you love me." She wouldn't say it, and it pissed me off. "Turn around, ma." Putting her in a doggie-style position, I knew I could get her to say it then. This time, I wasn't gentle. I slammed my dick in her harder and harder. Sliding my thumb in her ass while I fucked the shit out of her, I asked again.

"Tell me you love me."

Slamming in her as hard as I could, she finally answered. "I love you, baby."

Still not easing up, I got her to say everything I wanted to hear.

"Tell me this my pussy."

Screaming out with each stroke, she responded. "It's yours. Fuck." This was the best feeling in the world, and there was no other place I would rather be. "What the fuck! Quick, look." She tried to get away from me, and I looked up to see what was wrong. This bitch Alaysia was lying on the floor on her elbows like she was on a mission in the army. This ho's arms were strong as fuck. How the fuck she get up the stairs? Laughing at the visual, I kept pumping inside Ash as I looked Alaysia right in her eyes. The bitch wanted to play and blackmail me. Now, I was gon' show her who was in control.

"Quick, stop. This damn girl in here looking like a damn roach. Let me up." Slamming my dick inside Ash hard as fuck, she stopped trying to move.

"Did I tell you to get up?" Slamming inside her again, she knew to answer.

"No."

"Then shut the fuck up and throw that ass back on this dick." I could see the tears falling down Alaysia's face, but I didn't give a fuck. Bitch in here trying to make mud puddles and shit. She wouldn't turn her face away, so I continued to look at her as I fucked the shit out of the love of my life. I felt Ash's body shaking, and I could feel my nut rising.

"Damn, baby, I'm about to come. Fuck, Quick, damn." Her body started going crazy, and I knew I was about to nut right behind her. Holding her tight so she couldn't pull away, I shot my nut all inside of her. Pumping harder and harder, a nigga was trying to make sure his nut made it up there.

As soon as I could gather myself, I pulled out and got out of bed. With my dick swinging all in Alaysia's face, I bent down to pick her up. This simple ho actually tried to get my dick in her mouth. Grabbing her body, I picked her up and threw her out of my room. Locking the door, I got back in my bed and kissed Ash.

"Nigga, you ain't shit." She laughed at me.

"Fuck her. The same way she got up the stairs, she can get back down. Do you have to go home?" She nodded her head. I watched her go and clean herself and get dressed. Then I threw on some shorts and a tank and headed out to take her back to her car. Alaysia's ass was still trying to make it down the stairs. I stepped over her ass and kept walking. When I got to the bottom, I pushed her chair away from the stairs. She was gon' be tired as hell by the time she got to that chair. I laughed when I looked back and saw her mean mugging me. Bitch was gon' learn real fast who the fuck I was.

Chapter 51

Juicy

Walking in the door, I was tired as hell. My mom has been sick, and even though there is nothing directly wrong, I sense something is going on with Face. He came home the other day, and he didn't want to have sex. He just held me. I tried to get him to open up, but he wouldn't talk about it. This was the worst I had ever seen him since Blaze died.

The nigga was looking like shit, and I had no idea what to do or say. I knew if I pushed him to tell me, it would only turn him away. As I thought about what I could do, I looked up and wondered what the fuck was going on. There was a note attached to the front door. Opening it, I walked in, closed the door, and started to read it.

"The first place you stole my heart, open the closet, that's where you will start."

Oh my God, I love scavenger hunts. I took off running to the bedroom. That was the first place he told me he loved me. When I walked in, I opened the closet door. A silver cocktail dress and a pair of silver Red Bottoms hung on the back of the door. I looked at the price tag. It read $2,000. Vera Wang was out of her mind, but the dress was so pretty. It dipped down all the way to the waist, it was fitted around my ass area, and then it flared out at the bottom. Grabbing it off the hook, I saw another piece of paper taped to the door.

"I stay to your left because everything about you is right. In this drawer, my love for you will shine bright."

I walked over to the dresser and opened the right one. There was a big velvet container. I opened it, and a diamond necklace and bracelet sat there blinding the fuck out of me.

The entire necklace and bracelet were diamonds. Tears ran down my face as I rubbed my fingers across it. Guessing that was the end of the hunt, I took my clothes off and walked in the bathroom and got in the shower. After getting my hygiene together, I dried off and noticed another paper taped to the bathroom wall.

"In the room you hardly use, you will find a key to my heart, soul, and mind."

Rubbing myself down, I quickly got dressed. Once I slid my shoes on, I ran downstairs to the kitchen. I knew how to cook, but I didn't do it often because he was hardly here. He would always grab something before he came home. He probably thinks I don't know how to cook. Walking around the kitchen, I looked for a key.

When I opened the first drawer, a car key was laying inside. Before I headed out, I ran back upstairs and got my red clutch. I dropped my ID, phone, and debit cards inside. Looking at myself in the mirror, I knew I looked damn good. Heading out the door to the garage, I almost passed out. An all-red Maserati with a red bow, sat right there waiting on me. Happy I didn't wear makeup, I wiped the tears as they fell. Getting in the car, I found another piece of paper taped to the steering wheel.

"To love me was a big sacrifice. Let me thank you in our own paradise."

This was the first clue I got that I didn't know what he meant. Turning my car on, I reached in my purse to grab my phone. When I looked at the screen, I saw that he had already entered the destination. All I had to do was hit start. Putting my phone down, I hit start and drove to where he wanted me to meet him. I entered the gates to some airport. When I parked my car, my baby stood there waiting for me outside of a helicopter. He looked so fucking fine in a suit that I couldn't wait to fuck him. I ran to him and jumped in his arms.

"Thank you, baby! This was the sweetest thing anyone has ever done for me."

"Don't thank me yet; we aren't done." We climbed in, and the pilot asked us to put on our seat belts. He flew us all the way to Wisconsin. A car was waiting for us there that drove us to a romantic restaurant. The entire time, I wondered what I did to deserve this. When we stepped inside, we were the only people there besides the live band and the servers. Our meal was already placed on the table as well as the wine. We sat down to eat; then Face spoke.

"I know I haven't been the easiest person to get along with, and I have done some things that even I'm not proud of, but one thing I do know is that I love you, and I'm sorry. I'm sorry for not being the man that you deserved, and I'm sorry for taking you for granted. Please don't ever give up on me.

"I'm all in, and I'm ready. I have never been this way with anyone. There are going to be times when I hurt you, and there's going to be times when you hurt me. All I want to know is if you are willing to stick it out with me no matter what?" He was pouring his heart out, but he didn't realize he just told me something loud and clear. He did something to hurt me . . . which means he cheated. Now, I can't prove it, but I know it. I also know it's eating him alive, and I'm making a choice to forgive him. We are going to start fresh right here at *this* moment.

"Whatever it is that you did, make sure you don't do it again. I love you too, and, yes, I promise to stick it out with you." The look on his face told me I was right. He leaned over and kissed me. Once that was out of the way, we enjoyed the rest of our meal.

He grabbed my hand, and we got up to dance. I felt safe in his arms, and I knew I would never love another man as much as I loved him. After laughing, talking, and dancing some more, we headed out. I couldn't wait until we got home so I could show him just how much I loved him. He was my everything, and I vowed to show him that. If he stepped out again, however, I was done.

On this day, I decided to give him my all. There would be no reason for him to cheat. If he does, he is just a fucked-up nigga. I was even going to start cooking. I would be his calm in a storm, his breath of fresh air, and his peace of mind. I would give him what I had given no other man. My all.

Chapter 52

Rico

Trying my best to hurry up, I grabbed my shit to get in the shower. Debra was going off as usual and asking me where the fuck I was going. The shit was getting old. She already cut up all my clothes and was mad as fuck when I made her buy me all new shit. She had me fucked up. Her mouth has always been bad, but she was worse in her old age.

"Nigga, you think you supposed to go out of this house every day and keep leaving me here?" Shit was starting to get on my fucking nerves.

"You know what the fuck it is to be with a street nigga. You forgot, we been here before. The shit don't change. I can't make money in the house. How the fuck you expect me to take over if I'm laid up with you all day?"

"Nigga, who the fuck gon' let your old ass take over? Sit your old ass down somewhere and let our kids do what they do best and take care of us."

"They take care of you, not me. They barely want to speak to my ass."

"And you still not wanting for shit. I just gave your ass $60,000. Tell me if you have made that much in these streets. What are you chasing? It has to be pussy cus we got plenty of money."

"And you have a pussy, so what you saying?"

"I'm saying stay your ass in the house sometimes. Damn."

Done with this argument, I jumped in the shower. She would go on and on saying the same shit. I couldn't wait until I got all the money I needed to pay that nigga off in Puerto Rico; then my ass was out of here on the first thing moving. After stepping out, I walked into the room to put on my clothes. She was quiet and not saying anything. I'm glad she finally shut the fuck up. After throwing on my clothes, I slid my feet in my shoes.

"Aaah—what the fuck!" Taking my feet out of my shoes, I looked inside them motherfuckers and saw a smashed up lightbulb and glass in them that her ho ass put in. "I'm about to beat your ass."

She took off running, and I couldn't even catch her. She fucked my feet up. Knowing I wasn't going anywhere tonight, I shot a text to Shirree letting her know we would meet up tomorrow. Taking my ass to the bathroom, I grabbed some tweezers. Easing my way back to the bed, I started pulling the small-ass pieces of glass out of my feet.

This shit hurt like a motherfucker, and I could barely get that li'l-ass glass out. Getting out as much as I could, I went to the bathroom and poured peroxide on my feet. As I climbed in bed, I wanted to kill that ho. It took me damn near two hours to get that glass out. I lay there pissed until I drifted off to sleep.

My ass must have been tired because I didn't wake up until twelve in the afternoon. Jumping my ass back in the shower, I threw on my clothes I took off from last night. Walking downstairs, from the smell, I could tell she was cooking breakfast. Not giving a fuck, I walked out the door. I was still pissed that bitch put glass in my shoes. Texting Shirree, I told her to meet me at the spot. She was bringing me money, but not enough. I needed the shit to come in faster. The only good thing was that I had Debra giving me lump sums of money as well.

Pulling up to the spot, I jumped out of my car and headed in. Shirree's car was outside, so I knew she was here. Walking in, I didn't see her, and I started to feel like the bitch was up to something. Grabbing my gun, I walked around the house looking for her. When I got upstairs, she had the money thrown all over the bed, and she was lying in it, naked. My dick jumped from the sight. Taking my pants and shoes off, I headed over to the bed. I lay down next to her, and I was ready for whatever she was about to do.

"Suck my dick, and you better not drop an ounce of nut or spit on my money since you doing the most with my shit."

"Yes, daddy." I hadn't even planned on fucking her anymore after the first time. I just wanted to blackmail her. She was on some different shit, though. Every time we met up, she was ready to fuck. She started placing kisses on the tip of my dick, and it jumped every time she did it. Licking up and down the base, she had me hard as fuck. Putting the tip in, she started sucking that motherfucker and swirling her tongue around it. Out of nowhere, she deep throated that motherfucker. Every time she went down, her mouth reached my balls. The gagging had her mouth wet as hell, and she never stopped her ass; she just kept going. The spit started running down her mouth, and I wanted to slap her ass for having us on top of the money.

As soon as I was ready to slap the bitch, she threw my legs back so fast that I couldn't stop her. When my legs flew over my head, her mouth sucked all the juices right out of my asshole. This was some nasty shit, but it felt good as fuck. Out of all the bitches I fucked, none of them licked my ass. I probably would have beat they ass had they asked, but this shit was intense. She kept stroking my dick as she fucked my ass with her tongue.

"Fuck, girl. Do that shit then." Climbing back up and releasing my legs, she started back sucking my dick. A nigga was ready to bust; then she stopped. Climbing up to my face, she sat on that motherfucker and started grinding. I loved when a bitch took charge. Shit was a major turn-on. While she rode my face, I felt someone's mouth go on my dick. This girl was trying to make me fall in love. I didn't even know she set up a threesome, but I loved every minute of it. As good as Shirree's head was, she had nothing on the girl she brought in the room. I take all that shit back I was just talking. This was the best head I ever had in my life. This bitch knew how to keep her mouth wet without dripping any, and her shit was tight as fuck around my dick. It's like I was fucking a virgin.

This is a skill most women would never accomplish. I couldn't stop moaning as I tried to keep eating Shirree's pussy, but I couldn't focus. My eyes were crossing, and my body was shaking. A nigga wasn't even about to nut yet, and my body was shaking like I was having a seizure. I guess Shirree realized I wasn't focused, so she took it upon herself to get her nut. She rode my face so hard that my damn lips were swelling.

I was so focused on my soul being sucked out that I didn't even care. When my nut shot down the mystery woman's throat, I think I became paralyzed. She kept sucking without ever removing her mouth from my dick. It didn't even take ten seconds, and that motherfucker was brick hard again. When she took her mouth off, I wanted to tell the bitch to keep sucking, but Shirree's ass was smothering me with her pussy. She wasn't moving until she got her nut. I tried focusing back on her clit until I felt the girl slide down on my dick. A nigga was taking her ass to the mall after we finished. I was even gon' propose to this ho. Her pussy was so fucking tight that I couldn't even think straight.

How a bitch pussy was this tight and wet at the same time is beyond me. My ass had to try to think of something else because as soon as she slid all the way down, I damn near nutted.

She was riding the shit out of my dick, and I was stuck and sprung. I finally felt Shirree shaking, and I was glad because I wanted to go balls deep in this pussy that was riding my dick.

I had to get control of the situation. Bitch wasn't about to fuck me like *I* was the bitch. When Shirree started creaming in my mouth, I gave her one last lick and slid her off my face. When I sat up to look at the girl, I almost passed out to see Tate's ass riding my dick like a pro. Shirree and I looked at each other like what the fuck! I was about to punch his ass in the back of the head when he gripped my dick with his ass.

A bitch can barely do that shit with her pussy, and this nigga did it with his ass. The deed was done, and my ass said fuck it. This was the best head and pussy I ever had in my life, so I may as well get this nut. Even if it was boy pussy, nobody would ever find out. Pushing him off me, I turned him around and slid my dick back in. Shirree's ass looked like she wanted no part of this shit, but she was getting involved whether or not she wanted to.

"Suck his dick," I demanded. She looked like she wanted to protest, but she did as she was told. Her ass actually had the nerve to look jealous, but she was getting fucked too; she just didn't know it. She leaned under Tate and started sucking him off. The sounds of her slurping had me slamming in and out of his ass hard as fuck. I couldn't take much more of this shit, and I shot my sperm all in his ass, but I still wanted some pussy. I couldn't leave here without fucking Shirree, and I didn't plan on it.

"Tate, come get this motherfucker back hard."

He slid over to me and put it back in his mouth. I played in Shirree's pussy as he got my shit back on brick. This motherfucker was hard in twenty seconds flat. Grabbing Shirree, I slid her on top of me. She must have felt she had a point to prove because she started riding that motherfucker like she was trying to go somewhere.

Holding on to her hips, I slammed in and out of her pussy like it was mine. As soon as I leaned her forward to put her breast in my mouth, Tate slid his dick inside her ass. She went crazy as usual. I never saw a bitch throw it back on two dicks like that at the same time. She was bouncing on these motherfuckers like we weren't ripping her in two.

"Somebody better make this dick come," I screamed out. The shit was feeling good as fuck, but I wanted extraordinary. After fucking Tate in his tight ass, I needed this bitch to twirl or something on this motherfucker. Tate slid out of her, and Shirree started bouncing on that motherfucker like she wanted to feel it in her throat.

When I felt Tate wrap his mouth around my balls, I fucking lost it. She was riding me like a pro, and he was sucking my sack. I knew it wouldn't be long before I bust. When he started sticking his tongue in and out of my ass while he massaged my balls, I felt my veins popping.

"Fuck, daddy about to come. Y'all make this dick come. Teamwork makes the dream work. Do that shit, y'all. Fuck. Here it come, baby." She started shaking with me, and we both came together. That was the most intense sex I ever had in my life. Five minutes later, nut was *still* shooting out of my dick, and she wasn't even on top anymore. They both were fighting to lick the nut. Two tongues on my dick at the same time had my shit jumping again. As they sucked the head at the same time, I knew I had to go one more round.

"Which one of y'all want this last nut?" They both screamed "Me," and I knew I wasn't gay, but I no longer wanted sex any other way than this.

Chapter 53

Shadow

This motherfucker was pissing me off. She would get a random phone call, and her ass would be gone. It's bad enough my dick wasn't working. I was feeling insecure like a motherfucker. I knew she said she wasn't trying again until she knew it was working for good, but that was fucking with a nigga's mental. Especially with her ass always gone. She was two seconds away from catching a fade and didn't even know the shit. Standing here looking at her getting dressed, I tried waking my dick up, but the motherfucker wasn't moving. His ass was lying in my hand like a loose damn noodle.

"Shirree, your ass ain't leaving out of this house today. We never spend time together, and I'm sick of it. You got a nigga over here whining like a bitch."

She looked at me and laughed. "Look at your dick." I looked down at this limp motherfucker and almost laughed myself. "What do you call a nigga with no dick? A bitch. That's why you whining like one. Now move. I have to go." This bitch had me fucked up. I knew my shit was making me look like a ho, but I wasn't tolerating disrespect. Grabbing her by her neck, I slammed her ass against the wall.

"Don't fucking play with me. I'll knock your eye through your fucking nose. You done forgot who the fuck I am, and I'm about to show your bigmouthed ass." She knew I wasn't playing, and she didn't say shit else smart.

"Baby, we about to have a girl's day, and I need it. Now, can I please go? I'll be back in a couple of hours."

Releasing her neck, I decided to let her go. One thing I ain't never been good at was chasing a bitch. A nigga got asthma; shit ain't good for my health. When she walked out the door, I looked through my phone for the chick's number I met at the store. She can talk all that good shit, but my dick gets hard. It just don't get hard for her ass. She was going out of her way to make me feel like shit, and I was gon' go out of my way to get her ass back. I'm a tit-for-tat-ass nigga. This relationship was slowly going down the drain, and it was time for me and her to have a talk. One thing I wasn't gon' do was be in a relationship with a chick I wasn't happy with. Dialing the number, I hoped she remembered who I was.

"Hello."

"Hey, this the nigga you met at the liquor store awhile back. We . . . ummm . . . kind of messed around."

She laughed into the phone. "Just say I sucked your dick. I remember even though I never caught your name."

"Shadow, what's yours?"

"Stacey. Quit beating around the bush. You trying to roll through?" Damn, her ass got straight to the point.

"Yeah, text me the address." As soon as the text came through, I jumped in my whip and headed out. It took me forty-five minutes to get to her spot. When I pulled up, I parked a little bit down the street. I didn't know shorty like that, and I didn't need a motherfucker to know I was in there. Knocking on the door, she opened it right away. She had on a silk robe, with nothing under it. She had it open so you can see everything. She stood there pulling on a blunt, and the sight was sexy as fuck. I didn't even like bitches that smoked weed, but I was loving how she was looking doing it.

"You gon' stand out there and stare?" This girl's mouth was off the chain.

"My bad." I walked past her and in her house.

"Fuck you do, catch an Uber or something?"

"Do I look like the type of nigga that rides in an Uber? Don't play yourself, shorty."

"My homegirl told me that the only nigga she knows named Shadow is a Hoover. Is that you?"

Wanting to make her feel like an ass, I told her. "Yeah, now recognize when a boss in your fucking presence. Don't ever talk to me like that again or your ass gon' regret it." I was tired of all the chicks in my life trying to walk over me. A nigga was a good guy, but they didn't appreciate that shit. A bitch would never talk to my brothers like that.

"I'm sorry. Can I make it up to you?" Liking where this conversation was headed, I pulled my dick out. I already knew she was 'bout that life; wasn't no sense in playing shy. She crawled over to me and started sucking my dick. The motherfucker was brick hard. Fuck Shirree. Bitch talks too much, and she couldn't get my dick hard. Stacey's head was good the other night, but it seems like now that she knows who I am, she was sucking as if her life depended on it. Shit was cool, but a nigga needed some pussy. It's been too long.

"Come sit on this motherfucker." She jumped up happy as hell and tried to slide down on my dick. "Hold up, baby girl." Reaching in my pocket, I grabbed a condom. I learned my lesson after Elise's ass. A nigga wasn't going through that shit again. I could tell baby girl had an attitude, but I didn't give a fuck. I made a mental note to take my condom with me. Blaze said if you don't trust a bitch, don't leave your nut with the ho. She slid down on that motherfucker, and her pussy definitely felt better than her mouth. She was riding the shit out of my dick, and I loved it. My ass had no intentions to ever cheat on my girl again, but she was on some bullshit, and I wasn't with it. She should have been trying to figure out why my dick wouldn't work, but instead, her ass was gone every chance she got. A nigga hadn't had no pussy in so long that I was about to nut already. Knowing I couldn't hold it, I would make it up to baby girl in round two.

"Fuck, this nut's coming, baby. I gotta let this shit ride." Instead of getting mad, she rode this motherfucker harder. My nut filled the condom up, and it was still on brick.

As soon as she started grinding again, someone knocked on the door. Grabbing my gun, I pointed it at the door. I didn't trust no bitch.

"Fuck you grabbing that for?" She had the nerve to question me. Pushing her off me, I pulled my pants up.

"Because I don't know who the fuck knocking on your door." She went and looked out the peephole and panic filled her face.

"Who the fuck is it?"

"My ex-boyfriend, Slick. The nigga is crazy. Fuck." Praying it wasn't a coincidence, I decided to ask her.

"Drea's brother?" She nodded her head. "Let him in. I promise he won't know I'm here. I'm going to hide in the closet and wait until he leaves." She was looking worried, but I didn't give a fuck. "Just act like you were asleep and be normal. I got you, shorty." Walking to her bedroom, I turned my phone on silent and hid in the closet. I started texting my brother as soon as I closed the door.

Me: Nigga, Slick just walked in this house where I'm at. Get to this address now.

I sent him the address, and he responded right away.

Baby Face: OMW. Stay out of sight. I'm close. About to hit up Quick.

Me: A'ight.

Taking my gun off safety, I pointed it at the door just in case this nigga was suspicious. I know my brother and them wanted to be here for his death, but if he opens this door, that nigga was going to the upper room. I could tell they had walked in the bedroom because I could hear them.

"You know you miss a nigga. I don't know why your ass be playing."

"Nigga, please. Your ass been gone for months, and I know you been laid up with a bitch."

"Your ass always think a nigga with a bitch. If I were with a chick, I wouldn't be needing some pussy this bad." I don't know what he started doing, but the ho was moaning like crazy. This ho was about to fuck him knowing she just had my dick in her. I hope the nigga ain't kissing her or eating her pussy. He was gon' have my dick all in his mouth. Laughing at the thought, I didn't even hear anybody else come in the room. I just heard her scream.

"What the fuck! Why are you in my house?"

"Your man about to go keep my brother company."

I guess Slick must have pulled his gun because Quick snapped. "Nigga, I promise you won't be able to get that motherfucker off." I slid the door open, and luck was on my side. Slick's back was to me. Not even about to play with his ass, I raised my gun and knocked his ass out.

"What the fuck, Shadow? Nigga, you got me fucked up. Who the fuck did you invite in my fucking house? This is *my* shit."

Pop. I shot the bitch right between her eyes.

"Damn, nigga, you didn't waste no time. I thought we was gon' have to convince you to let us kill your string bean." Quick was laughing at my ass.

"I told her if she disrespected me one more time, she was gon' catch a fade. I'm sick of these bitches. These hoes ain't got no manners. The fuck is a string bean anyway?"

"A side dish."

Laughing at these niggas, I walked over to Slick and kicked his ass. Groaning, he rolled over.

"Wake your bitch ass up, lucky charm." Quick was talking like Damon on *Friday After Next* when he was trying to rape Money Mike.

"You better not be trying to fuck this nigga."

"Nigga, I'll shoot your ass and that li'l crooked-ass dick of yours. Have your ass looking uncircumcised. Dick gon' be looking like a turtleneck." Knowing he was trigger happy, I shut my ass up. He and Blaze have always been the ones to do the most. When Slick opened his eyes and saw Stacey lying there deader than a motherfucker, he knew he was next.

"Where that bitch-ass nigga Tate hiding?" Baby Face was trying to question him before we sent his ass to the moon.

"I don't know. The nigga been on some other shit lately. He don't even come to the safe house no more. He has a new witness and said he don't need me anymore."

"Who is the new witness?"

"I don't know, all I know is it's a bitch."

"Is it Alaysia?" Quick was trying to find out if that bitch was playing both sides of the fence.

"I don't know, I swear. Just don't kill me. I'll help y'all get that nigga for playing me."

"I got something more important than that. We can definitely use you on our team, though." The nigga got happy as hell listening to Baby Face talk . . . until he raised his gun and shot him in his dick.

"Aaah! What the fuck!"

"I need you to go keep my brother company. He lonelier than a motherfucker, and I promised to send him some company." Before the nigga could say anything else, we all raised our guns and fired. We were lighting his ass up, and it sounded like the Fourth of July in that bitch. We didn't stop shooting until all of our guns were out of ammo.

"I'll be right back. I need to run to the gas station." We knew what Baby Face was going to do, so we sat there and waited until he got back.

"The fuck was you doing messing with this bitch? I thought you was back on your faithful shit?" I knew they were gon' have questions. I told Quick as much as I could without telling him that my dick wasn't working.

"Shirree been on some other shit. Her ass always gone, and I hadn't had no pussy in a minute. A nigga needed to release, or I was gon' explode. My ass too old to be jacking off."

"Bro, you have to give her some time. All of our attitudes changed since Blaze died. It's rough on anybody in our lives. They have to deal with us and our mood swings and shit. That shit ain't easy."

Understanding what he meant, I felt like shit. Instead of cheating, I should have been making sure my fiancée knew my condition had nothing to do with her. A nigga was gon' do better. Baby Face walked in the door and started pouring gas on their bodies and all over the room.

"Fuck, I forgot the lighter."

Quick reached in his pocket and pulled out a Bic. "I been carrying this since that night. It helped me feel closer to him."

He lit that motherfucker and threw it. We ran out of the house.

"That's a damn shame how long it takes the police to come to the hood." I laughed because I swear not a siren could be heard.

"They don't give a fuck about us, but let's get the fuck out of here before they slide up on our ass and pick a day. I'm ready."

"Ready for what?" I was lost.

"To throw Blaze's remains." This must have given him some closure.

"A'ight. Bet. I'll hit y'all up."

We jumped in our whips and headed out. I was going home to try to make up with my girl.

Chapter 54

Quick

I couldn't wait to figure out a way to off this bitch. Ever since the night I fucked Ash in Alaysia's face, she been threatening me like crazy. If I didn't come home by a certain time, she was picking up her phone acting like she was about to make a call. If I didn't help her, if I didn't fuck her, if I didn't promise to leave Ash alone the bitch was threatening me. There was no way I would ever stop seeing Ash, but I kept her away from the house. This ho was making my life miserable, and I was ready for this shit to be over. Killing Slick meant I was one step closer. It also made me feel like I avenged Blaze in some way. I refused to throw his ashes, and we hadn't sent him any company yet. It was still going to be hard, but I asked Ash to come with me when we go later on. She told me yeah and asked if Paris and Panda could come as well. That was fine with me. They all loved my brother, and I felt it was only right. Walking down the stairs, Alaysia was sitting at the bottom waiting on me.

"I thought I told you we were having breakfast this morning. We are going to act like a regular couple, and you are going to *love* it. Are we clear?"

Walking past her, I went into the kitchen and sat down at the table. How this bitch rolled over to me and carried my plate is beyond me. I laughed, and she threw my plate at me.

"I'm glad you think this shit is funny. Your ass won't be laughing if you in jail getting fucked by Big Dick Willie." She grinned, and I wanted to slap that motherfucker right off her face. This bitch was pissing me off.

"You get a kick out of threatening me, but how does it feel to know you a lonely, miserable, no-leg-having-ass bitch that have to force a nigga to be with you?" Tears started to form in her eyes, but I didn't give a fuck. "Aww, you're about to cry. Your bitch ass want to take off running to your room, don't you? Damn, you can't run off and cry. You can't even make a dramatic exit. It's gon' take too long to roll your ass off." Standing up, I walked away from the table.

"I'll be back. Go do some push-ups or some-thing." Slamming my door, I jumped in my whip and drove off. I needed some air. I called Ash to see where she was and if we could link up.

"Hey, what's up, Zavier? Did the plans change?"

"Naw, they haven't. I just wanted to see if we could link up now. This bitch is driving me crazy, and I'm about to lose it."

"Everything will work itself out. I'm actually in the middle of something, and I can't come right now, and Panda can't come later. She has her baby."

"She can bring the baby. It's just us, and we only going to the lakefront."

"She said she doesn't want to, but I'll see you in a couple of hours. Just try to stay away from her as much as possible."

"Okay, ma. I can't wait to see you." Since I couldn't hang out with Ash, I headed over to my mom's crib. Using my key, I walked in, but I stood at the front door and screamed her name.

"Ma, where you at?" She walked down the stairs, and she looked good with her real hair. Made her look younger. "You riding with me, or you driving?"

"Rico gon' drive. I'm gon' ride with him, whenever he gets his ass here."

"OK, I just wanted to check on you, but make sure you change. We are wearing all-white."

"I know, boy. I had this on earlier. I'll see you in a li'l bit."

Kissing her on her cheek, I left. Needing to clear my mind and be away from Alaysia, I drove around for hours. A nigga had a lot on his plate, and the shit was starting to wear me down.

I finally decided to head home. We were meeting up in a couple of hours, and I needed to get ready. Driving to the house, I wondered what Ash had to do that she couldn't hang with me. Even though I knew she had a man, the shit bothered me knowing she be going home to that nigga. I hope her ass was pregnant and she had no choice but to come back to me. I was a petty nigga, and I could admit that. Pulling up to the house, I headed in.

When I walked in the door, I damn near fell over Alaysia's wheelchair. She had her ass sitting right out the door.

"Your ass can't keep rolling up on me like that. You scared the fuck out of me."

"What time are we leaving tonight? You know it takes me awhile to get ready."

I looked at her like she was crazy. "You think you coming to some shit for my brother? You must have rolled over your fucking brain." I knew if she could, she would stand her ass up and slap my ass.

"You keep forgetting you don't have a choice. Now, what time are we leaving?"

"At nine. Your ass better be ready too, or you gon' be rolling that motherfucker all the way there, and be in all-white." I turned to walk off, but she stopped me.

"Take your pants off."

This bitch was stressing me the fuck out, and even though Ash had a man, it had me feeling like I was cheating on her. Alaysia didn't know I was still fucking her, and I needed to make sure she never found out. Ash has the code to my door, and one day, she might decide to pop up. I couldn't have that shit. Knowing I didn't have a choice, I pulled my pants down. She rolled over to me and started massaging it. No matter how pissed and disgusted I was at her, my dick always stood up. I never could understand that shit.

"I don't know why you fight this shit. You know we are meant to be."

Ready for her to just shut the fuck up and suck, I didn't respond. She caught the hint, and her mouth slid down on my dick. Don't get me wrong. I always nut, but I swear I don't be into this shit at all. When I zone out and think about Ash, I think that's how I always end up coming. Alaysia's head was bouncing up and down, and I just wanted her to stop. If she thinks I was fucking her tonight, she had another think coming. Taking my mind back to Ash and I having sex, my dick got brick hard, and my nut shot down her throat hot and fast. Alaysia tried to keep sucking, and I knew that meant she wanted to get fucked. I slid back, and her ass fell out of the chair.

"We have to get ready." Jogging up the stairs, I laughed as I pictured her ass on her elbows trying to get back in the chair.

Going to my closet, I pulled out my white True Religion shorts and my all-white Gucci shirt. Grabbing my all-white Gucci high tops, my outfit was complete. Jumping in the shower, I washed Alaysia's slob off my dick first. Shit was starting to feel like rape, and I wanted this shit to be over. After washing everything else, I got dressed and headed downstairs. Surprisingly, Alaysia's ass was ready. To kill time, I turned on a movie, and we sat there in silence until it was time to go.

When I pulled up to the lake, I noticed they had the brother line going. Drea must already be here because Blaze's truck was lined up as well. Pulling in behind them, I grabbed Alaysia's wheelchair out of the trunk and placed it by the door. Not bothering to help her, I stood there until my brothers got out. Once they did, we walked off. Heading down to the beach, I wondered how the hell Alaysia was going to roll that chair over all that sand. Laughing, I noticed my mama, Rico, and Drea were sitting on the sand waiting for us. We walked over and joined them.

"Bro, your ass going to hell. You know that damn girl can't get across that sand." Shadow was laughing, but Baby Face was dead-ass serious. "You really trying to call her bluff like that?"

Thinking about all the threats the bitch had been throwing, I walked back to where we were parked. Looking at her stuck in the sand, the bitch was sweating and crying. Laughing my ass off, I went over and helped her. She didn't say shit as I pushed her. There was no way she would have made it on her own. My ass could barely push her through. When we got to the bottom, I put her directly by the water where we would be doing the ceremony. I wasn't about to do this shit again until it was time to go.

Heading back over to my brothers, we stood there waiting for everyone else to arrive.

"Hey, did y'all know that Drea's ass is pregnant?" Shadow asked out of nowhere.

"Fuck, no. That shit crazy, but that means Blaze will always be here with us." I was shocked, but the baby would fill some of the void.

"Yeah, I knew." That was all Baby Face said, and that was strange.

"Well, why the fuck you didn't tell us, nigga?" He acting like he was the only uncle.

"I told Mama. I just knew she would call everybody." That's true, but Mama been too busy chasing Rico's ass.

Paris and Ash were walking across the beach, and my dick started playing double Dutch all in my shorts. That motherfucker was jumping all over the place. She had on a long, white, see-through dress. The shit was flowing and blowing in the wind right with her hair. It was a sight to see. I grabbed my phone and took a picture. I caught her laughing while she pushed the hair out of her face. The shit was beautiful as fuck.

"Fuck is y'all staring at? I know my big ass is cute as the fuck, but, damn." Paris's ass was always going off.

"It's cute as fuck, Paris. Who the fuck taught you how to talk?" We laughed at Shadow's proper-talking ass. He knew she was country, and that's why she talked like that.

"Nigga, it's whatever the fuck I say it is." We all laughed, but I never took my eyes off Ash.

"Hey, y'all."

Everybody hugged them. I hugged Paris and waited on Ash to give me a hug. When she finally got to me, I held her longer than I expected to. She smelled so fucking good.

"Damn, nigga, you gon' fuck her on the beach with Strong-Arm Sandy sitting over there?"

We all looked over at Alaysia, and she was burning a hole through me. Laughing at Baby Face, I let her go. Juicy and Shirree ended up walking up together. We said our hellos and headed down to the water. Baby Face looked like he was finally happy. They were holding hands and laughing like some schoolkids. Shirree and Shadow looked like they were uncomfortable and two days away from a breakup. Without thinking, I grabbed Ash's hand and placed her next to me. Baby Face had the urn, and he stepped up to talk first. Holding the vase out, each person walked up and said something about Blaze and then placed their hand on the urn. Once we all were done, Baby Face used his other hand to remove the top, and we let our brother fly free. Everybody's hand was on the urn except Alaysia's. She couldn't reach it. Once all of his remains were flying over the lake, everyone's face was filled with tears. Never wanting to accept that he was gone, this made it real as hell. I broke down and was about to lose it. Ash grabbed me and started whispering in my ear.

"It's going to be okay. I'm here. You have me, Zavier. I'll help you through this." Not responding, I just nodded my head.

"Nigga, you just gon' keep disrespecting me like I'm not sitting here?"

Pulling back from Ash, I looked at this bitch Alaysia like she lost her mind. It was obvious all of us were going through it, and this was *not* the time.

"We will discuss this later. This is *not* the time."

"You keep fucking with me, ain't gon' be no later. Your ass gon' be in a cell. You must think I'm playing with you. I told your ass to stay away from this bitch, and you bring her here. You got me fucked up." With the emotions I was already feeling and her going off on me, I just snapped. Without thinking, I walked over to her and snatched her out of the chair.

"Bro, what the fuck are you doing?" Ignoring Baby Face, I walked into the water until it was deep enough and tossed that ho.

"Quick!" Ash was screaming my name, but I didn't give a fuck. Taking my shirt, I wiped my prints off the chair.

"I'm sick of that bitch. I couldn't take it no more."

Shadow and Baby Face were laughing so hard they were on their knees in the sand.

"Nigga, your ass going to hell."

As we looked at her ass flapping her arms, the shit was funny as fuck, and I had to agree with

Shadow. A nigga was going to hell with gasoline drawers on.

"Somebody toss her the chair so she can be rolling on the river."

When Baby Face screamed that, none of us were good any more. My mama walked over, and I just knew she was about to go off.

"It's about damn time. What the fuck took you so long? Let's go."

Once I saw Alaysia's head go under the water and stay there, I walked off. That bitch's arms were strong as shit, and I had to make sure her ass didn't make it out. Grabbing Ash's hand, I apologized.

"I'm sorry, but it needed to be done. You leaving with me?"

Nothing else needed to be said when she nodded her head. She was going to be mine, and I was going to make sure of that.

Chapter 55

Ash

Watching Quick throw that damn girl in the water had me at a loss for words. I planned to tell him about Zavi Jr. the next time we met up, but I was now convinced he would kill me. I intended never to see him again. When Paris, Panda, and Drea said they wanted to go to Hoover Nights, I should have followed my first mind and stayed my ass at home. My girls swore the brothers hardly ever came in there, but it was just my luck they were there that night. I wanted to die when I saw Blaze come set Drea on fire. If he was there, then I knew Quick was too. A part of me wanted to run out and say fuck Drea; she will be okay. But I knew I couldn't leave my friend like that. All this shit was happening so fast. The night Quick and I had sex, I went home and tried to act normal, but Jason was all over my ass, and things went downhill.

***

Walking in the door, I tried to head straight for the shower, but he was sitting on the couch waiting for me.

"Where the fuck have you been, Ashanti?"

Rolling my eyes, I tried to act offended. "You already know where I've been. Why do we have to go through this every time I walk in the door?"

"Because I think your bitch ass lying. You gon' make me fuck you up."

Shaking my head in disbelief, I headed up the stairs to shower and lie down. As soon as I walked into the room, he was right behind me.

"I want some pussy. Take this shit off." I was shocked because he hadn't touched me in so long. We barely even slept in the same room together.

"I'm not about to do this with you tonight. I just want to lie down and get some sleep." I tried my best to stay calm.

"Bitch, I don't give a fuck what you want to do. I said take your clothes off and give me some of my pussy."

Before I could protest again, he grabbed my clothes and started snatching them off. "Now, I know I'm a slow nigga, but either you done turned gay or your ass been fucking another nigga." Looking down, I noticed Quick left hickeys all over my body. Nothing I could say would hide the guilt that was all over my face.

"I'm sorry." That was all I got out before he damn near slapped me to sleep. I tried to take off running, but he grabbed me by my hair and started punching me all over my body. He avoided my face I'm guessing to leave no evidence. Whatever the reason, I was grateful. Knowing I was small, I tried to fight back any-way, and that only made it worse.

He was punching me like I was a nigga, and I did everything I could to get him to let go of me. Dragging me to my son's room, it was finally over. He tossed me and snapped.

"Get your ugly-ass son, all of your shit, and get the fuck out of my house. Whatever you don't have in an hour, you won't have." He left, and I didn't have time to sit and cry. Grabbing my phone, I called Drea and asked her to come help me. Running to the kitchen, I grabbed the box of garbage bags. Heading back upstairs, I dumped all of my clothes and shoes in bags. Going into Zavi's room, I did the same thing. Packing up his games and toys, I was ready to go.

When Drea pulled up, she didn't ask any questions. We packed our cars in silence. Going *back in, I grabbed Zavi and carried him to my truck. Once I was finally on the road driving, I allowed myself to cry. Not because my relationship was over, but because I allowed him to stop my day care, and now, I didn't have anything. Not to mention, I knew I couldn't prevent Quick from seeing his son.*

Sitting next to him now and seeing him in rare form, I lost the nerve to tell him. I knew I couldn't avoid telling him for long, but for now, I would wait. I prayed he would understand once I did, but deep down, I knew that everything we were building would be torn down once he found out about Zavi Jr. Knowing my skeletons would fall they ass out of the closet soon, I would enjoy tonight.

Chapter 56

Drea

After that night with Baby Face, I went into a deep depression. Yes, I was missing Blaze like crazy, but I should not have allowed myself that weak moment. He deserved better than that. I was a mess and couldn't tell anyone what was going on with me. The fucked-up part is, I didn't even see Baby Face like that. When we went to spread Blaze's remains, I thought it would be awkward to see him, but I looked at him and felt nothing. The only emotion that ran through me was shame. Once Ash moved in, I had to get myself out of my funk. My baby needed me, and I planned on getting myself together for whatever was growing inside my stomach. It's been a long journey getting here, but I was finally okay. I wasn't over Blaze, but I was ready to pick up the pieces and move on. That was the only thing I took away from Baby Face's and my night together. It was a good thing Paris and the girls ended up canceling because it never even crossed my mind they were on the way. I got so wrapped up in him that I forgot the girls and I were supposed to go out. I dodged that bullet, and I thanked God for that.

Getting dressed, I was headed to the doctor to find out the sex of my baby. Well, my girls would find out. These hoes convinced me to have a reveal party. I didn't want to do it because I thought it would be strange to have one, and the father was not going to be present, but my baby deserved the best. Paris would definitely make sure it was the best too. Jumping in Ash's truck, we all headed to the doctor.

"TT Drea, how is it a baby inside your stomach?" I looked over at Ash like *Bitch, you better have this conversation with your son.*

"Easy, to get a baby in your stomach, you lean back and shut your ass up. That's how." We burst out laughing at Paris. She didn't care what she said to kids.

"TT Paris, you mean."

"And you can't whoop me. So, sit there and be mad."

"That's why your hair nappy."

We laughed at Zavi.

"Paris, are you really gon' sit here and argue with this child?" Panda was on her save-the-world shit. I thought it was funny.

"Gah, I'll argue with your grandma if she came at me wrong. The fuck!"

Laughing at her crazy ass, we pulled up to the doctor's office. When we walked in, it was nothing like last time. It was empty as hell, and we were grateful. My ass was hungry, and I was ready to get some food. I filled out the paperwork and was called to the back ten minutes later.

"Hello, Mommy. Let's hope today the baby lets us see what you are having. Are you ready?"

"They are. I'm not. I'm going to close my eyes while you do the ultrasound, and you can show them what it is. We are going to do a gender reveal party."

"Back in my days, we didn't know the sex of the baby until we gave birth. These days, everybody's doing the reveal party. Okay, let's get started."

I closed my eyes as the doctor rubbed the cold gel on my belly. I could hear the heartbeat, and the anxiety was killing me. I almost opened my eyes at least five times. When I felt her wipe the gel off, I knew she was finished. Not taking any chances, I kept my eyes closed for a while longer.

"Bitch, are you waiting on one of us to kiss your ugly ass or something? Get your ass up so we can go eat."

I hated Paris's ass sometimes. She had no chill. Panda was just sitting there with this goofy-ass smile on her face, and Ash was crying.

"You hoes so dramatic. Let's go." We headed out to grab some food. Deciding on the Cheese Cake Factory, I was glad it wasn't as packed as it usually is. Once we took our seats, these hoes started ordering liquor. They knew how badly I needed a drink and couldn't have one. Shaking my head at them, I ordered a soda; then we all ordered our food. Paris talked the entire time we ate about what she was going to do regarding this party. I stopped her, though, when she started talking about locations.

"Bitch, I can't wait. I know a hall we can have it at too."

"We are going to have it at the main house. That way, Blaze can be there."

"Drea, I thought we agreed no more séances."

I looked at Panda like she lost her mind.

"Gah, I did a whole shrine of him in the main house. The whole wall is his picture and shit. Your ass must be high."

"I stay high, and fuck you, bitch. I didn't know." I was about to say something when we were interrupted.

"Excuse me, can I talk to you for a minute." It took me awhile to answer because this man was fine as fuck. He was light-skinned with dreads, and he had the cutest eyes ever. He wasn't big, but he wasn't small. He was a work of art, and my pussy woke up at the sight of him. Before I embarrassed myself, I stood up so he could see my belly, and then I sat back down.

"The baby father here or are y'all like a gay couple trying to be all proactive and shit?" He was dead-ass serious.

"Nigga, we not gay. Shit, but you might be with them flashy-ass eyes. You got us fucked up." Paris cut up as usual.

"My bad. You have to ask nowadays. So, what's your name, shorty?" His smile was causing my pussy to have a heartbeat.

"Her name Deez Nuts. Nigga, fuck you want? Don't you see she pregnant?"

I wanted to slap Paris out of her chair.

"Damn, Paris, can she speak for herself? Shut your ass up and eat this damn dinner roll."

I appreciated Ash, cus Paris's ass was cutting up badly.

"Thank you, Ash. I'm Drea."

"I'm Mack. Now that we figured out you're not gay, where is your baby father?"

"He's deceased."

"That's fucked-up. Sorry to hear that, shorty. Look, let me get your number. I know I should have moved the fuck around when I saw you was pregnant, but something about you pulls me to you, and I'm gon' make your ass mine. You feel me?"

I didn't know what to say. I was stuck.

"Bitch, say something." Ash nudged me, while the others looked at me like I was crazy.

Paris snatched his phone and put my number in it.

"She don' turned into a mute. Maybe you should start off texting her."

I laughed at Paris, but I wasn't stuck. My ass was scared. Moving on to another guy would mean moving on from Blaze, and I didn't know if I was ready to do that.

"I'll hit you up later, is that cool?"

I nodded my head, and he walked off.

"Damn, bitch, you get all the fine-ass niggas. Shit, I need to be like you." Ash was talking that shit, but I knew her secret.

"Girl, stop. Everybody knows how fine Quick's ass is, and you done eased right back in."

Paris and Panda looked at her like she was crazy.

"Let me pay my check and get the fuck on. Bitch, that nigga gon' kill you, and I don't want to be anywhere around." Paris was actually standing up to leave.

"Who gon' kill my mommy?" Zavi asked.

"Deez Nuts. Mind your business, chile."

Laughing at her, we stood up to leave. Thinking to myself, if Mack calls, I'll answer, but I wasn't going to expect it to go anywhere serious. I don't know any niggas out here trying to wife pregnant bitches. Maybe I was in denial, or maybe a bitch wasn't ready to move on. Either way, I was hoping his ass didn't call. If he did, I was a goner. That nigga was fine as fuck.

Chapter 57

Baby Face

Juicy and I have been on really good terms lately, but a nigga was feeling guilty as shit. She knew I cheated, but if she found out with whom, she would kill me. That's why a nigga been going all out of his way to show her that she is all I want. That was the truth, though. I didn't want Drea's ass and hadn't thought about her since that fucking night. Only time she crossed my mind is when I think how fucked-up it was. It was strange, though; after all this time, she hit me up out of the blue and asked me if we could meet. I'm glad she didn't want to meet at the house because even though I didn't want her ass, I was still a nigga.

Pulling up to Priscilla's Soul Food, I got out and went in. Everybody knew my brothers and me, so normally, I would be in and out. Today, I was sitting down because we were there to talk.

She was already seated and eating. Walking over to the cashier, I told her to bring my usual to the table I would be sitting at. I could have gotten in line and got it myself, but I was a boss, and I didn't have to.

"What's up, ma? How you been?" Looking at her now, I don't even see how that shit happened. Don't get me wrong. Drea was fine as fuck, but I wasn't feeling shit sitting here with her now.

"I went to the doctor to find out the sex of the baby, but they told it to Paris. She wants to do a gender reveal party, and I wanted to know if we could have it at the main house."

"Girl, you could have shot me a text and just told me the day. You know it's all good." The waitress brought my food, and I started eating.

"I know, but I wanted to talk to you about what happened. Shit is different now, and I don't want it to be."

"Girl, we straight, I promise. It was a lapse in judgment. I'm trying to get shit back on track with my girl. Drea, I promise, we good. I don't look at you like that, and I hope you not looking at me like that cus the shit would never work."

"Boy, don't flatter yourself. I was coming here to tell *your* ass that." We laughed, and I could tell something else was on her mind.

"What's on your mind?" She looked up at me like she was wondering if we were really good. "Girl, what's on your mind? I got shit to handle. If I get done eating and you still ain't said shit, your ass is fucked." She knew I was just joking, but she started talking anyway.

"I met this guy like a week ago. We been talking and stuff, but I don't know if I can move on."

"I know you loved my brother, and my brother died trying to save you, so I know he knows how you felt about him. At the end of the day, he gone and life has to move forward. It would be selfish of us to expect you to stay single. If he seems legit, give him a chance. Especially if he willing to be with your fat, pregnant ass."

She slapped me on the arm. "Shut up. For real, though, thank you. My girls didn't understand why I felt so guilty, but you just showed me it's okay to live."

"Just because Blaze is gone don't mean you had to die as well. Just take your time and make sure that's what you really want."

"Okay, well, I'm about to get out of here. Me and him supposed to go on a date, and I have to get ready. You got the bill, right?"

I couldn't do shit but shake my head. "Yeah, I got it with your gold-digging ass gone and don't forget to text me the date of the party."

She said okay and walked off. After I finished eating, I left a hundred-dollar bill on the table. Not really having anywhere else to go, I headed home. When I walked in the door, Juicy had the house smelling good as fuck. Now, a nigga was pissed he just ate. Noticing a trail of rose petals, I followed them all the way upstairs. I still didn't see Juicy, so I jumped in the shower. When I got out, I wrapped a towel around me and walked back in the room. My baby was standing there in a red thong and bra looking fine as fuck.

"Lie down."

Doing as I was told, I climbed in the bed and lay on my back. She grabbed a blindfold and tried to put it on my eyes.

"Hold the fuck on. I ain't with no stupid shit. If I let you put this on me, your ass better not be on no gay shit and don't be beating me and shit." She responded by slapping me in the face. Then she went to put the blindfold on me again, and this time, I let her.

"We are going to have some fun, but you must follow the rules. Am I clear?"

"Yes." My dick was hard from the excitement.

"Rule number one. You are never to remove your blindfold. Rule number two. You can't touch. Keep your hands still at all times. Rule number three. Don't come quick."

I had no idea what the fuck she was about to do, but I soon found out when I felt two mouths on my dick. I knew Juicy's mouth. I didn't have to see her to know what she was doing to me. She was sucking my dick, and the other person was only allowed to suck my balls. Every now and then, I would feel the other girl run her tongue up Tsunami, but she would go right back to my balls. Juicy rose up to kiss me, and the girl started sneaking licks in. I laughed because Juicy must have given her rules as well. Once my baby went deep into a kiss with me, the girl started going to work on my dick as fast as hell. She must not have wanted to get caught. Her head wasn't as good as Juicy's, but she was deep throating the shit out of Tsunami. I had never met a girl that was able to do that shit.

I wanted so bad to grab my girl's ass while we kissed, but she said I couldn't touch her. As soon as Juicy leaned back, the girl went back to sucking my balls. I felt the girl stop, and she cradled me. The only reason I knew it wasn't Juicy is because her ass was smaller. She leaned forward, and I thought the bitch was gon' try to kiss me. This shit was gon' stop if she did that shit. When she leaned forward, she put her breast in my mouth. A nigga was kind of scared to suck it until I felt Juicy slap me.

"Suck."

Wrapping my lips around her nipple, I started getting into the shit. She leaned back and put her other breast in my mouth. Doing the same thing, I sucked the shit out of that motherfucker. Juicy's hand wrapped Tsunami, and she started slapping it against the girl's ass.

"Mmmm. That dick so big." When she spoke, I realized it was a white girl. This would be a first for me. I've never been with a white chick. I thought Juicy was going to slide my dick in her, and I was gon' beat her ass. My dick don't go in randoms without a condom. The white chick wanted my dick in her bad as fuck because she kept trying to slide into it when Juicy smacked it.

"You want my dick, don't you? Your pussy throbbing at the thought of it, ain't it?" This side of Juicy was turning me the fuck on.

"Yes, please. I want it so bad."

Juicy laughed, and I didn't know what she was going to do next.

"Get up." The white girl climbed off me, and I lay there trying to figure out what they were doing. When the white girl's mouth hit my dick, I could tell Juicy was guiding her. The rhythm seemed forced. The girl was gagging like a motherfucker, and that caused her mouth to get sloppy wet.

"Fuck," I moaned out because the shit was feeling good as hell.

"Did I say you could talk? I see you need something in your mouth." Juicy better not put that bitch's pussy in my mouth. I knew that wasn't happening when the girl started sucking my dick like her life depended on it. She was swallowing my shit, but I was scared to moan again.

As soon as I got ready to say something else, Juicy sat on my face. I wanted to grab her ass and guide that motherfucker all over my tongue, but she said I couldn't touch her. My baby started riding my face like she was on my dick. Trying to eat her pussy off her body, I was all in it. My dick was swelling up, but a nigga was scared to nut. I felt the girl's mouth come off my dick, and she sat on my lap. I prayed this girl didn't try to stick my dick in her. She didn't. She just grinded on it, like she was trying to come from the friction. The bitch thought she was slick. She damn near slid him in when she went back on it. I made him jump so it would miss her hole. She wasn't about to get me killed in here. Juicy started shaking on my face, and the girl climbed down and put my dick back in her mouth. When Juicy creamed all on my tongue, I was ready to fuck her. The girl climbed down, and Juicy climbed on top of my dick. The way she slid down with ease had me ready to nut.

The girl kept sucking my balls, and this shit was driving me crazy. She started licking up and down, and I knew when she licked past my balls, she was eating Juicy's pussy. A nigga was ready to snatch the blindfold off. This shit I wanted to see, but I couldn't, or they would stop. Juicy started moaning like crazy, and I realized the girl was no longer sucking my balls at all. She focused solely on Juicy's clit. My baby started bucking like crazy, and I couldn't hold it any longer.

"Fuck, I'm about to come!"

When Juicy slid off my dick and let the white girl catch my nut, I shot a dumb-ass load down her throat. White girl wasn't playing cus she never missed a beat. She caught all my nut without stopping to swallow. She kept right on sucking. Tsunami was back on brick, and I had no idea if there was a round two in the picture. Next, I heard a paper wrapping and then Juicy again.

"You earned yourself a ten-minute ride. After ten minutes and you still on top, I'm going to knock your ass off."

I felt Juicy slide a condom on my dick, and the white girl jumped on my shit so fast, she damn near bent it. A nigga never had a bitch ride my dick this fast. She planned on making this ten minutes count. Even though I didn't think it would be, her pussy was tight and good. She was doing moves I hadn't felt before. Juicy leaned down and kissed me while ol' girl rode me like I was the bitch. She was gripping her muscles so hard against my dick that I thought she was trying to ease the condom off. I damn near nutted every time she did that shit.

The bitch started spinning on my shit. Literally spinning, going in circles. She was about to be mad because I wasn't about to make it ten minutes. She did her swirl one more time and started bouncing up and down. She bounced my nut right up out of my ass. When she realized I was done, she slid back some and used my dick as her personal dildo. She started rubbing it against her clit and sticking it in and out of her until she came. When I felt the liquid hit my feet, I knew she had squirted all on my shit. What fucked me up was that she started doing it again. I guess she said Juicy gave her ten minutes, and she wanted all them motherfuckers. The friction against her clit woke Tsunami back up. As soon as she realized that, she slid right back on it and started bouncing again. A nigga was about to be embarrassed because I was about to nut again. When I felt the hot liquid shoot all over my dick, that was all I needed, and I nutted again.

"A'ight, that's enough. Get your pissy ass up." I couldn't do shit but laugh at Juicy's ass. I felt my baby pull the condom off my dick and walk off. When she came back in, she took the blindfold off. The girl was gone, and Juicy was standing there looking at me like I was crazy. I should have known this shit was too good to be true. How the fuck was she mad at me when *she* the one that set the shit up?

"What's wrong Juicy?"

A smile spread across her face, and I was confused. "You got another round in you? I wanna feel you in my guts." She climbed in the bed and got on all fours. Tsunami stood straight up, and I climbed in my pussy and did what I do best. No bitch could ever top my Juicy. This girl had me sprung as hell, and I loved every minute of it. Giving her all that I got, I fucked her like it was my last time. She screamed as I tried to reach her soul with the tip of my dick.

Chapter 58

Shadow

I was trying my best to get on one accord with Shirree, but she was making this shit hard. I've been doing everything in my power to make shit right with us, but it was like she just wasn't hearing it. Tonight, I was determined to show her what she means to me and get back on track, but when she walked in the door, I could tell she had a fucking attitude.

"Hey, baby. I need you to get dressed. We going out and don't ask where because it's a surprise."

She rolled her eyes, and I almost slapped them motherfuckers out of her head.

"Do we have to? I'm tired, and I just want to lie down."

"I can't make you do shit, but if you want me to stay and keep trying to make this shit work, then you should. The choice is yours, but a nigga ain't about to be unhappy in his own home." You could tell she was thinking it over.

"How am I supposed to know how to dress if you won't tell me where we're going?"

"Just dress nice."

I already had my clothes on, and I was ready to go. It took her about an hour, but when she finally came downstairs, she looked amazing. *This* was the woman I wanted to spend the rest of my life with. Beautiful and smiling. Grabbing her hand, we walked out the door and hopped in the Phantom. She was silent as I drove toward downtown, but it didn't bother me as long as she wasn't snapping and going off. We pulled up on Michigan, and I gave the valet my keys. When she saw the horse and carriage, she lost her mind.

"Baby, is this for us? I have always wanted to ride one of these."

"I know, and that's why I chose it." I helped her up and allowed her to sit down before I climbed in. The view was amazing as we rode all over downtown. The horse finally stopped in front of the John Hancock Building, and we got out. Heading to the ninety-fifth floor, we walked into the Signature Room like we owned the place. Once we sat down, I ordered a bottle of wine and soup for an appetizer. This was the first time I had seen her smile in a long time.

"How did we get here?" she asked as she stared into my eyes.

"In a damn horse. The fuck you talking about?" I was confused. We just walked in the door.

"Not here in this moment, dummy, but *here*. Our *relationship*."

Realizing what she meant, I thought about it for a minute. "It started with the constant disrespect and arguing. Me cheating with Elise wasn't cool, but you have to admit you pushed me there. Then you cheated, and I figured we were even, and we could move forward.

"Shit was going good until my brother got killed. My mental fucked up, and it's affecting our sex life. Knowing I can't please you been fucking a nigga's head up, and you leaving all times of the day ain't helping shit, either. I just want to get back to us and move forward."

"I agree, and I apologize for the parts I played in all this. Do you think there's a chance for us?"

"There is, if we want it and work hard at it, but we both have to want it, Shirree." Before she could respond, the waitress brought our soup and took our order. When she walked away, there was an awkward silence. I grabbed her hand and kissed it.

"I love you, and that's all that matters to me. Anything we have done up to this point is forgiven, but we have to start working at that shit, or I'm gone." She smiled at me and agreed. The rest of the dinner we laughed and talked about everything. She took me down memory lane all the way to when we first met. It was a great night, and hopefully, a new beginning for us. Leaving, we were hugging, kissing, and laughing like it was our first date. We climbed back into the carriage, and it took us to my car. As soon as we got home, I was determined to end this night with some mind-blowing sex. There was no way my dick should be getting hard for another bitch and not her.

As soon as we stepped in the door, we both started removing our clothes. I chased her up the stairs, my dick was bouncing around, and life was coming to it. When I laid her on the bed, I didn't try to eat her pussy first. I needed to go to work while my shit was working. Kissing her, I slid my dick in and started tearing her ass up. My shit was finally on brick, and I was happy. Spreading her legs, I went balls deep in her shit. Changing positions, I pulled her on top of me, and she started riding that motherfucker like a pro. She ain't never went crazy like this on my dick before. I lost my mind when she slid off and started sucking my shit. Letting it hit her tonsils, she deep throated every time she went down.

Going to my balls, she started sucking like crazy. A nigga was ready to get back in her pussy and bust . . . when this bitch pushed my legs back and started licking my ass. I was so pissed I supersocked that ho on the top of her head. She jumped up, holding her shit. The bitch actually had the nerve to be crying.

"Why you punch me like that? What the fuck is wrong with you?"

"Bitch, when have I ever gave you the vibe that I wanted somebody playing in my ass? Ain't shit about me gay, and if you ever even look at my ass like that, I'm gon' knock your ass out. Simple-ass ho. The fuck made you do that shit anyway?"

"I thought we could try something new."

"Ho, you about to try your way into a black eye. Do that shit again, issa woman beater." Jumping off the bed, I went to get in the shower. Looking at her shitty-mouthed ass was pissing me off. Walking past her, I shook my head at her and went to wash my ass. There was no way this bitch wasn't out here fucking another nigga. I'm trying to make shit work, and she out here sucking turds and yesterday's meals out of some fag-ass nigga booty hole. When I got out of the shower, I grabbed the cover and a pillow and took it in the bathroom and made a pallet on the floor.

"Why you putting that in the bathroom? What's wrong with your ass?"

"Bitch, since you like shit so much, now you sleeping next to the fucking toilet. I don't wanna even look at your ass tonight." She thought I was playing . . . until I got up to drag her ass. Walking to the bathroom, she stomped all the way there and slammed the door.

"And brush your teeth with your nasty-mouth ass." Lying down, I grabbed some oil and jerked my dick until my nut came out. I would have gone to Stacey's house, but I killed the bitch. A nigga went to sleep right after. This ho was getting out of control, and I knew I had a decision to make. I didn't think I could be with her anymore. She changed, and I didn't like the changes she was making.

Waking up the next morning, I had all kinds of low alert messages on my phone from my bank. The only money we put in the bank is the money from the clubs and real estate, but there was no way them motherfuckers should have been low. Calling my bank, they informed me that Shirree had been withdrawing all of this money. This ho was up to something, and it was time to get to the bottom of it. Grabbing my phone, I called Baby Face.

"Hey, nigga, do you still have the number for that private investigator that will follow a motherfucker?"

"Yeah, but what you need that for?"

"I'll explain it later; just text me the number." I'm about to find out what this ho up to. I had played dumb long enough. It was time to get to the bottom of this shit finally. If this ho was living foul, she was about to find out who the fuck I really was. This nice guy shit wasn't working, and I was done being that nigga.

Chapter 59

Debra

Today, I was hanging out with Drea, Ash, and Juicy. I wanted Shirree to come, but she had some business to handle. Walking around the mall, we tried to find something to wear for the gender reveal party. My old ass was tired of walking, and they ass was just getting started.

"How long y'all ass gon' be? I'm trying to go home and get some from my man before he hit the streets." They looked at me and laughed.

"It's not weird for you, Mama D? He been gone all these years, and just like that, y'all back together?" Juicy had this serious-ass look on her face. I know my son better not fuck up because I can tell she is zero tolerant of bullshit.

"It was easy for me because he was the only person I ever gave my heart and pussy to. He was the only man I craved, and I never messed with anyone else after I thought he passed away."

Drea started to look sad, and she turned to me. "I met a guy. We haven't had sex or anything, but we been hanging out a lot, and I really like him. He is everything, but it feels like I'm cheating on Blaze."

My heart hurt for her. "Look, everybody ain't built like me. You aren't cheating on my son. He is dead. You have to move on with your life. If this guy seems like he's the one, then leap, bitch. What you waiting on?" Everybody laughed, but I was dead ass.

"Ash, I know that you and my son are back messing around. All I'm going to say to you is don't hurt him. He needed you to heal him, and you have done that, but when I look at you, it doesn't seem like you are all in. Be honest with him, or it will hurt him more in the end."

"Mama, I love Quick with all of me, but I have done some things he may not understand. Even being up front with him will only cause him to be hurt. There's no way around it."

"Listen, everybody has a past. My sons wasn't no saints, and you bitches wasn't no virgins. We fuck up from time to time, but if you love that person like you say you do, then love will help you forgive."

"That shit is easier said than done. Certain things can't be forgiven. Some shit is just too much to deal with. I hear you, Mama, but I ain't with all that *you hurt me I forgive you* shit."

Baby Face had his work cut out for him. Juicy didn't play.

"Then that means you never loved them like you thought."

"I can love somebody and not be weak."

She done lost her mind. "Who the fuck you calling weak? You young bitches don't know what it means to love someone with your whole being. I loved Rico so much my soul bled when he died. He was a part of me, so when he died, half of me went with him. Staying by myself didn't make me weak and taking him back didn't either. Now, weak would be me sitting here letting you disrespect me and that ain't gon' happen in your sleep. You can feel how you want, but you gon' watch what the fuck you saying to me. You think them niggas you fucking with is a savage, but *I* raised them motherfuckers. Don't get shit twisted." She had me fucked up.

"Girl, I wasn't even talking about you. I meant it in general. You just did the most for nothing."

"Oh, in that case, I agree."

Everybody laughed, and I had to join in. She was about to get her ass tapped for no reason. "My sons have never loved a woman before other than me. Be patient with them, I know it gets hard, but in the end, it will be worth it. You all have their hearts, but if you break it, you have to answer to me, and you *don't* want that." They took in what I was saying, and we went to the last store. Grabbing my outfit, I was done and ready to go.

"I'll see y'all at this fancy-ass baby shower. Paris's ass do the fucking most. We could have had hot dogs and passed out gifts." They hugged me and laughed. We all went our separate ways, and I took my ass home. When I walked in the door, Rico was sitting in the front counting money. I'm glad some was finally coming in, and he could start giving me my shit back. I'm a down-ass bitch, not a sugar mama.

"Hey, baby, is that for me?"

He looked at me like I was crazy. "Damn, can a nigga make a profit before you start begging?"

He had me fucked up. "Begging? Was it begging when I done gave your ass damn near a million dollars? My sons would kill me if they knew I was giving your ass all that money. Don't play with me. You won't get another fucking dime if you even think you gon' play me."

"My bad, baby. I had a rough day, and I need some pussy." Pulling his dick out, he sat on the couch and started rubbing it, trying to get it hard. I got on my old-ass knees and started sucking that motherfucker. It was getting hard, but not all the way, and I was sucking for dear life. Trying to get that motherfucker to stand up, I started sucking on his balls. This nigga lifted his legs.

"Lick my ass, baby, while you licking my balls."

The fuck this nigga say to me! "You a fag? Damn, it all makes sense now. You were in jail for twenty years; you had to be fucking something. Well, I can tell you now, bitch, you can go be a burrito in the Mexican jail if you want your ass ate. Ain't shit going in my mouth unless it was killed and cooked." Standing up, I looked at his ass in disgust. He stood up and slapped the shit out of my ass.

"Bitch, ain't shit gay about me. Don't ever disrespect me again."

"You the one flipping your legs back like a two-dollar sissy. What the fuck am I supposed to think?"

"You heard what the fuck I said. You pop off at the mouth cus you think your sons are untouchable. One already got touched; don't have the other ones going to meet they Maker." He walked out the door, and I was left with two thoughts. One, nigga gon' and leave with your loose booty ass. Two, the fuck did he mean one already got touched? That shit didn't sit right

with me. If I find out he had something to do
with Blaze's death, I will kill him myself. It was
time for me to quit sitting back and accepting
what he was telling me. I was too old to be a fool,
and I wasn't about to start that shit today.

Going upstairs, I lay down. When this nigga
got back, I was going to put that tracking app on
his phone. This would be the last night he left
this motherfucker, and I didn't know where he
was going. We were about to get to the bottom of
all these disappearances.

Chapter 60

Rico

A nigga was already irritated, and this bitch wanted to talk shit. When I met up with Shirree a little while ago, she brought me some money, and I tried to fuck her, but I couldn't get into it. The only way I could keep my dick hard was to think about Tate, and that shit was fucking with me. I thought it was a mishap, but the same shit was about to happen with Debra. When she started calling me gay, it hit home. A nigga can't be gay in this line of business. As soon as I got all the money I owed the cartel, I was headed back to Puerto Rico. They would kill me if they found out I was into niggas. You can't be the nigga in charge and be gay. I've never had feelings for a man. I never even looked at a nigga in that way. Had Tate tried that shit, and I knew it was him, I would have killed his ass. The nigga had me feeling shit I didn't think was possible sexually before I even realized it was a man. Now I was craving that shit, and I couldn't do shit about it. Grabbing my phone, I called Tate to see where he was.

"Hey, where you at?"

"I'm at home. I thought you didn't need me at the meeting today."

"I don't. I need to talk to you about something else. I'm about to come over."

"Okay, the door will be unlocked."

Hanging up, I headed to his house. Everything in my being that was still manly was telling me to turn around, but my dick was driving me straight to his house. I pulled up and threw all fucks out the window. Walking in his house, he was sitting on the couch drinking a beer. He must not have figured out the real reason I was there. He was about to find out, though. I walked in front of him and pulled my dick out. He looked at me, and no words needed to be said. Taking his beer, he started pouring it over my dick, then started sucking. Closing my eyes, I knew this was a craving I would never be able to get rid of. I didn't know what the fuck I was going to do, but I needed this shit like I needed air to breathe. His jaws were so fucking strong and wet against my dick, and he deep throated without gagging each time he went down. Massaging my balls while he sucked, he slid them in his mouth with my dick when he went down the last time. The grip he had on my shit had precome shooting out.

"Fuck. Suck daddy's dick."

Grabbing me by my ass cheeks, he started slamming my body against his mouth. He had me fucking his mouth, and that shit was feeling good as fuck. Once I knew what he wanted, I took over. Using his finger, he started sliding it up and down my ass and massaging my asshole. I didn't want to be penetrated, but the feeling had my dick harder than it's ever been. When he slid his finger in and started fucking my ass, I nutted and couldn't even stop or control it. He never stopped sucking, and my shit was back hard. He continued to slide his finger in and out of my ass, and I was about to nut again, so I pulled my dick out of his mouth. I wanted to feel his ass, and he was trying to make me nut.

"Come ride this dick." Sitting on the couch, I rubbed my dick until he climbed on top of me and sat down. Once he started riding that motherfucker, I knew I was a goner. Maybe when all this shit was over, I could convince him to leave with me and act like he my security. He grabbed my hand and placed it on his dick as he rode me to the ends of the fucking earth. I had never been with a man before, so I didn't know what to do, but I knew what I would want. I started stroking him, and it had him going crazy. He leaned back to kiss me, and I let him. All you heard was balls slapping and moans.

"Fuck, daddy; your dick so big, I'm about to come. Make me come, daddy." I gripped his dick harder and started stroking the shit out of his ass. His moans drove me so crazy. I could feel my nut rising as well. As soon as his nut shot all across the room, my nut shot all in his ass. My body was shaking, and I knew I was sprung.

"You ever been to Puerto Rico?"

Chapter 61

Drea

Whew, this man was giving me life. Every time I tried to be down and depressed about Blaze, this nigga did something to bring me right out of that shit. Most people can't find true love once, and here it is looking like I may have found it twice. He still couldn't compare to the love I have for Blaze, but he was definitely trying. My ass in here now trying to get ready for my gender reveal party, and he insisted on coming with me. I tried explaining to him that I didn't know how Blaze's family would handle him coming around, but he told me he was good. Still nervous, I gave in and told him that he could go. The last thing I needed was for him to think it was something else. Grabbing my clothes, I started getting dressed. I wanted it to be a girl, so I had on a white button-up, blue jean capris, and a pink bow tie and suspenders. I threw on my all-pink Huaraches and waited for Mack to get here. My ass couldn't do shit but smile as I thought back to our last date.

When I got in the car, I had a million questions.

"Where are we going? I hate surprises. Just give me a hint." He laughed at me and kept driving.

"A surprise means you're not supposed to know. Just sit back and let your man take care of you."

"Uuughhh. Just tell me the area."

He turned the radio up on my ass and kept driving. When we got out, we were at some park. He went to the trunk and grabbed a bag out and said, let's go. It felt like we were walking for hours. If I went any farther, I was gon' go my fat ass into labor. Seeing that I was struggling. He bent down and let me get on his back.

"Get your big lazy ass up here."

I don't know if he was playing, but I jumped my ass right on up there. He stood up and kept walking. When he finally stopped, we were by the lake, and he placed me down right by the water. Unzipping his bag, he pulled out a *blanket and laid it out. He started placing food on top of it, and my heart melted. He even put rose petals all over. Helping me down to the ground, I sat there and stared at this man that came in and healed me at my weakest point. When I thought I would never be able to pick up the pieces, he helped me put my shit back together. Then he handed me a Kindle, and I looked at him confused.*

"Read to me," he said so sweetly.

"What am I supposed to read?"

"Take a pick. I already downloaded Love the Way You Thug Me *by KB Cole,* Cherished by a Boss *by A. J. Davidson, and* Beautiful *by Tyanna."*

I looked at the book covers and read the synopsis. I didn't want to pick one over the other, so I knew I would read all three. I started with Love the Way You Thug Me. *The entire time I read, he listened intently while he fed me at the same time. We ended up out there for hours. Walking back to the car, I knew tonight would be special. When we got back to my house, he came in, and I just knew we were about to have sex, but he stopped me.*

"Not yet. I wanna fuck your mind first. It will happen when the time is right. Not because you feel we had a great date." He kissed me on my

forehead, and the nigga left me with dripping panties. He and Blaze were complete opposites. I loved the gentle side of Mack, but I loved the rough side of Blaze. Both men touched my heart, but Blaze still owned it.

Hearing the bell ring, I got up and walked out. As I climbed in the car, I noticed Mack had on a blue jean button-up, some jeans, and some dark blue Gucci high top sneakers.

"You think I'm having a boy?"

"No, I think *we* having a boy. I know I'm not his real father, and I could never take his place, but I'm gon' do whatever I can to make sure the baby never misses his presence." Tears slid down my face as we headed to the party. He slid his fingers through mine, and we rode in silence.

Pulling up to the main house, I could tell Mack was in awe.

"Goals." I laughed at him as we got out. The whole outside was decorated in pink and blue and accents of silver. When we walked inside, the memorial was decorated as well, and a plaque hung on the wall that said, *"Always a father, forever in our hearts."* I couldn't stop the tears from falling. Mack just held me and let me have my moment. I leaned toward the wall and kissed Blaze right on the lips.

"I love you always."

Walking into the rest of the house, I noticed everyone was outside. Pink and blue floating balloons were everywhere. A big-ass tier cake stood on a table. Each layer was a different color. A pink picture frame photo opp and a blue one stood on a table. You could take a pic in the frame of the color you thought it was going to be. Right in the middle of it all was a flame going with a pic of Blaze next to it. I had no idea why that was there, but it looked amazing. When everyone noticed I was there, they were happy . . . until they saw I wasn't alone.

"Drea, you done lost your damn mind?" Baby Face was pissed.

"You told me to move on with my life, and that's what I'm doing."

"I said move on, but I didn't say move that shit over here. You know we don't do this fuck shit, but since it's your party, I'm gon' let you be great."

Mack stuck his hand out to shake their hands.

"I'm Mack. I ain't here for the bullshit, but I won't duck it. I just wanted to be a part of the shit since I'm choosing to be with Drea and the baby. I have a right to be at the shower just like anybody else, but this y'all shit, and if y'all want me gone, I'll leave." I loved how Mack handled it.

"You light-skinned niggas be sensitive as fuck. Pull your skirt down, B."

We all laughed because Shadow was the only dark-skinned brother. They all shook his hand, and the tension died down. We partied, ate, and enjoyed ourselves until it was time to reveal the gender. Everybody was happy except Debra and Rico. They looked like they were going through it.

"OK, I need everybody that think it's a boy on one side of the flame, and everybody that think it's a girl on the other. Hurry the fuck up. This fire hot shit."

We laughed as Paris snapped out. Everybody took their places except me.

"OK, you and Blaze gon' pop this big-ass balloon, and whatever color fly out is the gender." Everyone looked confused.

"Hey, P, how the fuck is Blaze gon' pop the damn balloon?" Quick asked, but we all were thinking it.

"If you shut the fuck up, I'll tell you. You motherfuckers slow as the fuck. Anyway, Drea, you hold the balloon over the fire. When it pops, the shit will fly everywhere. We all know that wherever fire is, so is Blaze, and that's how he will be a part of it."

The fact that she found a way to include Blaze touched my heart. I walked over and held the balloon to the flame. When it popped, pink and silver shit flew everywhere. Out of nowhere, pink-colored doves were released. The shit was beautiful. I hugged Paris and cried as I watched the pink birds fly around us.

"Awww, shit. Mama, you finally got your girl. This baby about to be spoiled as fuck." Everyone agreed with Quick. My girls and I mingled, and I noticed Mack was talking with the fellas.

"Bitch, you bold, and you must got magic in your pussy. How the fuck you convince that nigga to walk into a death trap?"

I laughed as I answered Paris. "He asked me to come. He said since he is going to be the one to step up as the dad, he had a right to be here."

"Girl, he is a fucking keeper." Once Ash said that, it made me think of something.

"Where is Zavi?"

"He's with Jason. He begged him to pick him up. I'm surprised he said yes. I'm going to get him when I leave." We hung out for a little while longer; then everyone headed home.

I was in the house for about thirty minutes when my phone rang.

"Hey, come outside and talk to me for a minute. I'm in my Hummer." Baby Face didn't even give me the chance to respond. He hung up in my face.

I should have known today went too smooth. There was bound to be some bullshit. I wobbled my ass outside to see what he wanted. This nigga better not be jealous of Mack. I thought we discussed this, and he knew I didn't see him in that way. If he was in his feelings, I was gon' have to ask him to stay away from me. The shit we did was consensual, but it was wrong as fuck, and it will never happen again. I was weak, lonely, and depressed. I'm not in that space anymore. Even if I were, I wouldn't mess around with Face. He better get over this shit quick if he wanted to be in his niece's life. I would hate to keep him away, but if he on some bullshit, I would have to.

Chapter 62

Debra

This nigga Rico had me fucked up. He walking around like he the fucking man. Every time I think about him asking me to lick his ass, I get pissed. Loose-booty-ass nigga. I bet he can't hold a fart in, his ass around here beat boxing and shit. He been leaving the house a lot lately, more than usual. He wouldn't even touch me sexually, but he can go upside my head when I won't give him no money. I needed to see what the fuck he up to before I told my sons. I know I'm dramatic, and they will kill him. Before I took that step, I needed to know. So, when we got back from the gender reveal, he said he was heading out. Tonight, I didn't give him any lip. I let him go. But a bitch was right behind his ass. My ass was too old to be out here dressed in all-black and shit, but here I was.

When he got out of the car, I stayed parked down the street. Trying not to be seen, I climbed the neighbor's fence and tried to approach it that way. Shit didn't work out how I planned it. As soon as I got to the top of that fence, baby, this knee went left, and my ass went right. I hit that ground, and I thought a ho was dead.

"A bitch too old for this shit," I said out loud to no one in particular. Getting up off the ground, I realized my ass landed in dog shit. That should have been my sign to take my old ass in the house. On top of that, my knee was throbbing, I was hunched over from the pain in my back, and I smelled like a fucking goat. One thing I learned in life, if a bitch wanted to find some shit out about her man, nothing would stop her, and it didn't. I limped my funky ass to that house and walked in the door. However, I was nowhere near ready for the sight before me. Rico was sitting on the couch as a girl rode his face, and a nigga was sucking his dick. This nigga was sucking his shit up like a vacuum.

"What the fuck!" They all turned around, and I almost passed out. "Shirree. have you lost your fucking mind?" Before anybody got a chance to move, I ran over to the couch forgetting all about my bad knee. I hit that bitch so hard she flipped over the couch. Not done, I walked around the couch and started stomping the life out of her ass.

Rico grabbed me by the li'l hair on my head. A bitch was already bald-headed, and now a ho was gon' have patches. He threw me to the floor, and I jumped up and grabbed the lamp, hitting his ass over the head with it. Then I punched him in the mouth. Running back to Shirree, I stomped her ass some more. Out of nowhere, the sissy ran up and round housed my ass. I blinked once, and then I was out.

The sounds of sex woke me up out of my power nap the sissy gave me. These motherfuckers tied me to a chair. I knew I shouldn't have left my gun in the car. Looking up, I was in the kitchen, but I could still see these nasty motherfuckers. Shirree was gone, but the man I didn't know was riding the shit out of Rico's dick as they kissed like they were in love. I started throwing up all over myself. Now a bitch was really mad. Not only did I have dog shit on me, but now I was covered in vomit. A bitch was gon' be smelling like a farm in a minute.

"That's right, fuck daddy's dick. I'm about to come," Rico demanded to the other guy, and he started riding that shit better than any woman I had ever seen. Who the fuck can compete with some shit like this? No wonder he didn't want my stiff old ass. I saw nut flying everywhere, and then Rico started grunting.

"I swear I love your ass."

It wasn't until he said those words that I realized I had fucked up. This nigga didn't want me. He was using my ass. Standing up, he walked over to me with his dick swinging. The dick I used to be so in love with. Now it was covered in shit, and I wanted to chop it off.

"I had no intentions of anyone ever finding out about this, but you didn't know how to stay in your fucking lane. Now I'm going to have to kill you and your bitch-ass sons." His phone rang, and he walked over to it before I could respond.

"What the fuck you mean? How? I'm on the way." He grabbed his gun and walked over to me. Hitting me over the head with it, I was out again.

Chapter 63

Shadow

The entire time we were at the reveal party, Shirree had a motherfucking attitude. I mean, she was pouting and stomping around like somebody stole her fucking bike. This bitch was in her last days, and she didn't even know it. After the balloon popped, the girls ventured off, and the fellas went and talked to this nigga Mack. Something was off about the nigga if you asked me. He was trying too hard. When everybody started leaving, I couldn't wait to get home. As soon as we got in the car, the bitch slammed my door, and it pissed me off.

"Open my door and close it like you got some sense. If you slam my shit one more time, your head's going through the window. You can think I'm playing and try me, but, bitch, you gon' die today. This car cost more than your fucking life, and you slamming shit." She thought I was playing about doing the shit over until she saw I wasn't pulling off. She opened the door and closed it regular this time. I pulled off and started right back up.

"What the fuck is wrong with you? This was supposed to be a happy occasion, and you got your ass around here acting like a li'l-ass kid."

"Nothing's wrong. I just want to go home and go to bed."

I left it alone and turned my radio up. I don't kiss ass. That's *her* nasty-ass department. She got a text and all of a sudden, the bitch wasn't pouting any more. A nigga didn't say shit. I just continued to drive home. She had a week to get the fuck out of my shit. I was tired of playing these games with her. I was done. There's plenty of bitches out here who would be happy to get with a nigga like me. I'm not taking shit else off this bitch. As soon as we pulled up, she got out and was in a different mood.

"Drea needs us to help her clean up. I'll be back in a little bit."

I didn't even respond. I walked into the house, and she drove off. Walking in the room, I started pulling all her shit out of the closets. Fuck a week—this bitch was leaving my shit tonight. She's lucky I wasn't throwing her ass out with nothing. I bought everything she has, but she can have it all as long as she got the fuck out of my house. My phone rang while I was getting all of her shit together.

"Hello."

"I need to meet up with you. Do you have a minute?" It was the nigga Jerome I hired to follow Shirree. He must have something.

"Yeah, where you want to meet?" After I got the address, I walked out and jumped in my whip. My stomach was doing knots as I wondered what it could be. The whole way there, so many different things went through my mind.

When I finally pulled up, my nerves were shot. He was leaning against his car with an envelope. Getting the shit over with, I walked up to him to see what he had.

"Hey, man, I hope you weren't busy, but I thought you might want to see this." He handed me the envelope.

"It's all good." Pulling out the pictures, I didn't need to see any of the other ones. She was sitting on a nigga's face, while another nigga was sucking his dick. Now I know where she got that fag shit from. This bitch was fucking some fairies. Putting the pics back, I didn't look at the rest. A nigga wasn't trying to see no gay shit.

"She goes to the bank every day and comes out with a bag of money. She meets up with the same two niggas, but she only gives money to one. As soon as he gets the money, she practically rips his clothes off and starts having sex. The other guy comes in late or don't be there at all."

That's fucked up. She paying a nigga to fuck her clown ass.

He saw the look on my face and apologized. "I'm sorry I had to bring this news to you. I hope shit works out."

"It's cool. You just doing your job. I'll wire the rest of your money in the morning." We shook up, and I left.

Putting the pics in my glove box, I was gon' let this bitch make it, but now, she about to go pay Blaze a visit. This bitch had me fucked up. I tried to call Quick and Baby Face, but neither was answering their phone. Hanging up, I headed to the house to wait for the bitch to come back. Shit was about to get real ugly. I had no idea what lie this bitch was gon' try to tell to get out of it, but I wanted to see what she would come up with. This ho had me fucked up in the worst way. She should have known I would eventually figure it out. I was the smart one, but this ho was treating me like I was short-school-bus slow. Thinking of the different ways I could kill her, I kept calling my brothers. These motherfuckers weren't answering, and I knew without them to talk me out of it, I was about to go off the deep end.

Chapter 64

Baby Face

I couldn't believe Drea brought some nigga to our house. She knows we don't trust a mother-fucking soul. Hell, I didn't even want my father over here, but she brought this nigga we didn't know. It was her day, though, so I would holla at her about it later on. He seemed like a cool-ass nigga, but we been through too much this year, and I wasn't taking any more chances. After the reveal, I was gon' talk to this nigga and see where his head was at. When Paris said that Drea and Blaze were going to pop the balloon together, the nigga was smiling . . . but his veins were popping out of his neck. He either really loved Drea, or he hated the fuck out of my brother. Either way, he knew how to put on a good front, and that's the type of shit you have to look for. I noticed he kept looking at Blaze's picture, and the shit was bothering me. As soon as the girls branched off, I took that as my chance to see what the fuck he was on.

"Hey, homie, let us talk to you for a minute."

He walked our way, but he looked back at Drea, and I was trying to figure out what that look was for.

"What's good? This was a nice party. Make a nigga want to have a baby and shit." He gave a lame-ass laugh, but I wasn't buying it.

"I thought you just said her baby is your baby. So, my nigga, you just had one of these parties." He looked at me, and I could see his eyes changing over. You know when a motherfucker gets pissed, and then in a split second, they smiling and that look gone. Yeah, that's what this nigga just did.

"You know what I mean. That's your brother's baby. I would never try to take his place."

"You can't take his place, nigga. Fuck is you talking about?" Quick was ready to go off. I knew his tone.

"Look, y'all picking apart everything a nigga saying. I thought shit was all good."

"Shit will never be all good until I know that you are who you making yourself out to be. What you do for a living?"

"I have a couple of buildings, but I'm trying to be like you niggas. Instead of going at me all night, you need to be putting a nigga on. With Blaze gone, y'all gone need a fourth man. I'm from the streets, so I know how to handle myself."

I looked at this nigga like he lost his damn mind, and Quick was pulling his gun. Motioning for him to put it away, I kept asking questions. There would be another day we would see Mack, but this wasn't the place.

"What you talking about, nigga?"

"The bank robberies. I want in. I'm not your brother, but I *will* have your back. Shit, there's enough money for all of us out here. Let's get this paper."

"Who the fuck told you some shit like that?"

He looked over at Drea. "Baby girl did. She was telling me what her nigga did for money. I wasn't trying to start nothing. I just want in."

Not wanting him to think anything of it, I let it go. "It's all good. We'll hit you up if we decide to expand. Fair enough?"

"Fair enough."

We stopped talking when the women walked back over. Drea was gon' have to answer to me tonight. I spared her life once, but this bitch wasn't about to get away with this shit twice. Once everybody started leaving, I grabbed Juicy and headed home.

"What's wrong with you, Face?" She was trying to read my mood.

"I'm good, baby, I just have to handle some business real quick after I drop you off. I won't be long."

"Okay."

I could tell she wanted to ask me what it was, but I wasn't about to tell her. When we got to the house, she got out of the car but didn't close the door.

"Can you come in for a second?"

I really didn't want to. I wanted to go beat Drea's ass, but I got out, so I didn't piss her off.

As soon as I walked in the door, she snatched my pants down and pulled Tsunami out. A nigga didn't have sex on his mind, but my dick always responded to her fine ass. She started sucking, and I had to hold the door because my knees started buckling. Lately, every time I left the house, she fucked me before I left. She must have thought I was meeting a bitch, and I wouldn't fuck if she fucked me first. Taking as much as she could in her mouth, she started beasting on my dick. Knowing I had some business to handle, this had to be a quickie.

Pulling her up, I lifted her around my waist. Leaning against the door, I pulled her dress up and moved her panties to the side. Sliding my dick inside her, I almost didn't want to leave. I was so in love with her pussy, a nigga could stay in it forever. I didn't bother taking my time, though. I started tearing her pussy up. Using my hands to spread her ass cheeks apart, I pushed Tsunami all the way in with each stroke. Picking up the pace, I fucked the shit out of her against the door. Her pussy juices were leaking all over my shit. As soon as I started kissing her, she came all over my dick. Once I knew she got hers, I started pumping harder. My shit got brick hard, and my nut shot all up in that pussy.

"Damn, girl, let me find out you trying to get me to stay here."

"Is it working?"

I laughed as I let her down to the floor. "Naw, baby, it ain't, but I'll be back in a few."

She tried to stomp away, but she was limping, so the shit looked funny as fuck. Putting my dick up, I walked out of the house. A nigga would have to shower when I got back. Jumping in my Hummer, I pulled off and headed to Drea's house. When I pulled up, I called her phone.

"Hello."

"Hey, come outside and talk to me for a minute. I'm in my Hummer." I waited for her to walk out. She finally came out and walked over to my truck. When she climbed in, I was about to go the fuck off when something caught my eye. In disbelief, I watched Ash walking down the street. If my headlights weren't on, I probably would have missed it. She didn't even look my way, and I guess it was because she never saw this truck before. I jumped out of the truck, and Drea was looking at me like I was crazy.

"What the fuck do we have here?"

Ash looked up and damn near shitted on herself. She had a little boy with her, and I know it was Quick's son. He was the splitting image of him.

"Baby Face, let me explain."

"Is that my brother's baby?" Even though I knew the answer, I asked because I wanted her to say it. When she didn't respond, I grabbed her around her neck.

"I asked you a fucking question. Is that my brother's baby?" Tears were rolling down her eyes, but I didn't give a fuck.

"Let go of my mommy." The little boy started punching me in my leg. I almost kicked the li'l nigga, but he was my nephew.

"Face, don't do that in front of him, please." Drea was begging me, and I let Ash go.

"Zavi, do me a favor and go in the house. TT will be in there in a minute, okay?"

I watched how Drea was talking to the boy, and I got pissed off again. As soon as he was in the house, I smacked the shit out of her.

"You knew?" She backed away from me, and I wanted to beat her fucking ass. I ran up on her and choked a booger out of her ass. "All you bitches knew and sat in my brother's face like it wasn't shit." A nigga was so pissed that I was shaking.

"I'm sorry." Ash was crying hard as hell. Letting Drea go, I walked up on her.

"I'm not gon' touch you; I'm gon' leave that for my brother, but you bitches better know this shit ain't gon' end well." Walking off, I jumped in my truck and drove off. Grabbing my phone, I called Quick. This nigga wasn't answering. I kept calling back-to-back until I made it home. When I pulled in my driveway, I realized I never asked Drea about the shit Mack said. Fuck. This shit was about to get messy. I walked in the door and found Juicy sitting on the couch.

"Did you know Ash had a baby by Quick?" The shocked look on her face let me know she had no idea.

"What? No, I didn't know that. What the fuck. Face, what the fuck is going on?"

Not wanting to talk about it, I grabbed her and carried her up the stairs. I needed to relieve some stress, or I would be back over there beating Ash's brains in. As mad as I was, I couldn't do that shit without Quick. It wasn't my place. Looking back at Juicy, I let the shit go for now. I was about to get some pussy tonight, but tomorrow, motherfuckers was gon' feel what the Hoover Gang was all about.

Chapter 65

Quick

A nigga ain't been this happy in a long time. I got Alaysia's nutty ass out of my hair, and Ash and I have been seeing each other non-stop. She got my ass wide open, and I loved it. There was happiness in the cards for a nigga after all. This morning, I was asleep, and I woke up to the smell of breakfast. My first thought was this bitch done army crawled out of the lake and made it all the way back to my fucking house. Jumping up, I ran down the stairs ready to drown Alaysia's bitch ass in the toilet if I had to, but when I rounded the corner to the kitchen, Ash was standing there cooking, and her ass was looking nice as fuck in them leggings. I walked up behind her and hugged her. She jumped.

"Nigga, you scared me."

"Shid, how you think I felt waking up to breakfast being cooked in my house? I thought your ass was gon' ask me if I like my pancakes dark, light, or fluffy." I laughed thinking back to ol' girl asking Martin that shit on *A Thin Line between Love and Hate*."

Looking at her ass jiggle every time she moved, I was ready to get in her guts. "Fuck that bacon. How about I eat you instead?" She blushed and continued cooking.

"Me and Panda gotta go help Paris set up for the reveal party."

A nigga was pissed, but I knew I could get that pussy whenever I wanted now. I'm going to leave her be for now, but later, I was gon' shoot some more nut up her ass. The first load must not have worked. My petty ass was determined to trap her.

"Why don't you move in?" The shit flew out of my mouth so fast, I didn't even know I was about to say it. She turned around and looked at me.

"Are you serious?"

"When have you ever known me to play around other than with my brothers? I love you, Ashanti, and I'm ready this time. I mean it. I promise I won't hurt you. Just give a nigga a chance to do right by you. I'll spend the rest of my life making up for the bullshit I did years ago." She looked sad when she responded.

"Give me a day to think it over. If we do this, we are gon' have to talk first. If you still want me to after our conversation, I'll give you my answer."

"Fair enough, but you know I'll always want you." I pulled her to me, but she pulled away to take the bacon out. We sat down and ate, and the shit just felt right. After we were done, she got up and cleaned the kitchen. If she didn't already have my heart, she would have it now. My baby was everything a nigga needed, and I was going to make her mine. Giving me a long kiss once she was done, she grabbed her shit and left. The rest of my day was boring, and I couldn't wait to get to the reveal party so I could see Ash again.

When it was time for me to leave finally, I called her phone like the thirsty nigga I was.

"Hey, girl, you wanna ride with me to the party?"

"Yeah, pick me up from Drea's house. I stopped over here."

Letting her know I was on the way, I hung up. Jumping in my truck, I headed to get my girl. That's right; she was mine, and I was claiming it. When I pulled up, she walked out looking good as fuck. She had on a dress that hugged her shit in all the right places. She got in, and my ass was ready to say fuck this party, but I drove to the main house to see what this girl was having. Shit didn't matter because we all were going to spoil it rotten. Nobody else had any kids, and with Blaze being gone, it was only right.

The party seemed to go on forever, but after our talk with Mack, everybody started leaving. I didn't like that nigga, but that shit was on Drea. It wasn't my concern or problem. He almost got his ass faded bringing up our business. I knew Baby Face was gon' holla at her about running her mouth, but if he said the nigga had to go, it was night-night for that nigga. Grabbing Ash, we headed out the door.

When I pulled up to Drea's house for Ash to get in her car, I pulled her over to my lap. Kissing her, I was surprised she kissed me back. Ash was shy and very conservative. When I noticed she wasn't protesting, I moved my seat back. Sliding my fingers under her dress, I almost came knowing she didn't have on any panties. Rubbing her clit, she was soaking my fingers. When she started grinding, I knew I had to release my dick. Unzipping my pants, I pulled Tsunami out and let her grind against that motherfucker. She leaned up and grabbed my dick. When she came back down, my dick slid in her like it knew her pussy belonged to me. She grinded on it like she been wanting it as bad as me. Grabbing her by her hips, I helped guide her up and down. When she started speeding up, I knew she was about to come. I kissed her and allowed myself to come with her. Our bodies came in harmony, and I fell deeper in love. She climbed back in her seat, and I started joking.

"Girl, don't get that nut in my seats. Fuck is wrong with you?"

"Shut up. At least if you put another girl over here, I will have satisfaction knowing she sitting in all my juices."

"No other bitch will ever get in my cars. You are it, and I'm going to prove it to you." She leaned over and kissed me. When she opened the door, I stopped her.

"Don't forget, we'll talk tomorrow, and then you will give me an answer."

"I'll be there."

"I'll be waiting."

She got out of the car, and I smiled all the way home. Shit was finally looking up for a nigga. I pulled in the garage and went into the house. As soon as I started walking up the stairs to go shower, someone knocked at the door. Walking back down, I opened it without thinking.

"Zavier Hoover, you are under arrest for the murder of Officer Alaysia Hampton. You have the right to remain silent, and anything you say can and will be used against you in a court of law. You have the right to an attorney. If you can't afford one, one will be appointed to you. Do you understand your rights?" At least twelve policemen stood on my doorstep. All of them had guns drawn on me, except the one that was cuffing me and reading me my Miranda Rights.

"The fuck you arresting me for? I haven't touched that bitch."

He punched me in the mouth and walked me to the police car. I knew they was about to beat my ass some more. Shit, they knew I bodied a cop. Hell, they might just kill me. All I could think about was the fact I wasn't gon' be able to see Ash again. As soon as I got her back, I was being taken away. This was some bullshit.

My phone started ringing, and they snatched it and turned it off. I should have listened to my brothers, but my anger and my grief got the best of me. Now, a nigga was going down forever if they didn't kill my ass first. Shaking my head at myself, I knew I had fucked up.

"You're about to have a long night, son."

That was the last thing I heard before the officer knocked me out with his billy club.

Chapter 66

Drea

"Why didn't you tell me he was coming over?" Ash was screaming at me like this shit was my fault as she slammed pots all over the fucking stove. She was about to cook for Zavi, but her ass was a mess.

"I didn't know. He called and said he was outside. As soon as I got in the truck, you walked up. I didn't even see you until he got out and approached you. You should have told him. What the fuck you think was gon' happen?" I was not about to let her play the victim and blame me.

"I was going to tell him tomorrow. I can't believe this shit is happening." She was crying hard, and I walked over and hugged her. Even though she brought this on herself, I felt bad for her.

"It's going to be okay. He loves you. He'll be pissed and maybe beat your ass, but he'll forgive you." She didn't respond; she just cried. After about twenty minutes of her crying and steady going off, she got it together.

"I'm about to take Zavi and go to a hotel. I don't want Quick coming over here acting an ass in front of my son. I'll go and talk to him tomorrow like I said."

I agreed. I didn't want that shit at my house anyway. When she left, I lay in bed just shocked at everything that happened today. I still didn't know what Face wanted with me. He got so mad, he left without telling me. Lying there trying to figure out what he could have wanted, my phone rang, and I answered once I saw it was Mack.

"Hey, what you doing?"

"Lying down; shit got crazy over here."

"You want some company?"

"Yes, please."

"Open the door."

I jumped up and ran to the door like a kid. When I opened it for him, he was standing there looking good as hell. We walked back to my bedroom, and I laid him on the bed. I took my robe off, exposing my naked pregnant body.

"You so damn beautiful."

Blushing, I leaned down to kiss him.

"Shorty, I told you already, you don't have to do this. We can wait until you have the baby. I don't want you to have any regrets."

"I promise I won't. I need you. I had a rough day, and I need you to make it better." I leaned down and kissed him again. This time, he didn't stop me. Laying me down, he started licking my pussy like it was his last meal. His head wasn't all that great, but that was okay. I could teach him what I liked. After being down there for about ten minutes, I was over it and ready for him to be inside me. Climbing on top of him, I grinded against his dick. Lifting up, I grabbed it and got ready to slide it in when suddenly, the smoke detectors went off.

"Fuck! Ash was cooking for Zavi. She forgot to turn the fucking stove off." Jumping up, I ran out to try to fix the shit, but it was too late. Flames were everywhere.

"Maaacckkkkk!" I screamed his name, and he ran out and saw the fire. I blanked out and forgot the house was on fire and fell to the floor crying. This day was supposed to be a happy one, and here it is, another happy day ending with me crying my heart out. This was the last thing I had of my mom, and Ash burnt it. In one night because her life was fucked up, she took the last thing I had. Mack came running to me with my robe.

"I know you're pissed, but we have to go. Is Ash here?"

"Nope, the bitch left and damn near kilt our ass." Standing up, I wrapped the robe around myself. When the ceiling started falling in, he snatched me, and we ran out the door. As I ran, it dawned on me that all my money was in the house. I ran back toward the door, and he screamed my name.

"Drea, the fuck is you doing?"

Turning around, I didn't know what the fuck to say. "Blaze," was all I could get out before I passed out.

To be Continued . . .

This was a compilation of Part 1 and 2 combined. Please check out parts 3 and 4 to find out what the Hoovers are up to now.

Other Books by Latoya Nicole

No Way Out 1–2

Gangsta's Paradise 1–2

Addicted to His Pain: A Standalone Novel

Love and War 1–4

I Gotta Be the One You Love: A Standalone

Creeping with the Enemy 1–2

The Rise and Fall of a Crime God 1–2

A Crazy Kind of On the 12th Day of Christmas My Savage Gave to Me

Love

Shadow of a Gangsta

14 Reasons to Love You

Love
AND WAR

The infamous Hoover gang—Baby Face, Blaze, Quick, and Shadow—have taken Chicago by storm. These four are not your average street thugs. Bank robbers by day and club owners by night, they have held on to their place at the top by never trusting anyone enough to allow them in their circle. The moment they do, all hell breaks loose.

Zayn "Blaze" Hoover has always lived by the code *Never trust a female;* hit and quit. Then he meets Drea and starts doing everything differently. He wants to give her the world, and he's ready to change his ways for her—until someone sets him up, and all signs lead to her.

Zavien "Shadow" Hoover is the youngest of the crew. He's never wanted the females that come along with their lifestyle. Engaged to his first love, Shirree, he's ready to make her his wife. After a big argument and a night of drinking, however, Shadow does something that could jeopardize their love forever. Out for revenge, Shirree might be crossing a line that puts them both in a difficult position.

Zavier "Quick" Hoover is not overly impressed by the ladies who surround him, but Alaysia sweeps him away with her beauty—at least on the outside. On the inside, she's ugly to the core. The harder he falls, the closer she gets to his circle. Unbeknownst to him, that's where she wanted to be all along. Not only do her scandalous ways affect Quick, but the whole Hoover gang may be at risk.

Zaire "Baby Face" Hoover has always been open to love, but when he finds it, will he get the chance to be happy? Being the oldest, he has to clean up the mess his brothers created, and he might lose his love in order to do it.

They say all is fair in love and war, but how do you fight when you don't know the enemy is the one you love? Will the Hoover gang be able to reign supreme, or will they fall at the hands of the women who are supposed to have their backs?

URBAN
Renaissance
WWW.URBANBOOKS.NET

U.S. $7.99 / CANADA $10.99
ISBN-13: 978-1-64556-097-5
ISBN-10: 1-64556-097-X

EAN

PRINTED IN U.S.A.

5 0799

9 781645 560975